Prologue

Auschwitz, 21 December 1943

'*Eins, zwei!*'

Gioele counted the steps between the dormitory and the doctor's office in German. The rhythmic tapping of his soles on the floor, between the cold, bare walls, echoed to the ceiling, painted a ghostly cerulean blue by the search-lights.

'*Drei, vier!*'

He hopped to the end of the hallway, to the only window that could be opened, clutching the drawing paper. Almost all the windows in Block 10 were barred with a heavy wooden beam but not this one: from here you could see the stark, whitened birches on the avenue, the barbed-wire fence that gleamed in the searchlights and a distant farm-house with a chimney exhaling puffs of smoke.

He stood up on tiptoe.

The snow was drumming on the glass. Cold and soft, it tapped the pane before sliding down and coating the entire avenue, the trees, the flower beds, the blocks and the watchtowers. He could see the soldier in the sentry box. Thick clouds of his warm breath scattered the air and he appeared to be shaking like a leaf just standing there, in the frost, behind his machine gun. Gioele wondered if he was longing for a cup of hot broth, a fireplace with a burning log or a family gathered by a crackling fire.

He began to hop again.

'Fünf, sechs!'

He stopped outside Uncle Mengele's office. He tried the door, but the handle was blocked and the accordion blind quivered against the glass pane with a hollow clatter.

On the wall behind the desk, displayed next to the collection of eyeballs, were Gioele's drawings. Gioele didn't have to open the door in order to see them, because by now he knew the room like the back of his hand. Mengele allowed him to go anywhere he liked, even in his private office. He treated him differently from the other children. For example, he allowed him to draw, then he'd put his creations up everywhere, give them to nurses and other doctors, and show them to SS officers with great pride.

When the Birkenau painter had come to sketch the twins, Gioele had stared at her with his mouth open the whole time. He was bewitched by the eyes and lips that emerged from the hazy, sooty pencil swirls, the faces that took shape as though alive. He thought Dina was much better than any other painter he'd ever seen in his life. That morning, Gioele had asked for paper and a little piece of charcoal and drawn the avenue outside the kitchens. One of the nurses had put his sketch up on the wall and Uncle Mengele had got annoyed. Afterwards, though, he'd taken a closer

ASHES
IN THE
SNOW

Oriana Ramunno (born Melfi, 1980) lives between Berlin and Bologna with her husband and three children. Following a number of prize-winning crime novellas and short stories in various magazines, she started writing her debut thriller *Ashes in the Snow*, inspired by the story of her great-uncle, who was detained in the Flossenbürg concentration camp. She dedicates this book to him, a book she describes as 'the last act of love in a long journey'.

ASHES
IN THE
SNOW

ORIANA RAMUNNO

Translated from the Italian by Katherine Gregor

HarperCollins*Publishers*

HarperCollins*Publishers* Ltd
1 London Bridge Street,
London SE1 9GF

www.harpercollins.co.uk

HarperCollins*Publishers*
1st Floor, Watermarque Building, Ringsend Road
Dublin 4, Ireland

Published by HarperCollins*Publishers* 2022
1

Originally published in 2021 by Rizzoli, Italy, as *Il bambino che disegnava le ombre*

Published in agreement with Piergiorgio Nicolazzini Literary Agency (PNLA)

Oriana Ramunno asserts the moral right to
be identified as the author of this work

Katherine Gregor asserts the moral right to be identified
as the author of the translation

A catalogue record for this book is available from the British Library

ISBN: 978-0-00-849553-4 (HB)
ISBN: 978-0-00-849554-1 (TPB)
ISBN: 978-0-00-856181-9 (Canada TPB)

Set in Sabon LT Std by Palimpsest Book Production Limited,
Falkirk, Stirlingshire

Printed and bound in the UK using 100% renewable electricity
at CPI Group (UK) Ltd

To Samuel, Elia and Emanuele

Note from the author

I was eighteen when I found out that my great-uncle had been in a concentration camp.

He had never told that to our generation. He didn't like to remember. I had only noticed that he did not like movies about concentration camps, he always changed channel.

The first time he told me his story he was misty-eyed and his voice was trembling; he had finally agreed to tell me more because I was close to my high school diploma. I had chosen to do an essay on the Shoah, and I wanted to interview someone who had experienced the horrors of war on their own skin. It was then that I found out about the Flossenbürg camp, where he had been deported from Durre – about the long road to get there, how he had to feed on the raw meat of animals killed by the bombs, and about the companions he lost along the way. And then later, about his transfer from the concentration camp to the death camp, for having imitated Hitler without paying attention to prying eyes. 'In that field I did not find people, but wandering shadows', says his scratched voice, still imprinted on the tape on which I recorded it. 'It was an atrocious imprisonment.'

Along with the painful tales of hunger, death and abuse, there was also a glimmer of light: he told me of German commanders who secretly tried to help. One in particular, a certain Michel nicknamed 'eight children', remained etched in my uncle's memory for his smile and humanity, and for the subterfuges with which he tried to make life in the camp easier.

On that sunny afternoon, spent collecting this precious testimony, was born the novel that I would write twenty years later. That day I understood that I had to look at History with different eyes, to dig, to search, to study it. At university, I took two exams on the Shoah, which allowed me to approach the subject in a more scientific way and to access academic documents. I began a journey of personal research not only regarding the concentration camps, the Holocaust and Nazism, but also regarding the German Resistance and its martyrs: the latter a story which often goes unnoticed. Finally, life took me to Berlin, where I live and where my path has found new life.

My novel saw the light after this inner gestation, when it and I were ready. It was the last act of love in a long journey.

look at the drawing and smiled. It was a barely perceptible smile, but a pleased one. He'd returned that afternoon with a wad of paper and some Lyra pencils. Gioele had never had such a fine box of pencils. From that moment on, this wing in Block 10 had been filled with his drawings.

'*Sieben, acht!*' he resumed, turning away from Mengele's office.

The corridor was long and dark. The patients in the block were afraid of it because rooms would open onto it like hungry mouths beyond which terrible things happened. Sometimes, you could hear dreadful screaming. But what was even scarier were the whispers in the night, the footsteps that were like a dull tolling, the moans that made you shudder. Some people said it was the ghosts of people who'd died during doctors' examinations. They infested the building and at night you could glimpse them in their long, milky cloaks, gliding along the walls and sliding over windowpanes, creating sudden condensation. Or else you could see them in the constant flicker of the light bulbs.

Gioele summoned up the courage.

'*Neun.*'

He stopped outside an open door. Inside, the light was off except for a faint glow at the far end, so the threshold seemed like a dark eye staring intently at him. Gioele looked up and in the semi-darkness read the inscription SIGISMUND BRAUN on the nameplate by the jamb.

The door moved with an eerie squeak, perhaps because of an open window. Gioele couldn't help thinking that the stories about the ghosts might be true, after all. He clutched the drawing paper against his chest to silence his heart, which was pounding in his throat. Instead of turning and running away, though, he stuck his nose into the liquid darkness of the laboratory.

When they were on the train and he called out to the SS men through the window to practise his German, his mother often said, 'You're too bright and too inquisitive a little boy, Gioele, and it'll get you into trouble. It'll bring you bad luck.'

Since he'd been in the camp, he had survived only because he was bright and inquisitive, and thanks to the genius that set him apart from the other twins, even his brother Gabriele. He was rewarded with lumps of sugar, chocolate and, every now and then, a used toy. He and his brother slept in Block 10 with the other select few and not in the Birkenau blocks, which he'd been told were cramped, dirty and swarming with lice. They wore the clothes in which they'd arrived at the camp and weren't forced to trek across miles of countryside from the Birkenau barracks to the Auschwitz laboratories to be measured and studied. That was lucky, he thought.

'Zehn!'

Gioele gathered all his courage. With a single, heroic stride, he stepped over the line between the half-light and the darkness in the room. It felt like leaping into a black, menacing abyss.

You couldn't see anything inside.

He searched for the switch, flicked it down and a cold light flooded the room. It was so bright that he had to squint before he was able to see anything. He held his hand flat above his eyes to shield them and looked around. This laboratory was like all the others in the block. Beneath the flickering light he recognized the granite floor and the white walls made of identical tiles. He let his gaze wander over the steel trolleys, the strange machinery and the tiled tables. It lingered on the cabinets full of medicines, the shiny sink and the photograph of the Führer hanging on the wall, looking at him with a grim expression.

The window was open but there was an odd smell in the air. It was neither disinfectant nor the formaldehyde the doctors used for preserving their exhibits. He thought he'd smelled it somewhere before, not only in the camp but also at home, in Bologna. Overwhelmed by the painful nostalgia of an elusive recollection, Gioele suddenly felt sad.

Silently, he walked to the middle of the room.

In some parts, the grout lines between the tiles were caked in blood. He looked up at the shelves and made out the clear jars in which floated a heart, a brain and kidneys. There was a foetus swaying as though asleep in its mother's belly and a basket of red apples that made Gioele feel hungry.

He looked for a chair he could climb on to get one but was distracted by the faint glow coming from the room leading into the laboratory.

He approached, then went in.

The office was lit by the soft, amber light from a table lamp that projected the colourful flowers of the leaded glass on the wall. He could hear a buzz in the air, like an electrical lament that permeated the walls. It was a rhythmic, constant rustling sound. Gioele looked at the desk, the microscopes, the velvet armchairs, the grandfather clock and the bookcase. In a corner, the gramophone was spinning non-stop. The stylus had reached the end of the record and there was no more sound coming out of the brass horn except for a scratching whirr, like a fly in distress.

He looked down at the floor. His attention was captured by a nibbled apple that had rolled down from somewhere or other. Gioele felt his heart catch in his throat as he made out a pale form between the desk and the Christmas tree. A white coat dumped in a corner.

Ghosts wear white sheets, he thought.

He nearly ran away but something held him back, rooted him to the spot. He felt his anxiety swell and his heartbeat echo through his entire body, down to his fingertips. It was not just a lab coat lying on the floor. It was a coat with a man in it.

Gioele recognized him immediately. Doktor Sigismund Braun's sleeves were rolled up to his elbows, as if he'd just finished working, and his turquoise eyes were blank. His mouth was open in a silent cry, his tongue hanging out like the SS men's dogs when they were thirsty. There was a dark bruise on his high, balding forehead.

Gioele tiptoed towards him and shook him, but the man did not stir.

He was stone dead.

Gioele sat down in front of him, cross-legged, licked his lips and put the drawing pad on his lap. Whenever he tried to swallow it felt like gulping fire, but despite this and the fact that his hands were shaking, Gioele started to draw. There could be no drawing more beautiful than that of a dead Herr Doktor Braun, he thought.

1

Judenrampe, 23 December 1943

The searchlights pierced through the darkness of the country-side, illuminating the siding, and casting a blinding light on the verge.

Leaning on his stick, Hugo Fischer got out of the car. The dry snow squeaked under his boots. At the same time, the rails screeched beneath the weight of carriages reaching their destination. They produced a sharp, drawn-out sound that gradually died down and vanished in the night's silence, among the birch forests that flanked the railway line.

The locomotive puffed out one last plume of smoke and an SS man jumped down, the hem of his leather coat flapping like the wings of an eagle.

Hugo sighed. The air condensed outside his mouth like a milky cloud, similar to the yellow cocoon swirling against the dark sky in the distance. There was a pungent smell in the air, just as they said in Berlin: a sickly-sweet smell reminiscent of burnt flesh.

He took out a cigarette and wedged it between his lips. He held it firmly with his teeth while clicking the lighter, his eyes seeking an SS man's approval. 'Who gives a shit?' the petty officer, his pose stiff, face taut and red from the cold, seemed to reply. In this cold that bit into your bones harder than a rabid dog's teeth, everybody turned a blind eye to the Führer's abhorrence of smoking.

The cigarette sizzled with unexpected warmth. The taste of tobacco stung his tongue and replaced the pungency dominating the countryside that even snow hadn't been able to wash away. Hugo sighed contentedly, voiding his lungs fully. Further ahead, the Alsatian on the SS officer's lead whimpered.

Hugo took another drag and leaned against the Mercedes to alleviate the ache in his back. Two days earlier, he'd woken up with a stabbing pain in his lower back and his arm numb all the way down to his thumb and index finger. He felt as though there were pins stuck in his flesh and a thousand ants walking under his skin, severing his contact with objects, so much so that everything risked slipping out of his hands. He knew that the acute phase of the illness would soon lessen, but not sensing the surrounding world and not being able to probe its consistency distressed him.

It was the same with every relapse. Whenever the illness started up again, nibbling at some hidden part of his brain and spinal cord, it left new marks on him, grooves on a record that played music off-key until someone repaired it.

After a while, the worst was over.

His sleepy leg, however, was a permanent scar. They'd told him that his nervous system was so damaged it would never go back to normal. At times, the leg was so unbearably heavy that he wished he could cut it off and feed it to the dogs, that way nothing would be left, not even a shred of flesh. But it was there, attached to his body, a phantom appendage that no longer obeyed his command.

Hugo slipped a hand into the pocket of his coat and the clinking of the morphine phial briefly made him relax. Whenever the illness came on strongly, he would start sweating, his veins throbbing like a drum, dilating and contracting under his skin. From that moment, and until he was able to stick the needle into a vein, there would be an unbearable wait that only increased his anxiety and made him short-tempered with everyone. Holding the phial helped calm him down. He'd discovered that it was the only way to control the tremors.

Hugo let go of the phial and took his hand out of his pocket. He turned up his coat collar to shield the clammy back of his neck from the bitter cold and pulled down the brim of his hat slightly. He took another puff at his cigarette to avoid thinking about his pain and darted a glance at the driver, nice and warm in the car. Good for him.

He looked around, lingering on the details of the train station. The ramp was long, interminable. The snow had been swept off, but more had accumulated over the past hour and now there was a thin coat on the gravel, crunching at every step. The odd flake fell from the sky. The searchlights made everything sparkle – the lorries, the vans, the helmets and the damp uniforms of the SS men who waited in line for the convoy that had just stopped. Even the dogs were on alert, whining and barking as they quivered.

He saw dozens of hands grabbing at the gratings of the carriages, which were still shut. Long, bony, dirty fingers, swarming like earthworms.

'*Eau!*' someone yelled from inside the train. No one answered, so they tried in a hesitant German, '*Wa-wasser, bitte! Wasser!*'

Hugo swallowed the smoke. He felt his heart miss a beat with an irksome arrhythmia.

He wasn't one inclined towards easy emotions. Over the past three years, since he'd been working with the Kriminalpolizei, he'd seen everything: bodies mutilated, women raped and killed, men strangled or brutally castrated, fresh cadavers and others putrefying, swollen, full of gas, shit and worms. The first few times, he'd vomited, had nightmares like those that torment children; then he'd got used to it.

He wasn't one inclined towards easy emotions, he mentally repeated while lapping up the aroma of tobacco to rid himself of the stench that permeated the station. And yet he felt he was about to witness something for which he wasn't ready. Something for which Arthur Nebe, the head of Department V of the RSHA – the Reich's Security – hadn't sufficiently prepared him. He could feel it in the air, compressed like a snowball in your hands, and in the smell of charred flesh that had started drifting over again in foul wafts now that the tobacco was burning away.

He could swear to it. This really was flesh bound for the crematoria, as he'd heard in the Berlin office. In the corridors of Prinz-Albrecht-Straße and in the new office in Werderscher Markt, they talked about Sachsenhausen and Dachau, but nothing beat Auschwitz. There were rumours that diseases and the SS-Totenkopfverbände's insane methods reaped so many victims that the SS men were forced to burn the bodies in state-of-the-art crematoria, stinking out the sky with clouds so dense you could never glimpse the sun. Here, the snow covered a thick layer of ashes.

The bark of an SS officer startled him. 'Bring the dogs!' He was holding a logbook and scanning it with his eyes. 'We're about to offload the cargo! A thousand pieces!'

The sky over the cattle wagons was dark, almost devastating.

The Alsatians curled their lips over their gums and scratched the snow with their paws. The searchlights made their sharp teeth glisten. Anybody would have stopped at the guttural snarling that came from their bristly bellies.

Hugo gave the cigarette – dying by now – one final drag and threw it into the distance.

A short-lived, luminous trail that then sizzled in the snow.

'Out!' an SS man yelled, beating a baton against the carriage walls. 'Out, you pieces of shit!'

The carriage doors opened one after the other with a deafening clatter that was drowned out by the shouts of the SS men and the barking of the dogs. A noxious smell flooded the station and Hugo instinctively stepped back.

'Out! Quick!'

Bodies, crushed beyond belief, swarmed out like bees from a broken hive.

Hugo felt as though he was in one of the circles of Dante's *Inferno*. He remembered the swamp of the River Styx well: it was where souls writhed in the mud, thrashing against one another. Some couldn't even reach the surface, but remained below, faceless, just bubbles rising from the mire.

The SS men tried to restore calm by administering blows with the butts of their rifles. Hugo's eyes met those of a woman who was carrying a suitcase in one hand and, in her arm, a baby girl only a few months old. She didn't want to let go of either. The viscous swamp sucked her back. In the crush she had to give up her suitcase and hold her daughter tight to make her way through the crowd.

Pushed by another woman, she fell to her knees.

An Alsatian snapped at the cold air right in her face. From his position by the Mercedes, Hugo could see her features deformed with terror. He felt uneasy at being this unexpected spectator, in his civilian investigator's coat, unable to do anything but watch. He took a step forward to help her, but the icy glare of the SS officer next to him stopped him in his tracks.

The woman got back up and looked around, lost. Now, the torrent of Jews with the yellow star pinned to their coats was following the SS men's instructions in an orderly fashion, with a meek murmur. Their eyes were full of questions, but no one dared breathe a word. Some gave the others quizzical looks but took care not to address the Germans.

Hugo felt uncomfortable. For him, Jews had never been a problem. But they were for the Party, to the point of obsession.

He had fond memories of Frau Mandelbaum, his neighbour in Berlin; she was like an aunt. In Nikolaiviertel, on summer afternoons, he would linger with her son Henryk. They'd go and play hide-and-seek at the back of the church or race on the banks of the Spree then dive in and swim to the other shore. A pleasant smell of apple cake would waft through the ground-floor windows, a warm aroma that covered the dank odour of the river. When the sky began to darken, Frau Mandelbaum would call them in for tea, her voice echoing throughout the district, bouncing off the boats that rocked on the water. Hugo and Henryk had attended a few university lectures together, and spent days among the stuccos and crystals of the Romanisches Café. Then the boycotts had started, Henryk had left, and Hugo never heard from him again. His mother, on the other hand, had died of a heart attack the same year, when the Gestapo had come to take her away, and all things considered, it was better that way, judging by what he was seeing on the ramp.

Hugo looked at the woman again.

'*Ma valise!*' she was screaming. She defied the crowd and the blows from the riding crops and tried to get her suitcase back.

'The suitcase stays here!' An SS man grabbed her by the collar and forced her to the side, where he was assembling women and children.

Prisoners wearing uniforms with blue and white stripes had arrived to pick up the luggage. They were stacking it in heaps that looked like unstable hills and loading it on trolleys and vans. In addition to the suitcases, they were unloading the bodies of those who hadn't survived the long journey. Hugo noticed that their gestures were brisk and confident: evidently, they were accustomed to doing this on a regular basis.

Meanwhile, the woman had broken free, stubborn, unwavering as only a mother can be. '*Ma valise!*' she insisted. '*J'ai besoin de ma valise!*'

13

'The suitcase stays here!' the SS man snarled again.

The young mother tried to make him understand how important it was for her. She touched her little girl's clothes, her woollen cap, and Hugo realized that the suitcase must contain the necessities for taking care of the child and cleaning her. The SS officer must have understood, too, but he continued to push her towards the group of women, where a man in a white coat was examining them.

She wouldn't give up. She stood her ground, even though she was so thin she looked about to collapse. The two of them carried on negotiating, one in French, the other in a German that was growing increasingly furious. And yet the SS man was showing no sign of taking up his rifle. He had the face of a decent young man who wanted to resolve the situation without using force.

'What's this racket?' An older SS officer, in gunmetal uniform, demanded.

He walked briskly over to them. The hem of his leather coat cracked through the cold air like a whip and the snow moaned under his boots. The beam from the search-lights cut his face in two, emphasizing his sharp, cleanly-shaven features. The skull and crossbones on his hat glowed as fiercely as his cerulean blue eyes.

'What's the problem with this Jew?' he asked.

'Heil Hitler!' The young SS officer stiffened in a salute. 'She doesn't want to leave her suitcase because it has things she needs for the child, Herr Sturmbannführer!'

'Let's solve this problem right now.'

The Sturmbannführer smiled, calm and icy. He flashed a row of strong white teeth that made him look like the Alsatians. He gently picked up the child and rocked her.

The mother froze.

Hugo leaned forward to look, leaving the side of the Mercedes for the middle of the verge. His spine stiffened with an odd premonition and, for a moment, he completely forgot about the pain.

An opening formed in the crowd and the officer put the baby down on the ground. He gave her a pat and a smile. The contact with the cold snow made her yawn, rousing her from the hunger and tiredness of the journey. Her mother watched her, wide-eyed, cheekbones piercing the skin like bramble thorns, mouth open in a silent scream she didn't dare let out. She was reaching for her daughter, but something was stopping her: perhaps the fear of doing the wrong thing.

Hugo held his breath, in the dreadful tension that had been created, and stared at the scene in dismay.

The officer took his semi-automatic out of the holster and pointed the barrel at the baby. The beam from the search-lights made the burnished steel gleam, its glow travelling to the manual safety lock which he lowered with a dull click. His finger slid down to the trigger so slowly, Hugo fell into an abyss that sucked the air out of his lungs as he waited, making his temples throb with a deafening roar.

There was no shot. Only the clicking of the trigger being pulled in vain.

'Damn,' the SS officer said.

The firing pin hadn't engaged the primer correctly. Hugo felt the tension rise, mouths getting drier.

The Sturmbannführer looked at the pistol, annoyed. He would have to unload it, throw away the faulty bullet and try with the next one. Instead, he put the pistol back in the holster.

'You just can't trust weapons,' he said with a laugh.

Hugo saw the mother reach out to pick up the child. Her face was rough and pale, as though all the blood had drained from her body, and she was shaking with fear.

The Sturmbannführer shot her a cold glance, as though ordering her to stop, then lifted his foot.

He stamped once. Twice. Three times.

The heel of his boot tore down furiously on the baby, with a sound that gradually became softer and more liquid. At every blow, Hugo shrank into his shoulders, unable to do anything to hold back the tremor that shook him to the core. A horrified silence engulfed the ramp.

'Now the suitcase is not a problem anymore,' the SS officer said mockingly. 'Let it be a warning to anyone who feels like wasting any more time.'

The officer cleaned the heel of his boot in the fresh snow and walked away.

The baby's mother was still crouching on the ground, her eyes staring into the void. The younger SS man prodded her with the end of his rifle, the tremor in his hands evident, his expression grief-stricken, and she put up no resistance. She got up and staggered away through the crowd of people who stood horror struck.

The prisoners woke up as though from a nightmare and resumed unloading the dead bodies from the carriages. They tossed them onto the platform like empty sacks, rag dolls that smelled of death. One of them almost knocked the woman down but she didn't appear to notice.

'Herr Fischer!'

Hugo was startled. He felt as though he'd suddenly come to after temporarily ceasing to breathe. He clenched a fist in the hope of feeling something in those numb fingertips and looked at the man running towards him panting. He was spitting clouds of vapour in the air while making his way among the Jews by waving his arms. Hugo struggled to make out his face. He still had before his eyes the horror of the ravaged little body, the mother's paralysed look. He summoned his courage and turned to look at the body. The SS men were walking past it, avoiding the mess so they wouldn't soil their boots or spread more residue on the rest of the platform. As if it were no more than a heap of dirt staining the snow.

'Herr Fischer!' the man, now close to him, repeated, startling him. Hugo could see him now. He was a tall, blond officer with grey eyes like pieces of dirty glass. 'Heil Hitler!' he added vehemently once he was in front of him.

'Heil Hitler,' Hugo stammered in a daze. He almost felt shame saying it.

'It's outrageous that you should have witnessed this kind of episode,' the man said apologetically, indicating the baby's remains. 'I am truly mortified. How come you stopped at the Judenrampe?'

'Weren't we supposed to meet here?' Hugo replied, still stunned. Remembering the sound of the boot stamping the baby triggered a retch he only just managed to hold back.

The SS officer shook his head. 'I was waiting for you at the station freight yard, but soon realized the misunderstanding. I'm Obersturmführer Tristan Voigt.'

'Hugo Fischer.' He shook hands, controlling the tremor in his own hand while pointing at the little body with the other. 'What happened—'

'Pay no attention,' the officer said, silencing him. He picked up Hugo's suitcase and motioned him to the vehicles parked on the edge of the platform. 'Every now and then these accidents do happen.'

Hugo followed him as quickly as his limping allowed, zigzagging between Red Cross lorries and vans as far as a Kübelwagen, the so-called tub-car. His heart felt about to burst in an attempt to rebel against the horror he'd just witnessed, and he had to ask his body for a huge effort to reach the vehicle.

When he saw them coming, the driver saluted and opened the doors.

'Welcome to Auschwitz,' Tristan Voigt said with a wink before vanishing into the car.

Hugo got in. He wiped the steamed-up windowpane with his hand and gave one last look at the Jews who were being made to set off, filthy and skinny as ghosts, and at the prisoners who were sorting through the luggage with a shadow of despondency in their eyes, paying no attention to those crying or asking questions, or to the mother, who was now lunging angrily at an SS officer.

Gunshots echoed in the silence of the night and the Jewess fell backwards, next to her daughter's remains. Her blood slowly spread in a pool and the snow drank it all, mixing it with the ashes.

2

The gaps between the clouds narrowed until the sky became a heavy mass.

The snow had started to fall in large flakes. The windscreen wipers were struggling to sweep them off the glass and the headlights made them glitter in the dark, like impalpable fireflies.

The road between the station access and the Auschwitz Stammlager was only a few kilometres long, studded with birch woods and the occasional farmhouse with light in the windows. The surreal whiteness in which they were immersed conveyed a peace Hugo found disarming for a place with such a sinister reputation.

The scene he'd witnessed had left a weight on his stomach he now couldn't shake off. Hugo had seen thousands of Jews board trains in Berlin, depart from Grunewald and Anhalter stations with their suitcases, yellow stars pinned to their coats, their faces almost cheerful at leaving a city that no longer wanted them and had become unlivable and violent. What he hadn't seen was where they arrived.

'I don't like this atmosphere,' Henryk Mandelbaum had told him one evening, several years earlier. They were strolling along Kurfürstendamm, past shop windows soiled with insulting slogans and humiliating drawings left by the storm troopers – the SA. They'd stopped at the foot of the Grünfeld building, covered with flyers demanding the Aryanization of the Jewish lingerie giant. 'What can I say, Hugo? I have a bad feeling about this.'

'Perhaps you're exaggerating,' he'd retorted. The SA had tried to boycott Jewish shops, posting signs everywhere and standing outside the entrances, blocking them, but people thought it was silly, outlandish even, laughed at this absurd demand and had gone in to do their shopping, as they did every day, as far as the crisis allowed it. There was no climate of terror yet, and even the utopia of an Aryan race was still sketchy, and yet Henryk didn't want to hear excuses; he'd given up his university teaching post in Criminology and fled to London. He'd done the right thing. Shortly afterwards, Ernst vom Rath, a German diplomat, had been murdered by a Jew named Hermann Grünspan and the SA had reacted with unprecedented violence: night-time Berlin had been filled with screams and torch fire, exploding windows in the shops and homes of prominent Jews; synagogues had been set alight, and Hugo saw through his window anger and hatred spilling into the street like the Spree bursting its banks. The following morning, Berlin lay devastated by Nazi fury, covered in ashes and blood. Almost a hundred Jews who'd come down into the streets had been killed, and thousands more had been arrested and taken to detention camps. After that night, radios and telephones had been seized from Jews, who were then obliged to wear the yellow star and prohibited from using public transport and lavatories, from going to school or keeping their jobs. Henryk would have lost his teaching post, anyway.

Hugo looked up through the windscreen.

The Auschwitz camp, the one where Henryk and his mother could have ended up, appeared before them, imposing, with a double barbed-wire fence, square poles with rounded tops, the watchtowers monitoring the zone like eyes focusing through the thick snow. Signs with crossbones ordered Halt: the fencing was electrified and if anyone so much as touched it, they would have died on the spot, even before the SS man on duty could shoulder his machine gun. This – and other places like this – was where Jews were taken.

'Needless to tell you that you must not reveal what you see here or in Birkenau to anyone,' Tristan Voigt said. He didn't even have to finger the small-calibre pistol in his holster to convince him. The skull and crossbones on his hat, which gleamed harshly in the headlights, was suffi-cient. 'Everything that happens in this camp is for the good of the Thousand-Year Reich, and the less people know about it, the better. The rest of the world isn't yet ready to understand our Führer's work, so we ask for your loyalty and discretion: we don't need publicity.'

'Of course,' Hugo assented. 'I've already been briefed.'

'I'll show you Dr Braun's body and where it was found,' Voigt said. 'Then I'll escort you to Kommandant Liebehenschel. He can't wait to make your acquaintance.'

The barrier slowly rose in the eddy of white flakes and the Kübelwagen drove through the gate with the wrought iron sign above it. The letters stood out, grim, outlined by the searchlights, wet from the snow. For some reason,

Hugo felt uneasy at the sight of that motto – work sets you free.

He leaned towards the window and peered out.

Illuminated against the night sky by searchlights, the branches of a large birch by the entrance were bending in the wind. A succession of silent buildings with neat masonry lined the driveway and, on the right, he could see a low hut with chimneys several metres tall. Such order was unexpected in a prison camp.

Outside the hut, prisoners were gathered in rows of five, standing in coats that looked too thin for the temperature of the harsh winter. They were so skinny, they swayed in the light of the lamp posts as if weightless. On one side, there was a heap of corpses, their greatcoats removed. All they had left on them was the striped uniform, their bellies were exposed and their arms spread out in the snow like sticks.

'That's—' Hugo couldn't complete his sentence. He felt as though he'd swallowed sand.

'That's—?' Voigt seemed to mock him. He gave a hearty laugh and adjusted the peak on his cap. He pulled the collar of his uniform slightly away from his neck and a strong scent of cologne wafted towards Hugo, though it couldn't erase the pungent odour of burnt flesh he'd smelled at the station.

'In Berlin there are many rumours about this place,' he confessed.

'What kind of rumours?'

Embarrassed, Hugo shrugged his shoulders. 'They say that Auschwitz has crematoria working day and night, and that there are more dead than workers . . .'

Voigt's lips spread into a wolfish smile that he turned

into a barely repressed laugh. 'Those aren't the crematoria chimneys,' he said, 'but the chimneys of the camp kitchen.'

Hugo swallowed a polite laugh. When Arthur Nebe had agreed to the Auschwitz Kommandant's odd request to send him the best criminologist around, he'd advised Hugo to stick to his job and not ask too many questions about the camp. 'Don't meddle in things that don't concern you,' he'd told him. 'The less you look, the better.' However, if there was one thing Hugo was good at, it was contravening Nebe's rules.

'Why are they keeping them out in the cold at this time of night?' he dared ask as they drove past the prisoners and turned into a side street.

'They're doing the roll call.' Voigt glanced at his watch while the Kübelwagen parked. 'They're definitely taking their time this evening. Maybe someone attempted to escape, or else the SS men on duty are in a playful mood.'

The engine stopped rumbling and Voigt got out of the vehicle without saying anything else. In the headlights, his shoulders looked broad and straight, chiselled by the leather coat of his uniform, and he stood out like a statue against the darkness of the night and the whiteness of the falling snow.

'To satisfy your curiosity, the crematorium is beyond that building,' he said, indicating an unspecified spot ahead. 'It's a rather primitive crematorium and isn't used anymore. It's been converted into a warehouse. But in Birkenau it's an entirely different story: we've improved the ventilation, so the bodies burn better, more of them and quicker. There's also a hoist. Nothing for the Sonderkommandos to complain about.'

23

Hugo got out of the car and carefully propped himself up on his stick to avoid slipping. 'Sonderkommandos?'

'The special unit of Jews who help with the bodies. You saw them at the station. The ones with the striped uniforms and the Jew triangles.'

Hugo looked at the horizon, where you could make out some kind of dawn and the malodorous yellow plume he'd seen from the station. Voigt didn't seem to mind his questions, so he asked another: 'Is that smoke coming from the crematoria?'

Voigt paused on the steps to Block 10 and licked his lips, cracked from the cold. 'Sometimes, our loads of bodies are too large,' he confessed. 'The crematoria are modern and efficient, but they're not enough. We make woodpiles with bitumen, a couple of Kobiór trees and burnt oil. The smoke you see is from a pile. You can tell by the yellow smoke.'

Hugo stared at him, astounded. This officer was admitting that so many prisoners were dying they had to be cremated outdoors. He had a faint smile and Hugo couldn't tell if he was baiting him or telling the truth. What he knew was that Nebe was right: his every remark about the camp would be damaging and compromising to his career. His task was not to judge the methods of the camp, nor the way it treated its prisoners.

'Tell me about Dr Braun,' he said, changing the subject.

Tristan Voigt threw the double doors open onto a corridor that smelled of disinfectant. He switched on the lights and led the way. His long shadow was dark against the white, chalky walls and stood out beneath the flickering electric bulbs.

'Sigismund Braun was a paediatrician specializing in

genetic diseases,' he replied, climbing the stairs to the second floor. His military step reverberated like a drumbeat. 'He obtained authorization to work in the camp from Reichsführer Himmler himself.'

What Voigt was saying tallied with what Hugo had managed to discover from the Berlin archives. Originally from Wupperhof, Braun held a degree in medicine and had worked in the children's department of the Kaufbeuren-Irsee Institute in Bavaria. He'd joined the Party as far back as 1931 and the SS in 1938. He'd fought in the war and returned from the front with a wounded leg, three lumbar hernias that had sometimes confined him to his bed for days, and two Iron Crosses. Because of his injuries he had been redeployed to work as a doctor in Auschwitz with the rank of Oberscharführer.

Hugo stopped on the stairs to catch his breath and rest his leg. He looked around, more from uneasiness than curiosity. At the top of the steps, in the first-floor corridor, there was a row of rooms set aside for patients. And yet it was too quiet for a camp hospital, and Sigismund Braun's curriculum vitae was a little too outstanding to land him in a position where he treated ordinary prisoners. Something didn't add up.

'Was Braun happy to be here?' he asked.

'Of course.' Voigt nodded and the skull on his hat seemed to sneer. 'This was a promotion for him, not a downgrade,' he added.

Hugo couldn't imagine an academic who would view working in a prison camp as a career move. Braun seemed like a strange character. 'Who found the body?' he enquired.

'A guest of the block.' Voigt's gloved fingers glided on the handrail. 'It seems the doctor choked on a mouthful of apple. Unfortunately, he was in his office outside working hours, so nobody came to his rescue. By the time the guest discovered him, it was too late.'

'By "guest", do you mean a prisoner admitted to this block?'

'A child,' Voigt replied.

'He must be terrified . . .'

'Do you have children, Herr Fischer?'

'Not yet. I'm not married.'

Voigt sighed. 'I had one.' A flicker of sadness dimmed his gaze. 'Children have an extraordinary ability to handle situations which we adults think of as dreadfully frightening. And, between you and me, here in Auschwitz, no child would be scared by a dead man.'

Hugo and Voigt exchanged a long look. He sensed the officer was about to tell him more about this place but then thought better of it, leaving him on tenterhooks. Hugo surveyed what he could see of Block 10, trying to absorb the vibrations of the place, as he carried on with his questions.

'Is the child a patient of Dr Braun?'

'Of Dr Josef Mengele.'

'So there are children in this block?'

'There's a small group of children Mengele brought here from Birkenau. The rooms on the first floor are occupied by a couple of hundred female prisoners waiting to be treated by Dr Clauberg, a gynaecologist. As you see, the rumours in Berlin are somewhat exaggerated. There are doctors here willing to sacrifice their careers to care for the prisoners and their children.'

For all the Obersturmführer's reassurances, Hugo couldn't shake off the feeling that there was something truly unpleasant about this place. He could sense it under his skin, like a shudder that made his hairs stand on end. It was a disturbing feeling, a shadow that hovered in the air, slowing down his movements. The place seemed more like a morgue than a hospital.

'If Dr Braun died from choking, why did Liebehenschel request my involvement?' he thought aloud.

'To prove that he really *did* die from choking.' Tristan Voigt resumed climbing the stairs with his rhythmic step. 'Rumours started after his death, and the Kommandant wants to silence them as soon as possible before they undermine the psychological serenity of the female prisoners.'

'What kind of rumours?'

Voigt stopped at the top of the stairs and massaged the fingers of his right hand. 'A nurse, Berto Hoffman, had a nervous breakdown when he heard about the doctor's death and remarked that it was his ghosts that had taken him back. An entirely inappropriate remark.'

'And this comment by a nurse in a state of confusion was enough to trigger panic?' Hugo felt his eyebrows rise in an expression of scepticism he immediately tried to wipe off so as not to appear disrespectful.

'There have been rumours about ghosts in Block 10 for a long time,' Voigt replied. 'And it's a short step between that and collective psychosis. That's why your presence was requested: to prove that it was merely a mouthful of apple that went down the wrong way. Ghosts have nothing to do with it.'

Hugo stopped three steps down from Voigt, leaning heavily on his stick. He couldn't believe that Liebehenschel would order him to enter a camp like this, shrouded in a curtain of silence, to lay a few ghosts to rest. His hands were beginning to itch with impatience.

'I want to speak to the Kommandant,' he demanded. 'And with the nurse.'

'I don't think we can comply with the latter request,' Voigt replied. 'Berto Hoffman is not in the best physical condition for talking and right now he's detained in the camp prison.'

'For scaring some female prisoners?'

'No.' The officer's eyes turned icy, and yet his voice remained calm. 'A female nurse, Betsy Angel, kept an eye on Hoffman because she was angry about what he'd said. She caught him having a conversation with another nurse, Adele Krause, saying that the doctor deserved to end up the way he did. At that point, the SS men felt it their duty to search Hoffman's bed. Under the mattress, they found many green triangles, which he was trying to substitute for the red ones of some prisoners.'

Hugo was surprised. 'Triangles?'

'Cloth triangles.' Voigt drew an imaginary triangle with his index finger on his own coat, over his heart. 'They're sewn onto the tunics. Green for common criminals and red for political prisoners. Hoffman was handing out green triangles to political prisoners. It's an unacceptable act of treason.'

'I still don't understand . . .' Hugo said apologetically.

Voigt let out a sigh. 'The green triangles,' he explained patiently, 'are for German criminals. Thieves, rapists, Aryan murderers. We give them the kapo armband and the task of overseeing the work of the other prisoners. They make excellent supervisors. They're capable of inhuman, ruthless acts, which is just what we need to keep the other prisoners under control. Hoffman supplied green triangles to Communists and opponents of National Socialism so they could be promoted to kapos: the aim was to have less aggressive or sadistic colleagues. Assistants who'd make the other prisoners' stay easier.'

'What will happen to him now?' Hugo asked.

'We're waiting to put him on trial. He will most probably be transferred to the Western front. The problem is that many people are convinced that Dr Braun didn't die of natural causes, and that Berto Hoffmann's words concealed an admission of guilt.'

'Could you be more specific?'

'The female prisoners may be convinced it was ghosts, but the SS men believe Hoffman killed him. Maybe Braun had discovered the business about the triangles . . .'

Hugo sighed. 'I see now. But if Liebehenschel wants me to discover the truth, whatever it may be, he'll have to put me in a position to talk to Berto Hoffman.'

'You can speak to him in due course,' Voigt replied, cold and immovable. 'Now I have orders to escort you to Dr Braun's chapel of rest and the office where his body was found.'

3

There was a makeshift chapel of rest in one of the rooms in Block 10.

Outside the door, tapers crackled next to fresh flowers, giving off thin strands of smoke that permeated the place with the sombre smell of a church.

Accompanied by Voigt, Hugo looked in from the doorway.

The unmistakable odour of death suddenly swept over him.

Dr Sigismund Braun lay on a stretcher that had been covered with a cloth to conceal its metal frame. Behind him, red and white emblems with the black swastika paid homage to his loyalty to the Greater German Reich, while black ones with runes recalled his honourable service in the Schutzstaffel. They'd dressed him in his uniform, his rank clearly evident in the sterile lamplight, the belt with the steel buckle gleaming proudly, the Iron Crosses pinned to his pocket with care, and the ornate dagger at his side. Greying hair, thinning at the temples, was visible under his hat. His face had recently been shaved and, now that he was no longer alive, his cheeks were sunken. His thin lips, protruding under a dark, well-groomed moustache, were drained of blood. Although he was lying down, Hugo was able to gauge his build: he'd been a tall, robust man. He looked about fifty and, when alive, must have been striking.

Hugo walked in softly, removing his hat as a show of respect, and placed himself in a corner, behind a group of people gathered around the body. He noticed a woman sitting near the dead man, next to the window secured with heavy wooden shutters. Tall and dressed in the dark-grey jacket of the SS-Helferinnen, she looked like a barely breathing statue. Her straight shoulders gave her the bearing of a general, and her angular features were something he would have expected to see in a Valkyrie. Her one indulgence was blond hair that came down in waves over the translucent nape of her neck and gave her a touch of femininity. She didn't make a single superfluous movement apart from constantly twisting her auxiliary uniform gloves, and yet her sorrow was evident and pervaded the whole room. Another SS-Helferin placed a hand on hers to stop her crushing her gloves so violently. Only then did she calm down and sigh, an act that finally made her look human and frail.

'That's Sigismund Braun's wife,' Voigt whispered in his ear, 'Brunhilde Braun. She works in Birkenau.'

'And who's the other lady?' Hugo asked, indicating the younger auxiliary. She was a peculiar woman, attractive, but with a large birthmark the colour of milky coffee marring half her face, from the left side of her jaw all the way up to her temple. She was trying to conceal the flaw with her hair, which was too short to hide the mark entirely.

31

'Anita Kunig,' Voigt replied. 'She supervises the work at the personal effects warehouse with Frau Braun. They're very close friends. Here in Auschwitz, you tend to form strong bonds. When you're in the *anus mundi*, you need to find distractions and a way to feel more human . . .'

Anus mundi.

Tristan Voigt had used an elegant turn of phrase to confirm that they were in the most obscene place on earth. Hugo gave him a long look, more questions cramming into his mind, but Voigt had already resumed his neutral expression and was now describing the other people present, naming them one by one. Every now and then, someone would look up as if sensing they were being talked about.

The doctor in civilian clothes who sat to the right of the body, Voigt explained, was Dr Carl Clauberg, a Brigadeführer. Short, with thinning hair and round glasses on a hooked nose, he'd been born in the same city as Braun. They'd gone to school together: one had become a paediatric geneticist, the other a gynaecologist.

'Braun was Clauberg's only friend,' Voigt whispered into Hugo's ear, a tinge of contempt in his voice. 'Clauberg is an arrogant man and half the doctors hate him.'

'You don't like him either, by the sound of it . . .'

Voigt took a deep breath. 'He's the sort that calls killing a young woman because she wouldn't go to a hotel room with him an *accident*. Should I like him?'

'I don't think so. How come he's ended up in Auschwitz?'

'He came to Poland after the *accident*. The fact is, he needed to flee Germany, and his good friend Himmler found him a position here in the camp.'

Next to Clauberg sat Osmund Becker, the late Sigismund

Braun's young assistant geneticist. He'd just graduated from Hamburg and moved heaven and earth to be sent to Auschwitz, considering it the path to a brilliant career. Once again, Hugo was surprised to hear that all these doctors thought working in the camp was an opportunity for development.

Tall, with jet-black hair and turquoise eyes, Osmund Becker was looking around feverishly. His eyes flitted from the nurses to Anita Kunig, and even to Braun's wife: Hugo surmised he was more interested in beautiful, living things than dead ones. And who could blame him?

The three women sitting together in the area furthest away from the body, Voigt finally explained, were the three nurses who'd worked for the doctor.

Betsy Angel was German. She was the one who'd secretly followed Berto Hoffman and shopped him to the SS. She was petite, like a small doll with languid eyes and carefully drawn lips that were as soft and inviting as a ripe piece of fruit. Brown curls cascaded onto her bosom, squeezed into her white coat. Everything about her was calculated to draw attention in this awful place where the only entertainment was the brothel in Block 24, known as the Puff.

'They call it "the doll's house",' Voigt muttered. 'It has beautiful women, but everybody here only has eyes for Betsy Angel.'

'Who are the other two?'

Voigt indicated Adele Krause, a German nurse from Irsee, with short, wavy, copper-red hair. She'd been a member of Braun's work team since before Auschwitz.

The other one was Bethany Assouline.

A Jew.

She sat with her hands crossed over her belly, an identity bracelet on her wrist. Her raven-black hair framed a pale face, and when she looked up, Hugo saw a flash of fear in her gloomy expression. Lacking Betsy's sexual allure or Adele's fresh complexion, hers was a beauty marred by something. Perhaps it was the deep, dark rings under her eyes, or the high cheekbones reminiscent of a person whose face has been hollowed by illness, or the fear he'd glimpsed earlier; whatever it was, he had the sense that she was in the grip of some shadow that seemed to devour her entirely. At one point, he saw her bend forward and wipe off a trickle of blood running down her calf with a handkerchief.

'That woman's not well,' he pointed out.

Voigt's eyes became two slits of liquid iron. 'She's a Jew,' was his terse reply.

'Then she's a Jew who's not well.'

'Trust me,' Voigt insisted, visibly embarrassed. 'She's better off here than in Birkenau. And now you should introduce yourself, don't you think?'

The Obersturmführer opened his arms to indicate the group of people looking at him. He'd raised his voice and everyone had turned towards them. Everyone except Bethany Assouline, who continued to stare at her ankles with a demure expression.

'Good evening.' Hugo clutched his hat and instinctively glanced at the doctor's wife. 'My name's Hugo Fischer. I think you all know why I'm here.'

'I was sure I'd be able to send the body to Berlin.' Beneath the grief, Frau Brunhilde Braun's voice had a hint of resentment. 'But they told us to wait for you . . .'

'You'll have to postpone by a day at least,' he said apologetically. 'I need to analyse the body. I was told I'd find a good anatomopathologist here for an autopsy – am I correct?'

'There's my Jew,' Dr Clauberg said, breaking his silence, 'or Dr Mengele's. We'll lend you one.'

Brunhilde Braun stood up abruptly and glared at them. 'Is that really necessary?' Her Aryan features had lost all their beauty, turning her face into a cold, impassive surface made nastier by the grey uniform. 'We weren't even allowed to set up the chapel of rest at the farmhouse,' she added with contempt. 'My husband is an officer, and I won't allow a Jewish rat to get his hands on him!'

'Brunhilde . . .' Anita Kunig touched her gently, to calm her down.

'Leave me alone,' the widow said, shying away from her.

Hugo gave an embarrassed cough. 'I have to verify that death was caused by choking, Frau Braun. That's what I was called in for; it's my job. I promise you that everything will be finished by tomorrow evening at the latest, but I'm afraid there's no way I can dispense with an autopsy. If you'd prefer, I can look for a German anatomopathologist—'

'There aren't any!' Clauberg interrupted with a burst of nasal laughter Hugo found deeply annoying. 'All the anatomopathologists here are Jews.'

'I want to speak to the Kommandant,' Frau Braun insisted, trembling.

She put on her leather gloves and touched Anita Kunig's elbow lightly, as a sign to leave. 'I will not allow the mockery of an autopsy by a Jew. You'll have to be content with a few minutes alone with my husband. I want him in the family tomb as soon as possible, with the honours he deserves!'

Tristan Voigt hurriedly gestured at those present, who left the chapel of rest one by one, as did Frau Braun. 'I'll wait outside,' he said.

Hugo was left alone with the body in the most absolute silence: if there was anything he valued about the dead, it was their ability to keep quiet, not complain and not raise an unnecessary racket.

Hugo put down his stick and sat on a chair.

He was still holding his hat and realized he was so tense he was wringing it. This was a bizarre situation. Before him lay a man on a stretcher, dead because a piece of apple had got stuck in his windpipe instead of going down his oesophagus. An apparently easy case. He'd picked a bad place to die, though, because here there was so much suffering it made ghosts real, and now he'd dragged Hugo here, too.

He sniggered. Nebe had sentenced him to quite a punishment, there was no doubt about that. He would rather have stayed in sooty Berlin and risked being hit in the head by a British bomb but, instead, he'd ended up in the *anus mundi*, as Voigt called it.

He heaved a loud sigh and massaged his jaw. After a day's travelling, he was bristly, or perhaps it was merely tiredness that made him feel so untidy. He pulled his coat away from himself and stuck his nose inside it. The dead man wasn't the only one who stank. He needed a hot shower, a dose of morphine to soothe the pain and several hours' rest. On the days when he had a relapse, he felt like a good-for-nothing old rag instead of a bloodhound ready for action.

Hugo put his hat on the chair and approached Braun.

He stared at the corpse for a long time before feeling

his belly and neck. There were no visible marks on his skin. The wedding band was missing from his ring finger, but you could see the thin white line left by it. Why had Braun removed the symbol of eternal love for his wife?

He squeezed Braun's mouth with his fingertips and prised open the jaw. At the back of the throat, between the tonsils, he could see the piece of apple. Too close to the surface to have caused choking, unless it had come back up during a late attempt at resuscitation. He smelled it but perceived no particular odour, except for the sourness of the by now rancid apple. He examined the mouth again and thought he could make out one or two lesions in the mucous membrane of the right cheek and on the tongue. He closed the mouth and continued to feel the neck, the lymph nodes under the jaw and the cervical spine. He moved the face left and right, forcing it a little. On the left side of the neck, just behind the ear, there were small scratches. He pulled the jacket collar away and saw light red hypostases.

Finally, he removed the dead man's hat. On the balding forehead, there was swelling, apparently caused by an object that had left a mark on the skin. A hard object, not very large, he thought, but with an irregular surface.

Hugo put the hat back on Braun's head, adjusting it as best he could, then smoothed the folds of the jacket and the insignia of rank in a respectful gesture. It occurred to him that Frau Braun was right: an autopsy would be a mockery. And yet something weighed heavily on his chest, a feeling that had alerted his senses. Sigismund Braun had died, that much was clear, but it had nothing to do with ghosts, even though the place was riddled with them. It had to do with the living.

Hugo put his own hat back on and left the chapel of rest.

He glanced at the shadows dancing on the walls, where the candles were now burning with a dying flame. One had gone out and the wick was giving off a strong smell of wax.

He walked down the corridor, which seemed oddly longer and narrower than earlier.

He wasn't the sort who believed in ghost stories and wasn't easily scared, but this block was undeniably gloomy and grim. The corridor looked like a narrow tunnel and a pale light came in through the few open windows, swelling the shadows and making them seem monstrous. The buzzing of the light bulbs was like the background to the most perfect horror story. In a place like this, it was unsurprising that tales about ghosts quickly took root.

As he was about to take the stairs, Hugo heard a sound behind him, perhaps the echo of his stick on the floor.

He stopped.

He thought he saw movement in the spot where the darkness was thickest, beyond the agitated candle flames.

'Is someone there?' he asked.

He saw two eyes and a lock of hair.

Then, as suddenly as it had appeared, the 'ghost' vanished.

4

Gioele flattened himself against the cold wall until he became one with it. He felt the icy chill against his thighs and held his breath.

He'd left the dormitory a moment earlier. He was the only one with the courage to leave his bed and face the dark corridors. Since Dr Braun had died, the other children were afraid to wander around even during the day. He'd told everybody what had happened, partly to act all grown up, and partly to scare them. He'd said that the doctor's tongue was swollen, his mouth open and his eyes so bulging they were practically popping out of their sockets to join Uncle Mengele's collection of eyeballs. He'd laughed while the others had cried, terrified by the macabre image.

That night, however, he'd dreamed about Braun and he'd appeared even more frightening. He'd heard that the body would be on display in a room for three days and wanted to see it again, to make sure he remembered it well so that his dreams wouldn't take the place of what he'd really seen. That was why he'd hopped off the bed and ventured into the block, following the women's voices.

Finally, he'd found it.

It was past a room full of flowers, with burning candles that cast their quivering, scary shadows on the wall. He'd waited patiently in the darkest corner until everyone had left.

The last one to leave had been a tall, young man who dragged his leg oddly, leaning on a stick. He wore a grey coat – not like the ones the SS men had, but an ordinary cloth coat, like his father's. Except for the red band with the swastika around his arm. When the man had turned to look in his direction, he'd also seen his face: pale, cold eyes; straight nose and sharp chin, just like the other Germans. And yet there was something about him that was less dangerous than the camp's SS men.

The man in the grey coat had looked around, then vanished at the end of the corridor.

Finally free to come out into the open, Gioele took small, nervous steps into the room.

Braun was lying on a stretcher and they'd put his uniform on him instead of the lab coat. His eyes were closed now and his tongue was no longer hanging out. His mouth was shut tight, his moustache looked freshly trimmed and he looked almost as if he was ready for a party. Gioele walked around him and stood on tiptoe to smell his face, his heart in his throat for fear Braun would wake up at any moment and devour him.

He no longer had the same odours as when Gioele had found him.

Now, Braun just smelled sour.

When Fritter, Gioele's dog, had died, his mother had told him that they'd have to bury her right away or she'd stink within a couple of days. Gioele had then realized that when life departs, it takes all that's good away with it; whereas death comes quickly and corrupts everything. Including smells.

That was happening to Braun too.

Gioele took a step back to have a better look at him, but caught a movement with the corner of his eye and glimpsed a shadow on the floor that made his heart leap to his throat. Someone grabbed him by the neck and, in his panic, he thought it was a ghost.

'What are you doing here?' the apparition howled.

It dragged him away from the body with such brutality that Gioele wasn't even able to turn around. He was hurled to the floor, his face slamming against the leg of a chair, his lip split. The ferrous taste of blood spread in his mouth and fear made his legs weak.

'You little worm!' the voice said. 'Filthy Jew!'

Gioele looked up. Betsy was glaring at him with such hatred, he truly did feel like a worm, so he tried to crawl towards the door. But she didn't let him. Instead, she slapped him so hard that his cheek burned and his eyes filled with tears.

'Jew!' she shouted angrily. 'Jew!'

'Stop it, Betsy!' Adele rushed in, her shoes clicking on the granite floor. 'Leave him alone. He's one of Mengele's children.'

Betsy quivered and Gioele knew she was about to hit him again, only something stopped her. Perhaps Adele's words. Or maybe the realization that, if she really hurt him, Mengele would be furious and have her dismissed.

'Lucky you that the friend of the Jews has arrived,' she hissed, adjusting her hair, which had got a little messy in the frenzy. She rubbed her hands as if to keep them still.

'Stop that nonsense,' Adele replied calmly. 'I cannot allow you to compromise Dr Mengele's test subjects. He needs them for his research.'

Betsy gave the dead body lying next to them a look of contempt. 'Braun pretended not to see the way you treat these rats, but from now on things are going to change. From now on worse times will come for you, too.'

'Stop it, Betsy.' Adele sighed then turned to help him off the floor. Gioele stood back up, his legs still shaking, and she brushed the lock of hair from his forehead. 'You're the boy who found the body, aren't you?' she asked.

Gioele nodded gingerly.

'You didn't find anything unusual in that room, did you?'

He shook his head vigorously, hoping his eyes, glistening and open wide, wouldn't betray him and reveal his lie.

'Now get out of here,' Adele said, more abruptly.

Gioele didn't have to be told twice, he dashed out and ran to his room, his breath stinging his lungs, his heart in his throat. He slipped under the covers of the bunk bed and licked his injured lip. The blood tasted odd, like iron, like licking a coin.

Gioele slipped his fingers into a gash in the mattress and took out a small, B-shaped, gold medallion. He'd found it under the Christmas tree in Braun's office. He turned it. There was a date engraved on the back: 4 December 1931. He rubbed the edge and the little diamond that glittered in a corner of the letter B, then put it back into the gash in the mattress.

That was his treasure.

A little treasure for when he left the camp with all his family.

5

The medical room where Dr Braun had worked smelled of chemicals and floor detergent. It was a large, tiled rectangle, with islands for dissections on one side, and burnished iron machinery on the other. There were neatly set out rows of formaldehyde tins on the shelves, with a basket of shiny apples and some anatomy manuals between them.

Hugo noted that the doctor's private area was more welcoming.

The bookcase and leather armchairs summoned an image of Sigismund Braun sitting and smoking a cigar, or reading a good book. On the other side of the room, there was a desk with microscopes and a photograph of the Führer, the decorated Christmas tree that gave off a scent of resin, and a cast-iron stove. No tragedy seemed to have taken place here: everything had been cleaned and the smell of detergent blended with that of tobacco, which still permeated the walls. The doctor's lab coat was hanging from a hook, the desk was tidy, all the books where they belonged.

Hugo sat behind the desk and looked at the microscopes. Everything had been put back in its place, because no one had thought it appropriate to treat this place as a crime scene. That meant he wouldn't find anything of interest here, neither evidence of choking nor a clue to support his own gut feeling: the room was a box emptied of any useful clues.

And yet he'd learned from experience that something always remained behind.

Hugo looked down. Next to a notepad lay a Kaweco Luxe fountain pen. He swiped his index finger over the letterheaded paper but felt nothing except the irritating tingling that had been numbing it for days. He tried again with his middle and ring finger and gave a start.

This time, he could feel deep furrows, as though someone had pressed down hard while writing.

He took the box of charcoal out of his suitcase and brushed some lightly on the paper. As the rough pores of the paper retained the blackness, a white inscription emerged:

DOLL O A B

'What the hell is this?' he muttered.

His heart raced. Again, that feeling of emptiness between his breastbone and stomach, which he called 'intuition'.

Braun, or someone else, had written these words on the sheet on top of this one, which had been torn off. The letters had been left behind as a relief on the sheet beneath, like the imprint on a plaster cast. Was it a message for someone?

Hugo carefully picked up the fountain pen with a handkerchief and looked at the nib. The tines were slightly bent forwards and the slit that carried the ink was widened, as though someone had pressed too hard when writing. He placed the nib in a paper bag and the message in another.

He stood up and examined the room one more time, then went back down to the ground floor and made his way to the front door of this gloomy place. He turned one last time towards the patients' rooms, a long row of doors that looked like closed mouths, and opened the front door, letting in the frosty air.

Outside, the snow was coming down thick. It swirled in the floodlights, coating everything and muffling sound.

The roll-call square must be empty by now. The prisoners were back in their dormitories and the SS men huddled in their lodgings. The soldiers on sentry duty were still on the watchtowers, scanning the illuminated area, and Hugo felt sorry for them.

Tristan Voigt was waiting for him at the bottom of the steps. He'd closed his umbrella and the snow had covered his coat and buried the skull and crossbones and the eagle with the swastika on his hat. He was smoking a cigarette, heedless of the wet filter, looking around as if he were standing on the edge of the most beautiful landscape.

'Did you discover anything interesting, Herr Fischer?' he asked, glancing at him.

'I can't say anything definite before the autopsy,' Hugo replied, turning up his collar. 'The piece of apple isn't wedged in the windpipe. It may have come back up—'

'But to prove that, you need a dissection,' Voigt said, proffering a silver cigarette case that gleamed in the searchlights from above. 'I warn you: Braun's wife has a lot of power here in the camp. Her father is a Gruppenführer in the Waffen-SS.'

Hugo took out a cigarette and lit it. 'I need that autopsy, whether Frau Braun wants it or not. A dead body is like the snow: sometimes, everything on the surface looks present and correct, perfect and clean. But it's underneath that the murkiest things are concealed.'

Voigt nodded, his gaze wandering down the driveway. 'It's true that snow makes even the worst things pleasant,' he said, still scanning the Stammlager, a barely perceptible sadness in his eyes.

Voigt was right, Hugo thought, this whiteness made Auschwitz look like a remote suburb in the snowy mountains. In some spots, the floodlights dispersed the shadows, in others, the darkness solidified, turning parts of the camp into an asphalted mass, and yet the atmosphere was still fairy-tale-like.

'If that piece of apple didn't cause Braun's death,' Voigt asked, 'what did?'

Hugo shrugged his shoulders. 'I must find out.'

'So it's not death from natural causes?'

'Let's just say that I have a gut feeling . . .'

Hugo took a drag on his cigarette. He felt snow crystals prickling his face, carried by gusts of wind that made them eddy everywhere. He thought about the doctor's cold skin, the group of people gathered in mourning around his remains, his wife, the two German nurses and the Jewish woman with frightened eyes.

Hugo indicated the door behind him. 'What was wrong with that female prisoner?' He couldn't shake off the memory of Bethany Assouline wiping the blood from her calf.

Voigt threw his cigarette down and crushed it under his polished boot. His gesture annoyed Hugo. He couldn't say why until the sound of snow crunching under the sole brought back the head of the baby, imploding under the fury of the SS officer's stamping.

'She's just a Jew,' Voigt replied, silencing him. 'If I were you, I'd avoid asking too many questions about the Jews. It could put you in a bad light. Your only concern is the Braun case.'

'Of course, Herr Voigt.'

Recalling Nebe's advice, Hugo swallowed the smoke along with his frustration. He stabbed the ground with the tip of his stick to calm himself down and clasped the handle tightly. He looked up at Block 10 and his gaze travelled along the locked windows and the wall that separated it from Block 11. There was something menacing in these two adjacent buildings. They seemed like hard faces, with piercing eyes, cruel mouths and skin made of coarse, worn bricks. They were concealing something Voigt either couldn't or wouldn't tell him. Something it was better not to investigate. Something that should be left undisturbed beneath the cloak of snow.

'I'd like to meet the Kommandant now,' he said with a sigh.

'That is a reasonable request,' Voigt said, smiling, less hostile, and gestured at the driver who was waiting for them in the Kübelwagen.

6

It was a brief ride in the Kübelwagen.

Through the steamed-up window, Hugo made out the orderly sequence of blocks, brick-built with sloped roofs. Along the street, trees reached upwards, majestic, with bare, whitened branches.

The Kübelwagen parked outside the Kommandant's building and Voigt escorted him to his office. Hugo knocked while mentally reviewing everything he'd learned about him before leaving Berlin.

Arthur Liebehenschel had been in charge for only a month and a half. He'd replaced Rudolf Höss, who'd been transferred to the SS central finance and administration office. There were odd rumours in Berlin about his transfer, the most tactless claiming he'd had an affair with an Austrian prisoner: a stain that had to be washed away quickly.

Liebehenschel had dealt with prison camps from the moment he'd joined the SS-Totenkopfverbände, the Death's Head Units. Everyone described him as a mild-mannered man, but self-confident enough to undertake a rise to power from common Scharführer to Kommandant of the Auschwitz camp.

Hugo opened the door and found him sitting at a mahogany desk. The light from a table lamp caressed Liebehenschel's slim form, his long, oval face and protruding eyes. The pomaded hair made him look more like a business-man than the head of a place with such a dismal reputation.

Hugo greeted him as soon as he came in. 'Heil Hitler!'

'Heil Hitler!' Liebehenschel echoed.

The contrast in temperature with outdoors was signifi-cant, obliging Hugo to unbutton his coat before sitting down. Melting snow dripped to the floor and formed two large puddles.

'I'm sorry,' he said.

'Don't worry,' Liebehenschel replied with a smile.

He invited him to take a seat and Hugo obeyed, shaking his hat and making himself comfortable despite his muddy clothes and the humidity gnawing at his joints.

'Hugo Fischer,' Liebehenschel began 'one of the Reich's best criminologists. Other countries would do anything to have you. I've heard that Harvard offered you a contract few would have refused. Your loyalty to Germany does you honour.'

'You flatter me . . .'

'Not at all. It's all written down here.' Liebehenschel tapped on a file he'd taken from a stack of papers. He opened it, cleared his throat and read, 'Graduated in Psychology from Friedrich Wilhelm University, first took a post at the University of Heidelberg, then again in Berlin, where he obtained a doctorate and wrote the manual *Kriminologie*. Has been working with the Reich's criminal police department and writes for the journal *Kriminalistik*, a beacon for any self-respecting criminologist. Enrolled at the faculty of medicine a year ago. Arthur Nebe says you have a brilliant mind and a rising career. An extraordinary education for one so young. How much Pervitin did you take to get this far?'

The Kommandant had spoken in one breath, concluding his last sentence with a little laugh, implying that Hugo had used methamphetamines to obtain all he'd earned through hard work and sweat in relatively few years.

Hugo looked at him, unperturbed. He couldn't understand why Liebehenschel had asked Nebe for the best criminologist on his team. Why was the man in charge of Auschwitz so certain that Dr Braun's death required the intervention of an outside investigator?

'You must be wondering why you're here,' Liebehenschel said, pre-empting him and saving him from embarrassment.

'I won't deny it, Herr Kommandant.'

Liebehenschel smiled benevolently. He got up and went to stand next to a small Christmas tree, motionless against a map of Auschwitz that represented the Stammlager Auschwitz I, Auschwitz-Birkenau, the detached camps and the Buna-Werke plant: a true colossus, a factory before it was a detention centre, where prisoners worked non-stop.

'Tell me a little about yourself,' he said, pouring coffee and handing Hugo a cup. 'You joined the Party only three years ago. How come?'

Hugo shrugged while formulating his response. He'd joined only to enjoy more benefits and to be able to work at the RSHA. He'd been a Hitler sympathizer when he was just a boy and the man who would then become the Führer was a soldier who went around talking to ordinary people, those who no longer had jobs, who'd been humiliated by the Great War. When France had occupied the Ruhr area as an act of punishment, Hugo was only thirteen and had felt fire raging inside him. It was his father who'd dampened his enthusiasm and shown him the intolerable side of this new party, the small acts of violence with which it was hoping to get ahead. When the Führer had taken full power, several years later, joining the Party was the only way to have a normal life, even for his father. For Hugo, on the other hand, it had been the only pass to working with the Kriminalpolizei, which had been absorbed by the SS and their central office.

Hugo looked at the Kommandant and considered which of those things it was best to omit.

'Better late than never,' Liebehenschel said curtly, delivering him from the fix. 'Do you have a family?'

'No. I'm not married yet.' Hugo sipped his coffee, feeling more at ease. It was top-quality coffee, with an aroma that made him forget the cold and the snow, his drenched clothes and the smell of burnt flesh. 'Otherwise, I wouldn't have had time to do everything you read in my file. Why do you ask?'

'Because Germany needs more children, now more than ever. Children with superior minds like yours, of pure German blood, with no genetic flaws . . .' Liebehenschel looked down at the lame leg.

'I had poliomyelitis,' Hugo said, lying before the Kommandant could ask if his limp was a hereditary defect, a flaw in the perfect Aryan machine. 'In any case, I was luckier than most. I've heard of people forced to live with an iron lung or in a wheelchair for the rest of their lives.'

Liebehenschel played it down. 'Apparently, Roosevelt suffered from the same disease.'

'So I've heard.'

'Once the war is over, the Führer will institute polygamy,' the Kommandant continued. 'Every Aryan man will be able to make more women pregnant, and the more children we give Germany, the better. This war has claimed too many victims . . .'

'I find it hard enough to handle one woman, let alone more than one!'

'The Führer commands and we obey,' Liebehenschel replied with a bovine stare, not picking up on the humour. 'We have a moral duty to give Germany more children.'

The Kommandant looked out of the window with sadness. Beyond the green curtains, the snow was so thick you couldn't see the rest of the camp. Hugo could easily guess his thoughts: at the front, soldiers were dropping like flies from the cold and the grenades, and more would die unless the increasingly daring British bombing raids stopped. Soon, repopulation would become a serious issue. That much, Hugo had to admit, was true.

'Why am I here?' he asked after a long pause.

Liebehenschel took a sip of coffee. 'I won't allow a German to be executed by firing squad for a crime he may not have committed, while the real killer is on the loose.'

Hugo put down his cup. 'Who are you talking about?'

'Berto Hoffman.' Liebehenschel opened a box of cigars and proffered it to him. 'Nobody liked his reaction to Braun's death, and some officers are convinced he's involved. But no one knows how. He'll be court-martialled because he tried to help political prisoners by selling green triangles, and I expect him to be tried for that crime alone, not for alleged ones. There's a big difference between transfer to the front and a firing squad for murder, don't you think? Höss would have had him executed by now – he was trigger-happy – but I will not permit hasty executions like his to continue under my command.'

'You seem certain that Dr Braun was murdered.' Hugo took a cigar and studied it. Like the coffee, it was of the highest quality. The leaves had been carefully rolled and gave off an unmistakable aroma. It was almost as though the Kommandant was trying to surround himself with beautiful, valuable things in order to survive a place considered the anus of the world.

'*Puro habano*, very hard to find,' Liebehenschel said, showing off. He lit the cigar and took a long, fragrant puff that dissipated in the air. Then, after a brief smile, he became serious again and took a paper envelope out of a drawer, placing it on the desk and motioning Hugo to open it. 'Do look at the contents.'

Hugo clenched the cigar in his lips without lighting it. He picked up the envelope and pulled out a piece of creased, coarse paper, the kind used for drawing. It was wrinkled from the humidity and there were halos over which the typewritten letters had faded. One corner was burned and concealed part of the writing. The essential fragment of the message was still legible, however:

THIS EVENING BRAUN WILL BE DEAD AND WE'LL BE FREE

As he read the words out loud, Hugo felt a shudder run up his spine to the back of his neck, which was still moist from the snow. A recollection surfaced from the discoloured images of his past.

When he was a child, his father would take him on holiday to Wattenmeer.

The first time he'd been there, the tide was low. The impetuous waves of the North Sea had given way to a long, interminable stretch of sand full of starfish, shells and sand worms. It was as though someone had drunk all the water and left in its stead a muddy bottom that blended with the distant line of the horizon. Six-year-old Hugo had stood shivering in his jacket and knee-length trousers – restless, impatient, disappointed. 'You need to be able to wait,' his father said. 'Sooner or later, the tide will come.' The sea arrived after a four-hour wait, which Hugo spent running along the water's edge, collecting shells smelling of salt. It came in gradually and majestically, foaming as though intent on eating all the dry land: the wait had truly been worthwhile.

Now, Hugo felt the way he had on that day.

The tide was coming in slowly, shaped like a tiny piece of paper. Suddenly, his presence in Auschwitz took on the form of a challenge. The gut feeling that had stung him a moment earlier was becoming a certainty: Liebehenschel wasn't worried about ghosts but about flesh-and-blood people.

'They call these messages "IOUs",' he said. 'Prisoners often use them to communicate among themselves, only they're usually handwritten . . .'

'Who in the camp has access to a typewriter?' Hugo asked.

Liebehenschel burst out laughing. 'Olympias are available to all the SS men and a large number of people have access to them.' He indicated his own, on a writing desk against the wall in a corner of the room, next to the bookcase. 'Braun's colleagues all have them for writing reports. I know it's not much help, but this note proves that Braun was murdered. He didn't die from choking.'

'You're right.' Hugo looked for the note he had retrieved from Braun's office and put it on the desk.

Liebehenschel nibbled at his cigar and puffed smoke through his thin lips. 'What is it?'

'"Doll OAB",' Hugo read out loud. 'Does that ring any bells? Someone wrote a message on the notepad with Sigismund Braun's letterhead and pressed so hard that the letters left an imprint on the sheet beneath. I managed to get the words by spreading a little charcoal powder over it.'

'"Doll",' Liebehenschel whispered without taking his eyes off the paper. 'And initials . . .'

'Do you recognize the handwriting?'

'It's Braun's.' Liebehenschel took a briefcase and looked for a certificate issued by the doctor. He compared the handwriting. 'It's undoubtedly his. Is it a message for us?'

'If Braun didn't usually press so hard when writing, he may have wanted to leave a coded message. Maybe the attacker noticed him writing and tore the page out to get rid of it. Only they didn't take the trouble to check the one beneath it. An oversight in a moment of panic.' Hugo made a calculated pause. 'Was Braun's office in disarray when his body was found? Was there anything strange?'

Liebehenschel shook his head. 'Nothing out of the ordinary. Everything was in order, but that doesn't mean there wasn't a struggle and the killer didn't tidy up afterwards . . .'

'So did the attendants, contaminating the crime scene,' Hugo said.

'Who could possibly have expected it to be murder? I gave the order to clear everything up and prepare Braun for the chapel of rest. I started having doubts only when I was sent this note. It was found near the personal effects warehouse. Yesterday afternoon, a non-commissioned officer who was having the area shovelled found it. The snow had fallen from a laden tree, along with quite a few branches and part of the rotting trunk, and buried it.'

'Someone wanted to burn it and get rid of the message,' Hugo remarked. 'They didn't wait for it to burn entirely, either because they were afraid of being discovered or else someone took them by surprise, so they left it there, not thinking that the snow would fall from the tree and extinguish the flame.'

Liebehenschel bent down to pick up something else. 'Here's the apple found next to the body. It might be of help.'

Hugo took the bag and looked into it. He noted the imprint of the bite, compatible with the size of the chunk stuck in Braun's throat. It already smelled sour and the flesh had turned brown.

'I have a good photographer here at the camp,' the Kommandant said. 'And also a good ophthalmologist.'

Hugo frowned, confused. He finally lit his cigar and took a deep drag that left a pleasant taste on his tongue and palate but didn't erase the sense of unease that had been oppressing him since his arrival.

'In order to analyse the retina,' Liebehenschel explained. 'The killer may have been impressed on Braun's retina, right?'

'That theory is out of date.' Hugo massaged the bridge of his nose. He hadn't been able to take even a single dose of morphine during the journey and the humidity was now seeping into his bones, aggravating the symptoms of his illness. 'The retina isn't really able to photograph the last image it sees. I consider these notions obsolete, now, like Lombroso's theories on criminal anthropology.'

'The Lombroso method is of indisputable value,' Liebehenschel replied, cutting him short. 'Italians are short and dark, and most of them are criminals.'

Hugo corrected himself. 'Of course.'

Too tired to hold his tongue, he'd forgotten he was talking to a man who interned Jews precisely on the basis of these theories. He'd spent months studying and debunking the notion of 'criminal by birth', according to which criminal behaviour was inherent to a person's physical characteristics, but this wasn't the right place to argue about them, he decided.

Liebehenschel extinguished his cigar and interlaced his fingers on the desk. He bit his lower lip, picking at the skin peeling off his chapped mouth, then stood up, took a shiny bottle of cognac and handed it to Hugo as though to seal a pact.

'Find out who killed Braun,' he said. 'Do it using every means available to you, including techniques you consider obsolete, if necessary. I don't want a murderer to remain on the loose in this camp, nor will I allow an innocent man to be executed.'

Hugo accepted the gift with a faint smile. The camp, from what he'd seen at the train station, was filled with murderers on the loose.

'It shall be done,' he replied. 'There are, however, a few prerequisites without which I cannot work. First and foremost, I need to perform an autopsy, even if Frau Braun is against it. The retina theories are outdated, but a good autopsy is the cornerstone of many cases. I must also ask your permission to question Berto Hoffman and have freedom of movement here and in Birkenau.'

Liebehenschel drummed his fingers on the desk and pressed his cigar into the ashtray again to extinguish the trickle of smoke still coiling in the air. With a nervous gesture, he spun the globe, which had pins stuck into the lands conquered by the Third Reich.

'You'll get a pass,' he finally said. 'But nothing you see in Birkenau must ever leave the camp. Do you understand?'

'Of course, Herr Kommandant. I've been told nothing else for days.'

'You can speak to Hoffman. As for Frau Braun, I'll make sure she sees sense.'

'Thank you.'

'One more thing: no one knows about the message found at the warehouse, except me and the SS man who picked it up. Make sure you don't broadcast this information and always watch your back.'

'It shall be done, Herr Kommandant,' Hugo said again.

7

The officers' lodgings in the camp were Spartan. The room allocated to Hugo had a bed, a desk and a blazing iron stove. Through the window, the beam of the searchlight split the darkness like a blade. Hugo glanced outside, then looked down at the desk, on which someone had left a cigar and a welcome note.

'It's not luxurious, but you'll be comfortable here,' Tristan Voigt said, putting the suitcase on the bed, which creaked. 'The Kommandant thought you'd find it more convenient here than in a farmhouse outside the camp or in the town of Auschwitz. This way you won't have to travel back and forth. In any case, you'll find everything you need here, from a barber to a dentist.'

'It's perfect, thank you.'

Hugo's gaze wandered. In a corner of the room, a young fir tree had been arranged, with unlit candles resting on the branches. It gave off a pleasant scent of resin, a fragrance that made him think of Christmases at home.

He was sorry to be spending the holidays in a place like

this. After the RAF bombings of Berlin, he'd promised his father they would be together. They'd decorate the house and light the candles on the tree in the lounge despite the black cloak that had soiled the city after the bombings. Adolf Hitler had attempted to eliminate Christian traditions in their entirety, but they were too deeply rooted. And so, this year, too, some people had hung wreaths on the front doors of gutted buildings and turned on the lights in spite of streets cluttered with debris, torn rails and carcasses of trams. The Kaiser-Wilhelm Memorial Church had collapsed, but the children's choir would once again be singing at the foot of the bell tower, which had miraculously survived.

Hugo shook his hat, which was dripping, and put it on the chair.

Whether he liked it or not, he was in Auschwitz and had to solve this case quickly if he wanted to return to Germany. He looked at the piece of paper on the desk and remembered the two notes in his coat pocket. What did 'doll' mean? What did the initials stand for? And why would a man about to die write such a mysterious message? There was no doubt about the other 'IOU': somebody wanted Sigismund Braun out of the way.

He rubbed his jaw and once again glanced at the snow-covered blocks outside the window. The fairy-tale landscape made him sleepy.

Hugo put a hand in his pocket. His fingertips caressed the morphine bottle. It wasn't yet time to rest, he decided.

He took his hand out of his pocket, fighting off tiredness and a desire to be alone. 'Tell me, Herr Voigt, what did you say the brothel in Block 24 is called?'

'The doll's house.'

'*Doll.*'

'What?'

'Nothing.' Hugo sighed. He took the bottle of cognac and ignored the pain, even though the only thing he yearned for at that moment was the needle of the syringe in his vein and that slow, warm tide, so similar to the one in Wattenmeer. 'Can you take me to the brothel? I need company while I drink, because this cold has seeped through my bones. I don't think I'll be able to get to sleep alone here.'

'As you wish, Herr Fischer.'

Block 24 was the first building on the left as you entered the camp, next to the kitchens and the roll-call square. It was identical to the other blocks, cubic, with red bricks and a small awning covered in a soft layer of snow that glistened in the light of a little lamp post.

From this vantage point, you could see the dark profile of the camp's communal gallows. There were two bodies hanging. A man and a woman swaying in the wind. Their hands kept meeting, as though wanting to clasp each other once more, even in death. They rocked slowly in the snow that was falling so densely it took your breath away.

Hugo walked past them, pausing for a moment, then followed Voigt to the brothel. The doors of Block 24 opened and music swept over them and spread across the camp, breaking the snowy silence. Hugo closed his eyes. He heard violins, trumpets, drums and a piano flirting with one another and blending with the clink of glasses and excited chatter. The air was thick with smoke. It was like being back in a bar on Unter den Linden or Friedrichstraße; at the Scala, before the bombs destroyed it, with its red neon sign and the dancers with feathered hats and sequins that caught the light; at the Eldorado,

61

before the Party closed it down, accusing it of being a homosexuals' club.

When he opened his eyes again, he was standing in a room with flaking walls and plaster bloated from the humidity and raised in countless bubbles. The SS men sitting at the wobbly tables were playing cards amid cigarette smoke and a stench of sweat. The prisoner musicians were at the far end of the room, in front of a window from which you could see the gallows, while prisoners with kapo armbands clapped in time with the music. On the stage, the conductor was beating time for a *Molto allegro* by Mozart.

'The brothel is upstairs,' Voigt explained, 'but it's only accessible to the inmates. Now if you don't mind, I'd like to go to bed. I'm sure you'll find good company.'

'Thank you,' Hugo replied.

He looked around. Braun wasn't just anybody, but a prominent figure, like all the other camp physicians, and the petty officers probably knew something more about him and, sozzled as they were, might be willing to talk to Hugo.

He went up to a table where two young men were arguing over a card game. The sleeves of their uniforms were rolled up, their legs stretched out under the table, hair tousled and cigarettes casually hanging from their lips. They looked quite cheerful, and there was nothing left of the harsh, ruthless attitude he'd seen on the Jews' ramp.

'Good evening,' he said, pulling out a chair and sitting down.

'Good evening.' The younger SS man didn't even look him in the face. He must have been twenty at most, clean-shaven, with a mop of very blond hair. He smiled, his lips curling to reveal wolf-like teeth. He slammed four aces on the table and, with a triumphant cry, reached out for the Reichsmarks he'd won.

'Fuck you, arsehole!' the other SS man yelled. He licked his cracked lips that protruded from under a prominently hooked nose, then gave Hugo a fleeting glance. 'This is the Reich's worst son of a bitch, you know? They should send him to the front with his arse in the snow!'

Amused, Hugo laughed. The two SS men burst into even louder guffaws.

'And who are you?' the fair-haired one asked.

'Hugo Fischer. I'm here to investigate the death of Dr Sigismund Braun. I imagine people have been talking of little else since yesterday – am I right?'

The young man shrugged his shoulders. 'Nasty business . . .'

The dark-haired one offered him a tankard of beer, but Hugo declined. Instead, with a theatrical gesture, he took out the bottle of cognac, which reflected all the light in the room in warm, caramel glints.

'French, one of the best reserves left around,' he exclaimed. He removed the cap, and an aroma of hazelnut and blackcurrant wafted around the table. 'Would you like some?'

'You must be joking,' the younger SS man said, embarrassed. 'That's expensive stuff . . .'

Hugo snorted. 'For heaven's sake! I've been given this bottle and a room in the officers' quarters, but I can't think of anything sadder than getting drunk on my own in such foul weather. Please keep me company.'

Overcoming his earlier awkwardness, the SS man picked up the bottle and drank in big gulps. Hugo could tell by his expression that Liebehenschel had given him a truly good reserve. When his turn came, he savoured the cognac

63

on his palate before swallowing it to warm his oesophagus.

He sighed. 'Powerful, elegant and well-balanced.'

'True,' the blond soldier said.

'You can't even tell the difference between beer and your own piss, Franz!' the dark-haired man said.

'You're a shitty bastard, Otto! Your mother cheered up half the army!'

Hugo let the bottle make a few more rounds between Otto and Franz, and waited for their laughter to grow even louder, their posture more relaxed, their eyes more vacant. There comes a moment when a drunk man is on the edge and it only takes a slight push to make him fall and lose all restraint, he thought. And these two were getting there.

'Did you know Braun?' he asked at one point, toying with the cards that were still strewn over the table. He unbuttoned his coat, loosened his tie and stretched his legs to make himself more comfortable. A sharp pain in his back made him grimace. The orchestra had started playing Wagner's *Ride of the Valkyries* and he tried to tap with his healthy foot to distract himself.

'Of course,' Franz replied. 'We know all the camp doctors. They're the ones who triage the Jews on arrival.'

'Triage?'

'Select those who can work.'

Otto gave him a dirty look. He was still too sober.

'It's not easy to choose,' Franz continued. He had the naive expression of one who has only recently come to know war and its cruelty. 'You can't throw the dice and decide. They're Jews, but they're still humans, aren't they?'

Otto shook his head and puckered his lips. 'Subhumans. They're not like us.'

Franz ignored his companion's menacing looks. 'The

doctors come to the ramp in their nice clean coats and triage them in a minute, without batting an eyelid,' he said indignantly. 'They take the place of God, that's what they do. There's one, Mengele – he's dreadful. We call him "the angel of death". He comes even when it's not his shift and chooses from the stack. He's obsessed with twins and the deformed . . .'

Otto looked around with an alert expression. Hugo sensed that this topic wasn't tolerated, not even in such a relaxed atmosphere, and that Franz was embarking on a conversation Otto considered to be dangerous.

'Did Braun also do this *triaging*?' he asked. He glanced at the bodies swaying in the blizzard outside the window. The two bodies seemed to be quizzing him with their wide-open eyes, screaming something at him through two abysses instead of mouths. The selection seemed to be about sorting those able to work from those who weren't, but there was something else in the young man's voice, a sinister barb Hugo couldn't decipher, but which clung to him like rough, uncomfortable skin.

'Yes,' Franz replied. His lock of hair fell over his forehead and he blew it off listlessly. He let an arm hang over the back of his chair and almost slid off it. 'Only he didn't come drunk. Actually, neither does Mengele. They're sober when they do it.'

'That's true,' Otto contributed this time. 'Klein's always dead drunk at the triage, and König and Röhde also drink like fish. But not Braun.' He shrugged his shoulders. 'He was a man of integrity.'

'A weakness for women, though!' Franz said.

Hugo leaned towards him. Like every other place on earth, Auschwitz wasn't immune to gossip and stories were quick to circulate and entertain prisoners and guards alike. It was these kind of stories he had to dig out.

'Dr Braun was married . . .' he remarked.

'So he was – poor doctor . . .' Franz thought aloud. 'Why?'

'Before Frau Braun arrived, he led the good life. He used to hang out here in secret. Some people pretended not to notice. Many people here pretend not to notice. I mean, only prisoners who've obtained reward vouchers have access to the brothel upstairs, and those vouchers are given only to important individuals who've distinguished themselves, like the barber and the cook. We ordinary soldiers are forbidden from setting foot there – let alone an officer. As a matter of fact, relations between an SS man and a female prisoner are strictly forbidden.' The young man's pupils widened. 'Otto and I are here just to drink, let's be clear . . .'

'What's the risk?' Hugo said, skipping over that.

'That depends.' Franz shrugged his shoulders. 'The bunker in Block 11 if you go with an ordinary person. But if you go with a Jew, they can send you to a special SS prison.'

'Did Braun often come to the brothel?'

Franz nodded, looking blank. 'Some people covered up for him. But he went with only one of the whores. A German, a real lady even if she's a Communist. They say he also had a fling with that nurse, the one with the big tits. What's her name?'

'Betsy Angel.' Otto licked the name from the tip of his lips, before moistening them with more cognac. 'The things I could do to her!'

Hugo glanced from one to the other. They were now both very drunk and in high spirits. If one of their superiors had been there, they would have spent a bad night, locked up.

'Betsy Angel,' Hugo echoed, focusing his memory on the attractive nurse he'd seen in the chapel of rest. A cheated wife might be capable of the worst kind of ill temper, but equally a lover who had to remain in the shadows would build up her own load of resentment. 'A woman who doesn't go unnoticed, I must admit . . .'

'The doll of Block 10!' young Franz agreed. He gathered his fingertips together and smacked such a loud kiss, it almost drowned out the drum roll. But what was most deafening of all was that nickname.

Hugo felt an electric shock travel up his back.

'There's no doubt: "Doll" is spot-on as a nickname.'

'It's the doctors who gave it to her,' Otto said. 'They melt as soon as she bats her eyelashes. What is it you say? A missy calls louder than a church bell.'

'It's a *pussy*,' Franz said, laughing so hard he almost fell off his chair.

'Tell me about Braun's wife.' Hugo tried to find a more comfortable sitting position but broke out in a cold sweat from the pain. He gritted his teeth and took a deep breath, only to inhale the thick smoke fogging the room. 'What happened after she arrived? Did he change?'

'Braun stopped coming here.' Franz scratched his nose and pulled a face. 'With his wife in the camp, he had to restrain himself.'

'I understand. And what's the name of the prostitute he used to go to?'

'Rose. She's on the first floor.'

'Can I meet her?'

Otto and Franz exchanged a knowing look. 'You must be feeling really lonely tonight, mein Herr!' Franz howled.

8

Rose was sitting on an unmade bed, behind a pale-coloured door with a spyhole through which an SS man monitored her having sexual relations with fellow prisoners.

She looked up as soon as he came in and her expression altered, from sad and worried to cheerful and affable.

'Good evening,' she said in a sing-song voice, motioning him to the bed.

She wasn't wearing a prisoner's clothes but a knee-length skirt, silk stockings and shoes with heels, a turquoise sweater and a string of pearls that shimmered around her neck. Even her face wasn't as emaciated as that of a prisoner. She had make-up on, her voluminous hair bounced on her neck, and she had a seductive, delicate perfume. But a shadow clouded her eyes, a hint of almost imperceptible sorrow beneath the eyeliner.

'Good evening.' Hugo remained standing in the doorway.

She smiled craftily. 'The guard won't say anything. He knows how to keep a secret for a few Reichsmark. Do come in.'

Hugo obeyed.

Before he could go up to the first floor, he'd had to face the landlady, a florid woman who'd asked him for his reward voucher, waving her flabby arms. He'd had to explain that he didn't have a reward voucher, that he was a criminologist and hadn't come for the prostitutes. 'Wash before you fuck!' she'd shouted from the bottom of the stairs, making him nearly trip from shame. 'And read the list of forbidden pleasures on the door!'

Rose tiptoed towards him, cocking her head in a pose she must have studied many times. She was short but her body was curvy like that of a film actress. She reached out to him then dropped her hand and clasped his groin. Hugo was startled, bewildered by her initiative.

'I'm not here to go with you,' he said, taking a step back to increase the distance between them. 'I'm investigating the death of Dr Sigismund Braun. Did you know him?'

Rose stiffened from head to toe. To Hugo, that meant yes.

'Are you German?' he asked.

'Bavarian. From Eggenthal.'

'That's not far from Irsee, where the hospital Braun used to work at is. Did you know the doctor from back then, by any chance?'

'No. I got to know him here, in this room.'

'I'm told he often came to see you.'

Rose shrugged her shoulders. 'A lifetime ago.'

'What was he like?'

'Friendly, polite . . . and a liar. A damned liar.'

She turned abruptly, walked to the writing table, looked at herself in the mirror and adjusted a curl on her forehead. She took a cigarette, lit it and inhaled the smoke. Her long fingers were trembling like blades of grass in the wind.

'How did you end up here?' Hugo kept his eyes on her, studying her delicate neck and elegant movements. She hadn't been a prostitute, or a criminal, outside the camp.

'They arrested me a year ago for illegal activities in a Communist organization,' she said, moving to the window. Her gaze wandered beyond the glass pane, to the snow-covered yard. 'When I came to Auschwitz, Sigismund noticed me because I was beautiful, healthy and German. He asked me if I wanted to work in the brothel and I said no. But when I arrived at the women's camp and saw the other prisoners . . .'

She turned to look at him. In her blue eyes, the pupils were inky lakes of bitterness. She went back to studying the snowy landscape and smoking slowly, tracing a shaky line on the clouded window at the same time.

'The women in the camp had shaved heads, they were thin, shapeless,' she continued. 'They looked like ghosts with their hollow cheeks. Their teeth were rotting. They were piled up on those bunk beds, in all that dirt and stench. My God, that awful stench. I didn't want to become like them. In the end, I accepted the job. I can wear make-up, use perfume, cologne and the clothes that come from the Kanada, and I have access to cigarettes, food and alcohol. I can wander around the camp freely. I sleep in a room without other prisoners, where it's warm. And all that for a few hours' lovemaking with those who need it most. Not bad, wouldn't you agree?'

'You said Braun was a liar,' Hugo said, steering the conversation back to the main topic even though he felt sorry for this woman. He could only imagine what she must have gone through. 'Why?'

'Because he told me he was in love.' Rose sniggered, tracing the word 'love' on the windowpane. She reminded Hugo again of a film actress, with teeth white as pearls, calculated movements, languid eyes lined with black pencil only slightly smeared from her last sexual encounter. A goddess in a place that smelled of death. 'He told me that once the war was over he'd take me away from this place. That we'd go back to Bavaria, that he'd leave his wife and come with me. Can you believe it? Me, a Communist, with a Nazi . . .'

Rose wiped the writing off with the palm of her hand, leaving only a wet trail through which you could see the thick, silent snowfall.

'Dr Clauberg was sure he'd sterilized me with radiation,' she continued. 'Then he discovered that radiation doesn't always work. I got pregnant and they took me to Block 10 for an abortion. There, I realized I wasn't the only one in Sigismund's heart. Or should I say pants?'

'Do you mean Betsy, the nurse?'

Rose took a nervous drag from her cigarette and her hand shook again. 'I mean Betsy, but not just her. He'd also done it with a Jew, the dirty pig, but that's something he didn't tell anybody, did he?'

'A Jew?'

'Bethany Assouline.'

Hugo recalled the Jewish nurse wiping blood from her calf. Her frightened eyes were etched in his memory like a scratch that wouldn't heal.

'Are you aware of the gravity of these allegations?' Hugo pointed his stick at her. 'You're saying that Braun committed a crime against blood purity . . .'

'I won't tell anyone else, if that's what's worrying you.

71

I don't hold any more grudges against Sigismund and won't soil his memory now he's dead.'

'Do you have evidence to back your claim?'

'While I was recovering in Block 10, I could hear noises at night. All the women on the first floor say that the block is riddled with ghosts. Ghosts!' Rose barked out a laugh and angrily extinguished the cigarette. 'One night, I got out of bed and went to check. I caught Braun mounting that Jew in his office. I kept quiet because I didn't want Sigismund to end up on the gallows, but, thinking about it, I could have reported him and got rid of the bastard much earlier.'

'You said you didn't hold any grudges against him . . .'

Rose gave a fierce smile. 'Maybe I was lying.'

'Do you think Braun's wife knew about these flings?'

'I think she asked to serve in Auschwitz because she knew perfectly well that Sigismund was incapable of keeping his cock in his trousers. As soon as she arrived, he stopped coming to the brothel.'

'Do the letters "O A B" mean anything to you?'

She shrugged her shoulders and pursed her lips like a little girl. 'Nothing. Now are you going to fuck me or not?'

'I haven't got time.' Hugo put his hat and coat back on and left.

'You'll come back to me!' she shouted after him.

Hugo couldn't help smiling. God only knew how much he needed, in that cold, a woman to make him feel healthy and fit and not a wreck who dragged himself on a dead leg, affected by an illness that never stopped hurting him.

He walked back down the brothel steps as the Overture from *Don Giovanni* drifted through the air.

9

Auschwitz, 24 December 1943

He was woken by the pale light of dawn.

Outside the hut it had stopped snowing, but clouds hung over the camp, emitting a dull glow that took away any inclination to go out and made you forget that it was Christmas Eve.

Hugo sat up in the bed.

His sick leg was there, and yet he couldn't feel it. It was as though it had been amputated. He was confronted with it every morning when he woke up, after the inconsistency of dreams gave way to the evidence of reality with unashamed brutality.

The pain, however, was something he couldn't come to terms with.

The nerve spasms took away the lucidity he needed for his work. Liebehenschel had been right about one thing: he had indeed used large quantities of Pervitin when he had to stay awake and study, but only morphine truly helped with the pain. And it could only get worse, year after year. He'd made up the story about poliomyelitis to avoid jeopardizing his tenure at the university and his job with the RSHA. If ever he got stuck for a word, was confused or saw double, he could always blame it on his heavy workload. But an illness that advanced, slow and inexorable like the tide in Wattenmeer, was another story. A story that had to be buried and kept concealed in a nation that didn't like imperfections.

Hugo took the syringe and filled it.

He held it in his teeth while rolling up his sleeve and tying a cord around his arm to bring out the vein. He inserted the needle into the blue shadow and pushed down the piston. The morphine spread a warmth that soothed everything, bringing with it a flush of heat that made him think of a woman's thighs. He thought about Rose and slumped on his pillows. He lay gazing at the damp ceiling of the room for a long time until the pain disappeared.

'Doll OAB,' he mumbled.

The spasms had ceased. But not his thoughts.

He pulled himself up slowly, in a daze, with the help of his stick. A basin of cold water had been left in a corner of the room, as well as a bar of Hellada soap and a razor. For Hugo, accustomed to shaving twice a day, it was like being served hot coffee in bed.

He rubbed his face with the soap and shaved with care, every now and then glancing out of the window. The prisoners were already at work, shovelling the snow that had accumulated overnight.

Hugo dried his cheeks, got dressed and felt ready to unravel the shroud of mystery around Braun's death. He'd woken up several times during the night, wondering about the notes in his possession and the doctor's far from virtuous life, but now that the morphine had calmed him down, he felt as though he was floating weightlessly in a bubble, with no performance anxiety, ready to think with a clear mind.

He picked up the little bag from the desk and took out the munched apple.

He turned it around in his hand, studied the brown flesh and the teeth marks in the peel. Then he put it back into the bag and took it with him.

The officers' mess smelled of coffee and was enveloped in a clattering of dishes and shouting SS men. The prisoners were distributing hot drinks, honey and Polish jams. The bread, fresh from the kitchen, spread an inviting fragrance.

Hugo noticed Tristan Voigt sitting in a corner. He wasn't wearing his coat and now the uniform with the runes emphasized his statuesque physique, offsetting his grey eyes. He had an Iron Cross pinned below his heart, a sign that he'd distinguished himself on the front. He glanced up from his coffee, saw Hugo and invited him to join him.

'Did you sleep well?' he asked.

Hugo sat down. A prisoner poured him some scalding coffee with milk. 'I slept very fitfully,' he admitted, sipping the drink.

'Was that because of the cot or because of Braun?'

'Both.'

'You see that man over there?' Voigt used the tip of his knife, heaped with jam, to indicate an SS officer. 'That's Dr Josef Mengele. The Jewish boy who found Sigismund Braun's body is a patient of his. I think talking to Mengele would be a good start if you want to throw some light on this issue.'

Voigt spread the jam on his bread, then bit into it. He licked his thumb, which was lined with cracks from exposure to the cold. He had long, tapered hands, like a pianist, but the ring with the skull and crossbones reminded you who he really was.

Hugo drank his milky coffee and finished his breakfast in silence. Then he said goodbye to Voigt and went to find Mengele outside the mess.

He found him smoking a cigar with other SS officers. He appeared to be in a good mood, judging by his demeanour – even his olive-black eyes were smiling – so Hugo approached and introduced himself without hesitation, as Voigt had advised him to.

'Good morning, Herr Doktor,' he said, holding out his hand. 'My name is Hugo Fischer – no doubt you've heard of me.'

'Most definitely!' Mengele replied with a rousing laugh. 'No one in the camp has talked of anything else since yesterday.' He clenched the cigar in his teeth and revealed the gap between his incisors, a distinctive feature in an already unique face. 'It's an honour to have you here,' he added.

Mengele felt the pocket of his coat and took out another cigar for him.

'Thank you.' Hugo lit the cigar and its aroma warmed him. The temperature had dropped and the abundant overnight snowfall had frozen. The warm tobacco immediately went down and clasped his chest like an embrace. 'I imagine you know why I've come to disturb you . . .'

'Because of Gioele.'

'Is Gioele the Jew who found Braun's body?'

Mengele nodded. 'You'll find him fascinating. A unique specimen.'

Hugo didn't think the doctor's smile and calm warranted the dreadful nickname 'the angel of death'. He looked like an affable person, and yet the flash of darkness in his eyes must have somehow accounted for that nickname. It was as though his pupils opened onto a void.

The doctor signalled to Hugo to follow him and they ventured into the deep snow.

Hugo looked around. The dogs of the SS men were bounding gleefully on the white heaps. They thrust their muzzles into them and sneezed with pleasure, following the Polish prisoners who were dragging the metal roller to smooth the road, shivering in the bitter cold. In some places, they sank up to their calves in the snow, so pulling the roller wasn't easy. You could tell by their features, tense from the effort, by their disorientated expressions, their sighs and their moans. For Hugo, too, the snow was anything but a delight, since it meant he had to drag his dead leg. He swore through his teeth and at some point almost got stuck.

'Gioele is an example of how, in an inferior race, genetics can produce an *error* which should actually be a norm,' the doctor continued, slowing down to wait for him.

'What does that mean?' Hugo asked, breathless.

'You'll see for yourself. Gioele has a twin brother. They're identical, like two drops of water, and yet I've never seen two people more different. Gabriele has dark eyes, while Gioele's are pale, affected by a typical pigmentation we call sectoral heterochromia. Basically, a small part of the iris takes on a different colour from the rest.

Apart from that, they're physically identical. Science teaches us that twins can be born from two eggs and be heterozygous, or from a single egg and a single sperm, as with monozigous ones. I'm certain that in Gioele and Gabriele's case, there was a single egg, but two sperms. It's just a supposition, of course, and not something verified by science.'

They strolled as far as the roll-call square, which was being vacated to the rhythm of the camp orchestra. Two prisoners were taking the bodies down from the gallows. A group of men was still in the square and an SS man was making them exercise.

'Jump!' he yelled sadistically. 'Turn! Bend your knees!'

The prisoners obeyed as best they could, tripping in the cold snow whenever their wooden clogs slipped off their feet. They were tired and their bodies looked like reeds bending in the wind. Even just one of these jumps must be excruciating, Hugo thought. The top of his stomach tightened and he felt an overwhelming sense of powerlessness.

'The differences between these twins don't stop at the eyes.' Mengele's voice reclaimed his attention. He was gesticulating with the hand holding the cigar, as though drawing something in the air. 'Gioele's been at the camp for a month. By the time he arrived in Auschwitz, he'd already acquired a good range of German vocabulary. His father taught languages at the University of Bologna before the racial laws, and at home they had many books. He says his father raised him bilingual and that during the journey he was able to practise extensively with SS men. As a matter of fact, he speaks German very correctly. He has an excellent memory and a marked ability for drawing, just like our Führer. And he's brighter than any other child I've ever met. As I told you, an error in an inferior race.'

'How old is your patient?'

'He's eight,' Mengele replied.

Hugo looked shocked. He wasn't surprised that a Jew should display the characteristics mentioned by the doctor, but that he should be such a young child.

'But let's speak about Braun now,' Mengele said. 'I've been told he choked on a piece of apple. Unusual for an adult.'

'Not really,' Hugo replied. 'There have been many instances of death by choking on food among adults.'

'Do you think it was an *accident*?'

'Don't you?'

Mengele produced one of his gentle, peaceful smiles. 'In the Grimms' fairy tale, the apple is poisoned.'

'That occurred to me, too,' Hugo replied, although the poisons he knew had a clearly recognizable scent and he hadn't smelled anything except the rancid smell of the rotting pulp. He took out the bag with the apple and held it up to the light.

'There's only one way to find out if it's poisoned,' the doctor said. 'Don't you think?'

'Should I do it, in your opinion?' Hugo glanced at the Alsatian running in the snow.

'For God's sake, Herr Fischer!' Mengele's eyes filled with indignation. 'Give it to me and we'll get one of the "zebra-striped" to try it.'

The doctor took the apple and approached the group of prisoners who'd finished exercising. He signalled at one of them and proffered him the apple with an inviting gesture. The man's eyes opened wide in disbelief. He probably hadn't had a square meal for days, judging by the bony shoulder blades sticking out from under his striped tunic and the way his wrinkled mouth attacked the apple, sucking it greedily. The man finished the apple in a heartbeat, thanked him and wiped his hands on his uniform, where a red triangle categorized him as a political prisoner and a letter marked him as being Hungarian.

Mengele smiled at him, like a kind benefactor, and walked back slowly.

'Now we know it wasn't poisoned,' he said, watching the Hungarian resume his position in the queue, waiting for orders from his kapo.

'Now we know,' Hugo replied laconically.

10

The tip of the pencil glided confidently on the paper, producing a dark groove.

Gioele was in the dormitory, alone.

The other twins were already in the doctor's office, but he'd feigned a tummy ache and started drawing the Bologna barracks, where the Nazis had taken him and his family before putting them on the train. What Gioele remembered most about that day was the shades of grey. It was early November, it had just stopped raining and the area outside the barracks had turned into a morass, with large puddles of water that mirrored the dark sky. The boots of the SS officers made a deafening noise. These soldiers wore grey uniforms and their eyes were like iron nuggets. Inside the barracks, a tall gentleman was tapping away at a typewriter with such a loud, rhythmical beat that it sounded like rain lashing the window. He was drawing up a list of those present in the large room, marking those who had to leave and those who could go back to their homes.

The door opened and Gioele put the pencil down on the paper, along with his memories.

When the doctor came in, he stood up from his chair, taking care not to scrape it against the floor, and saluted with his arm outstretched, as he had been taught to.

'Good morning, Uncle,' he said.

Mengele came forward with another man. Gioele recognized him: he was the gentleman with the stick and the ordinary person's coat, even though he wore the armband with the swastika. He'd seen him the night before, in Dr Braun's chapel of rest.

'Good morning.' Mengele searched his pocket and handed him two lumps of sugar. 'This is Hugo Fischer. He's here to investigate the death of Dr Braun and wishes to have a word with you.'

'All right.'

'Can he really understand us?' Hugo said.

Gioele stared, transfixed, at the man's right eye, which was darting from side to side. He couldn't work out if it was a tic or if he was doing it on purpose to intimidate him. Well, he wouldn't succeed. He wasn't scared of him.

'Of course I understand,' he finally replied.

'Where did you learn German?' the man asked.

'From my father.'

Gioele stood to attention like a little soldier. It came naturally whenever he talked about his father. 'He was a German language lecturer at the University of Bologna before he was suspended. He said he was teaching me German because it would turn out to be useful in life to know the language of a great nation.'

That wasn't true. His father's actual words had been:

'You have to speak German because it will turn out useful in life when dealing with those Hun bastards.'

After Benito Mussolini had sealed his pact – the one adults called the Rome-Berlin Axis – with Adolf Hitler, his father became convinced that teaching German to his family was important. And he was right. German was useful. When, questioned at the barracks, he'd said he was a language teacher, an SS officer had told him that interpreters were urgently needed where they were taking him.

During the journey, he and his father had revised everything Gioele knew, while Gabriele had refused. From the age of five, Gabriele had categorically refused to take part in the lessons and, after a while, had forgotten everything. Gioele, on the other hand, had carried on studying and reading books, and on the journey exchanged a few words with SS officers whenever they stopped at a station; this way, he'd discovered that some of the 'bastards' were nice, others as nasty as their dogs, but that they were generally better disposed towards those who spoke their language.

'I'll leave you together,' Mengele said. He took a few steps, then stopped and turned to look at him. 'How did you crack that lip?'

Gioele touched the crust with his fingers. 'I slipped,' he lied.

The doctor ruffled his hair affectionately and left, closing the door behind him. Gioele sat back down on the chair, beside the desk. The three-level bunk bed next to him was unmade and empty, and gave off a bad smell because someone had wet the bed that night.

'So,' Hugo Fischer began. 'It was you who found Dr Braun, right?'

'Yes,' he replied.

He paused to study the gentleman's face. Faint wrinkles formed around his eyes when he smiled and he was probably the same age as Uncle Mengele, more or less. His short haircut was impeccable, like that of all the Germans in the camp. He had a bright smile, with straight, white teeth, and a dimple that cut his right cheek lengthwise. Gioele didn't know why, but he associated dark, crooked teeth with bad people, even though almost all the SS men had perfect ones.

'Let me tell you about my job.' Hugo put his stick down and sat on one of the bunk beds. 'Usually, when a man dies, we try and find out if his death was natural or if somebody killed him. If there are any doubts, they call me. Now, they think Dr Braun died because he was eating an apple and a piece went down the wrong way. Your mother has probably told you many times to sit up straight when you eat, right?'

'Yes.'

'If a mouthful goes down the wrong way, you choke to death. That may have happened to Braun. However, the other possibility is that somebody may have hurt him. My job is to work out if this suspicion is correct or not.'

'And what can I do?'

'The room where Dr Braun died was cleaned by the staff after the body was removed. They tidied it up and I need to know what it was like when you found the body.'

'Do I have to describe it?'

'Yes, please?'

'Will a drawing be all right?'

'What?' Hugo looked at him in surprise.

Gioele wanted to help him. He was a nice man, without

fake politeness like the doctors in the block. He seemed different, like his coat. The boy got up, opened the desk drawer, took out his drawing pad and handed it to the man, who looked at the contents and stared in astonishment.

'Did you really do this?' he asked.

Gioele nodded proudly.

11

Mengele was right. The boy's eyes were extraordinary. On his tiny face, they were like two green lakes, with paler shades in the centre. In the left eye, the bottom part of the iris had a dark brown mark, like an island amid the green. It was what captured your attention the most about that skinny face.

Hugo studied him for a long time. He thought he could detect a storm in those unique irises and wondered what they might have seen. He remembered the Jews crammed into the livestock train carriage, the stench and the crushed bodies, the dead sliding through the doors of the train like water from a burst dam. He had on occasion witnessed arrests in Berlin, and seen groups of Jews escorted onto trains heading to prison camps. He'd watched them leaving with crammed suitcases, carefully labelled so they wouldn't lose them, wearing clean garments to make a good impression; but the ones he'd seen arrive were larvae hollowed out by hunger and thirst, by hours spent travelling in a cattle wagon, clothes soiled with excrement and vomit.

As for the suitcases that contained the hope of a new place where they'd live free from oppression, they'd been snatched away from them.

Gioele's voice roused him. 'So?'

Hugo looked down at the drawing again, created with minute details. It was an unbelievable sketch for a child of eight, but so would it have been for many an adult.

'It's brilliant,' he said.

'I've got others, more detailed and of the whole room.' The boy was excited. His little legs were swaying back and forth on the chair. 'I'll show them to you, but you must do something in return. If I help you, will you help me?'

Hugo frowned.

Gioele tensed from top to toe, his little body contracting under his matted jumper and short trousers. His knees were blue from the cold. Maybe he wanted long trousers or a coat, or extra food rations.

'You must look for my mum and dad,' he said.

'What?' Hugo said on an outbreath, taken aback.

'My brother Gabriele is here in Auschwitz,' he explained. 'Uncle Mengele is keeping him in the infirmary because he caught typhus. They're treating him, so I can't see him. But Mum and Dad are in the other camp.'

'In Birkenau?'

Gioele nodded and the lock of brown hair quivered on his head. 'Dad knows languages, so they must have taken him as an interpreter. Mum's a dressmaker, so she might be sewing the other prisoners' uniforms or working in the laundry. Uncle Mengele says they're well and that I shouldn't ask after them anymore, but I want to see them.'

Hugo leaned towards the boy and looked him straight in the eye. 'Why do you call him "uncle"?'

'He asked me to. He asks all the twins who come here to.'

'How many of you are there?'

'Four pairs here in this block, but there are many more in Birkenau. They come and go, they're never the same ones. So,' he insisted, his eyes boring into Hugo, 'will you look for my parents?'

Hugo drew in a long breath. How large was Birkenau? There were rumours in Berlin that it could hold two hundred thousand people, but that a large number of those died from typhus, pneumonia and hunger, even though the Reich's propaganda painted life in the camp as decent and humane. That meant the camp was never truly full, but huge nonetheless.

'So?' Gioele prompted.

Hugo gave in. 'All right.' The boy responded with an awkward smile and he felt a pang of guilt. He knew it was impossible to grant the request, but he'd chosen to give the boy hope. After the hell he must have been through, it was the least he could do. 'I'll try and help you, but first you must tell me their names.'

'My dad's name is Aronne Errera and my mum's Noemi.' Gioele opened a drawer and showed him the other drawings. 'A promise is a promise: here's the doctor's room before it was cleaned.'

Hugo picked up the drawing and studied it attentively. Gioele had drawn every detail with precision. On the desk, there were microscopes, books and papers. You could make out the letterheaded notepad and the fountain pen. There were the armchairs, the side table with the phonograph and the bookcase in a corner of the room. The grandfather clock indicated 11 p.m. On the rug on the floor, there was the apple. Braun was lying in his lab coat, sleeves rolled up to his elbows, between the desk and the Christmas tree. There were two tiny red drops on the floor.

'What are these?' Hugo asked, gently brushing the drawing with his fingers.

'Drops of blood,' the boy replied readily.

Hugo picked up another drawing. It was a close-up of the doctor. His eyes were wide open, the pupils black against the turquoise of the iris. His mouth was open and his tongue hanging out – perhaps longer and more monstrous than in real life. Gioele had drawn the bruise on the forehead, giving it an original shape that looked like a face.

'Are you sure there was blood on the floor?'

'Yes. Maybe the attendants cleaned it up, but it was there. Small, round drops.'

'Was the doctor wearing his lab coat or did you make that up?'

'Everything you see is real.' Gioele pointed at the drawing. 'He was wearing his lab coat and looked like a ghost.'

The boy opened the drawing pad and took out another sketch. A deep-blue ridge.

'And what's this?' Hugo asked, turning it under the ceiling lamp. The light quivered, faint because of the wooden shutters that prevented the sun from coming in through the windows.

'It's the smell Dr Braun had,' Gioele replied. 'One of the smells.'

Hugo smiled. He hadn't smelled anything, but some poisons are quick to disperse. 'Interesting,' he said. 'Do you want to tell me about it?'

'This blue is a perfume.' Gioele tapped on the sheet with his finger. 'A nice perfume, like what men and women wear when they're all dressed up for the theatre or a walk.'

Hugo took a sheet coloured in the same tone as clouds heavy with snow. 'And what about this grey?'

'That was in his mouth. It was a strange smell. At the same time bitter and sweet. I've already come across it somewhere, only I can't remember where.'

Hugo felt an electric shock go through him. There was a tingling sensation from the back of his neck to the base of his spine. He leafed through the drawings then returned to Braun's face. Gioele had drawn his own reflection in the doctor's pupils: the detail of a true artist.

'Try to concentrate,' he said. 'Mengele says you have an excellent memory and, from what I can see in these drawings, it's quite true. Where did you smell that odour before?'

Gioele swung his feet and looked up at the ceiling, sad. 'In Birkenau,' he finally replied. 'A week ago, Uncle Mengele asked me to go with him to translate for two Italian girl twins who were refusing to speak to the interpreters. There was a strong smell in the camp, as if they were grilling something.'

'And is that the smell you mean?'

'No. After speaking to the twins, Mengele asked me to go with him to a warehouse, so we could choose a pair of trousers that would fit me better than the ones I had on. There was a woman there, fiddling with hair. She was dividing it by colour. When I went close, I smelled a strong, sweet odour.'

'Was it the same you smelled from Braun's mouth?'

'Yes.'

Hugo picked up his stick and stood. He tapped it on the floor and took two steps forward and two back in the narrow room, which smelled musty. His heart beat faster than usual, he could hear it in his ears, and his stomach tightened as he searched for a pattern.

A friend of his, an employee at Degesch, one of the main pesticide factories in Germany, had told him of a large consignment of a fumigant called Zyklon B, which the Auschwitz Kommandant that year had ordered in vast quantities – almost five thousand kilograms – to address the problem of parasites. If the owners of that hair had had lice, they would probably have been shaved and their hair treated with cyanide.

'Is that smell by any chance like bitter almonds?'

The boy's face lit up. 'Yes,' he replied, excited. 'It was exactly like the smell of bitter almonds! My mum used to make a cake with bitter almonds. And amaretti!'

Cyanide, a very potent poison, was derived by dissociating cyanuric acid from its salt, and had the same smell as Zyklon B: bitter almonds.

'Death by cyanide provokes a kind of chemical asphyxia,' he said out loud, not so much to involve little Gioele as to convince himself. 'The pupils dilate excessively. Did you know Sigismund Braun personally?'

'Yes.'

'Do you think he was an educated man?'

'I think so.'

'Cunning?'

'Probably.'

Of course, he was. Educated and cunning. He'd realized that if he didn't leave a message, nobody would know what had really happened to him. Everyone would think

91

it was a death from natural causes. He also knew that, in order not to alert his killer, he had to write an incomprehensible message, a kind of riddle.

'Why did you draw your reflection in his pupils?' Hugo asked, sensing his intuition take shape.

'Because they were like a sort of mirror,' the boy replied.

'Were they dilated like in your drawing?'

'Yes . . .'

'Good.' Satisfied, Hugo put a hand on his head.

Braun knew Latin, he thought, and in Latin, *pupilla* – pupil – meant 'doll', because the other person's image is mirrored in it like a small doll: had the doctor sensed that someone was about to poison him with cyanide?

Hugo looked down at Gioele. 'Did you touch the body that night?'

The boy hunched his shoulders, like someone caught with his hand in the biscuit tin.

'I just want to know if he was rigid,' Hugo said to reassure him.

'He was hard as a rock.'

'It's called rigor mortis. In your drawing, the clock indicates 11 p.m. Is that when you found him?'

'Yes.'

Hugo did some quick mental arithmetic: Dr Braun must have been killed at least three hours earlier, at around eight. Exactly the time needed for the muscles to stiffen to the point of making him seem like a wooden log.

'And now tell me about the ghosts in the block,' he said. 'Do you know anything about them?'

Gioele stretched his neck and sat up straight on his chair. 'I'm the only one who's not scared of them. The girls on the floor below think the block is full of ghosts because at night they hear breathing and something like screams or moans, as if someone's crying. But I know what they are.'

'And what are they?'

'It's people doing grown-up things.'

'Did you see them with your own eyes?'

Gioele nodded. It was most probably Braun and Bethany Assouline. Or else Braun and Betsy Angel.

'Can you tell me who they were?'

'I didn't see their faces. They were in the medical room and it was dark. I came close to the door, but I was afraid they'd discover me.'

'Never mind. You've been very helpful.'

'Thank you,' the boy said with satisfaction. 'Remember your promise.'

Hugo smiled bitterly then put the drawings back. He noticed another one on the desk. It looked like barracks. Through the open door, you could see SS officers, their uniforms sketched with precision.

'What's this?' he asked.

'It's a place in Bologna, where I come from. It's called *Caserme rosse*. They put us there before taking us to the camp on the train.'

Hugo gave an embarrassed smile. Places like those were called holding camps and were used for triaging people towards prison camps. You'd leave as a family and arrive decimated, as in the boy's case. Hugo tried to distract him from these painful memories. 'You have a great football team in Bologna. Six championships and one Paris Expo trophy. What is it they say when you play?'

'*The team that makes the world quake*,' the boy recited. 'Árpád Weisz's family arrived here in October last year. Adele, the nurse, told me.'

Hugo nodded. 'Árpád Weisz.' He wasn't a great football fan, but everyone knew the Bologna coach. A Hungarian Jew, he'd turned every team he'd touched to gold, and yet that hadn't been enough to spare him the camp.

'The German soldiers arrested us during the Shabbat holiday. Dad says they did it on purpose.' Gioele shrugged his shoulders and indicated the barracks drawing. 'They took us there in the afternoon, kept us for a few days, then put us on a train. Just like the Weisz family.'

A shadow darkened his eyes beneath the thick eyelashes. In his pupils, Hugo saw once again the French mother at the station looking at the remains of her little girl, while the camp prisoners tossed lifeless bodies around her.

'It can't have been a pleasant journey,' he muttered.

Gioele shook his head and pursed his lips. Hugo wondered at his eyes still being so beautiful even after witnessing so much grief.

12

Block 11 was grim.

Everything in Auschwitz was, but Block 11 looked like a scrunched-up face with evil eyes and a mouth ready to devour you. When Tristan Voigt rang the large bell, he and Hugo heard the measured footsteps of an SS officer. Two stony eyes appeared in the spyhole, then the door opened onto a half-lit, cold, bare corridor. At the end of it, dimmed by the darkness, you could make out a grating: the waiting room to the camp jail, the place where anyone who'd attempted to escape ended up and where – forgotten for months on end – were those criminals detained by Katowice Gestapo while awaiting a verdict. So Voigt had told him as they skirted around the 'death block' – the name alone provided ample introduction.

The guard saluted. 'Heil Hitler.'

'Heil Hitler,' Hugo and Voigt echoed.

Without another word, the SS man accompanied them to the grating. Their visit had been sanctioned by Liebehenschel himself and that was all he needed to know.

The keys clanked as he unlocked the gates. He led them down a long, damp, icy corridor where dark patches stained the whitewashed walls. The air was musty. The whole place was permeated with a melancholy that made 'death block' seem an apt name for it.

The SS man opened the door and let them in.

Berto Hoffman was sitting on a cot at the end of the room, his back to a walled-up window. He was leaning forward, hunched over, as though his shoulders were crushed by a load only he could feel. The light bulb on the ceiling was flickering on the bare walls, the black floor and the bucket that gave off a pungent odour of urine. Voigt slapped the glass bulb and the light stopped flickering, though it continued to buzz loudly, filling the emptiness of the cell.

Hoffman lifted his face.

His lids were so swollen and bruised that his eyes disappeared between two folds of flesh, lips puffy, encrusted with blood. His face had been knocked about so much that Hugo couldn't reconstruct a single feature to make out what he looked like; he could only stare in horror at the tumefied mass with disproportionately enlarged bruising, all black and blue.

'You were right.' Hugo propped himself on his stick on the coarse, dirty stone floor, and glared at Voigt. 'He's not in an ideal condition to talk.'

Berto Hoffman lifted his nose to the ceiling and sniffed the air like a rat. Unable to see who had entered his cell, he sought him by smell.

'My name is Hugo Fischer and I'm investigating the death of Sigismund Braun,' he said by way of introduction.

Berto puckered his lips and Hugo really did think of a

rodent with a swollen face or an old print of Quasimodo, the deformed character in Victor Hugo's novel.

'You're one of Braun's nurses, aren't you?'

'Yes,' the man managed to mumble after repeated attempts to move his lips. Saliva trickled down the sides of his mouth and he tried to wipe it off with his cuff.

Voigt stood in a corner, his hands behind his back. He looked impeccable in his uniform and was watching the scene with a detachment that gave Hugo a bitter taste in his mouth. Voigt had before him a man beaten to a pulp, a German like himself, but he wasn't expressing an ounce of pity.

'I've been told you said something after you learned of Braun's death,' Hugo said, returning to Berto. He wished he could spare him this torture, but he was running out of time. '"It was his ghosts that took him back." May I ask what ghosts you meant?'

'It was just a joke.' Berto took a breath and leaned forward, struggling to talk. He broke into a coughing fit that made him stiffen with pain before he was able to add, 'A joke in very bad taste.'

'Were you referring to the ghosts that moan at night?'

'I don't understand . . .'

'Is it possible that the rumours about ghosts started because of strange amorous encounters at night?'

'I don't know what you mean.'

Hugo struck the floor with his stick. The air in the cell was unbreathable, heavy with tension. He was certain that Berto Hoffman was aware of Braun's many flings and that his comment about 'ghosts' could have referred to those who, with their whispers and moans, frightened Mengele's children and Clauberg's women. Either that or the past

97

infidelities Braun had had to confront. In both cases, the question of Braun's lovers was key.

'I'll speak more plainly,' he said. 'Did Braun have relations with other women beside his wife?'

'No.'

'Did you and Braun get on?'

'Yes.' Berto looked straight ahead. Like a newborn baby, he probably couldn't see anything but shadows, only he was at the other end of life, slowly heading towards death.

'Where were you on the night the doctor died?'

'In my room. I was tired. I'd been working all day.'

'What had you been working on?'

Berto searched for something in the air. Hugo noticed he was turned towards Voigt, waiting for his permission to speak freely.

The officer reassured him. 'You may continue, Herr Hoffman. Fischer is bound by secrecy and discretion on all that concerns Auschwitz.'

Hoffman nodded, licked his lips and went on. 'I was transferred to Birkenau some time ago, with another doctor.'

'How come?'

'There had been minor misunderstandings between Braun and me, and we both chose to take a break from each other.' Berto spat out a clump of saliva and blood, and took a noisy breath. 'I was assigned to Dr Schulz.'

'You said you had a good working relationship . . .'

'That's right.' Berto puckered his lips. It was obvious from his expression that pain was crushing every part of his body like pincers. Hugo knew the feeling only too well. 'We did have a good working relationship,' he insisted. 'The misunderstandings were trivial. Nothing of importance.'

'Please elaborate.'

'Just squabbles between academics . . .'

'Between a nurse and an academic,' Hugo said, correcting him.

'Yes, Braun's very words.' Hoffman tried to laugh but couldn't. 'I sometimes tend to be too proud and forget I'm just a nurse. I didn't agree with some of his methods, so he called me arrogant and sent me to follow one of Dr Schulz's experiments in Birkenau, to change my mind and see how much more humane Braun's were.'

More *humane*. Hugo felt uneasy standing up. He looked for a chair and sat down. He rested the tip of his stick on the floor and looked at the man beyond the bone handle. Auschwitz concealed unfathomable secrets and he was torn between the desire to unearth them and the necessity to act as though nothing was happening. Nebe's voice ordering him not to meddle in what was going on in the camp restrained him.

'Someone heard you say that the doctor deserved to end the way he did,' he continued. 'Was that connected to your misunderstandings?'

'I was still upset with him because of his phosgene experiment.' Berto coughed and his voice became phlegmy. 'Do you never say something you don't really believe when you're angry, Herr Fischer?'

Hugo decided not to engage. 'At what time did you go to bed?' he asked.

'I think it was eight o'clock. Straight after dinner.'

Hugo stared at the light bulb, which had started flickering again. Soon, it would burn out altogether. He raised his arm and glanced at the Junghans watch on his wrist. Braun had been found at around eleven, but he must have been dead for at least three hours to be as rigid as Gioele said he was. The time of death must therefore have been around 8 p.m.

'Did no one see you after that?'

'No.'

'Not even a colleague?'

'I told you: I went to bed straight after dinner.'

'Heavens,' Hugo said with a sardonic smile. 'The work Dr Schulz was making you carry out must have been truly exhausting!'

'It was.' Berto's voice grew stern. Hugo could have sworn that, had he been able to open his eyes, he would have given him a piercing look. Only, he kept them shut as they were too swollen. 'At the beginning of December, the Luftwaffe bombed an American ship in an Italian harbour,' he began. 'It was a ship loaded with mustard gas and phosgene, so Schulz was ordered to fine-tune the experiments already being carried out by Dr Hirt in the Natzweiler camp.'

Hugo felt the air become denser. 'What kind of experiments?'

'I had to select a number of prisoners.' Berto shifted slightly on the cot and let out a groan of pain. 'Schulz wanted deep wounds, because those of our soldiers at the front are very serious. So we made the Jews stand in a row and had them bitten by dogs. We then treated them all with phosgene and mustard gas. To some we administered urotropin, as suggested by Hirt.' He stopped to cough again and pulled his shoulders in, as though overwhelmed by spasms and the images that must have been flashing in his mind. 'In the subjects treated with urotropin, the phosgene had lesser ulcerating and scalding effects. We had to wait for the outcome of the experiment and photograph all the subjects, every hour, for a total of fourteen hours. There, Herr Fischer: that's the reason I was so tired and went back to my lodgings early. You'd have done the same.'

Speaking had demanded a superhuman effort of the prisoner. He now looked worn out and was once again hunched over, crushed.

Both Hugo's hands were numb from the story. He felt a tremor and realized his mouth was dry. He tried to swallow, but it was like ingesting sand from Wattenmeer.

It's illegal to conduct this kind of experiment was what he wanted to say.

To his side, Voigt was staring at them in silence, his dagger gleaming in the light of the bulb, the butt of his pistol peering silently from its holster. The skull and cross-bones on his hat alone was enough to make Hugo refrain from uttering that statement and asking just how many other kinds of experiments took place in Auschwitz and in other camps. He swallowed the bitter pill, as Nebe would have ordered him to, and returned to Berto.

'What can you tell me about the cloth triangles?' he asked, his voice less certain than earlier.

Berto Hoffman locked himself in a protracted silence where you could only hear the hum of the light and the rasping, phlegmy breath that inflated and deflated his chest like bellows.

'I'm innocent,' he said at last. 'They weren't mine.'

'That's all I need to ask you for the moment,' Hugo said, putting an end to the interrogation that was clearly taking an unbearable physical and psychological toll on Berto. 'It's Christmas Eve and I think you're entitled to some rest.'

Berto didn't reply. The light bulb buzzed and let out its last breath, leaving them in total darkness and with a strong smell of burning.

Outside, the snow glistened in the sunlight peering through the clouds.

Hugo filled his lungs with clean air. He still had on him the foul odour of the jail, of the rancid blood and urine left in the basin, stinking out the cell. The cold stung his nose, anaesthetizing him.

'Did you find the answers you were after?' Tristan Voigt asked.

Hugo sighed. 'No. If the SS men hadn't got the nurse in this state, he would have been much easier to interrogate.'

'You're too tender-hearted.'

'And perhaps you're too harsh.' Hugo realized he'd stepped over the line and spoken without restraint. He decided to continue. 'Hoffman is a German, a free Aryan, not a camp prisoner. He deserved to be treated differently.'

Voigt's voice turned as cold and sharp as his stare. 'Believe me, I personally made sure that Berto Hoffman received treatment appropriate to a German. You have no idea what Block 11 is like. You have no idea what's in the basement. Without my intervention, they would have stuffed him in a hole so small he would have drowned in his own excrement.'

Hugo bit the inside of his cheek. 'I beg your pardon, Herr Voigt.'

'I understand you,' Voigt said, 'but hold your tongue.'

They resumed walking in silence. Voigt proceeded straight ahead, hands behind his back, the snow creaking at his every step. After that exchange, Hugo no longer had the courage to utter the request he'd been gearing up for all morning. He knew it would be met with a refusal along with another icy look and a reprimand.

Still, he tried. 'I have a favour to ask you.'

'Go ahead. The Kommandant has ordered me to help you.'

Hugo took a deep breath. 'The twin who found Braun's body has asked me to look for his parents in Birkenau.'

Tristan Voigt gave a start, but his military stride remained unaffected. 'Herr Fischer,' he said, still walking ahead, not bothering to wait for him. 'Why are you telling me this?'

Hugo decided not to give up. He pushed his stick into the snow and limped after him.

'I wouldn't have told you if it weren't important to the investigation. The boy promised to provide me with all the details of that night in exchange for a favour. If I tell you their names, perhaps you could find them in the archives—'

'Are you telling me that you're using a Jew to find the culprit?'

'He was the only one who saw the crime scene before it was contaminated,' Hugo clarified.

'You mustn't trust him. I thought you'd be speaking to Mengele, not with his Jew.'

'He's just a child.' Hugo couldn't help laughing. 'He wouldn't lie on purpose. Why would he? Unless you think *he* killed Braun?'

Voigt stopped abruptly and looked at him with a blend of astonishment and anger. 'Let me give you a piece of advice: do not give the Kommandant the words of a Jew

103

as evidence. It would be the end of your career and – being in charge of the block – I don't want to look like an idiot because of you!'

'I'm not naive. Of course I won't.'

Voigt squinted. Hugo sensed the danger but forced himself to hold his probing glare. He glimpsed an unexpected dawn in what seemed like a dark, stormy sky.

'Do give me those names,' Voigt said, 'but be careful. Don't breathe a word of it to anybody. Here, your life and your career can end from one moment to the next. Don't take this as a threat, but as advice from a friend who's older than you.'

Hugo nodded, aware of the risks involved in revealing himself too much and coming across the wrong way. That was why he'd kept quiet for years. That was why he carefully pinned the red swastika on his coat. Many, like him, kept quiet because they knew the danger. He'd realized it back on Kristallnacht, when the SA had burned down the Berlin synagogues, destroyed the Jews' shops and ransacked their homes. The police had looked on. The firemen had merely stood on alert to make sure the flames didn't spread to Aryan shops and homes. Only Wilhelm Krützfeld, a dear family friend, had tried to save the new synagogue. In the days that followed, he'd been hunted down like the worst of criminals.

'Aronne and Noemi Errera,' he murmured after a lengthy silence.

'I'll see what I can do,' Voigt replied. 'But I can't promise you anything.'

13

Rabi Guttmann, the anatomopathologist, was waiting for him by the dissection table.

He was short and thin, with round glasses resting on a hooked nose, and protruding ears. The left-side comb-over suggested a tidy person who, despite his age and imprisonment, still cared about his appearance. Next to him, on the white tile table, lay Sigismund Braun's naked body.

'Herr Fischer, it's an honour to assist you!' Rabi exclaimed when he saw him come into the mortuary.

He was so anxious to make an immediate good impression that his hands trembled in the air. On his wrist, he wore a yellow band with COURT JEW written on it. Hugo had noticed identical bands on Bethany and other Jews, all doctors, architects or engineers. He'd heard other prisoners call them 'two left hands' with a tinge of envy because they hadn't been assigned to hard labour.

Hugo smiled, doing his best to appear affable. He didn't have the aura of a Nazi, but he was still a German and had inherited from his mother irises the colour of dull steel that made his eyes look hard and sharp. 'The Kommandant has assured me that you're an excellent anatomopathologist,' he said. 'Possibly the best in the entire camp.'

'Thank you, mein Herr, you're too kind.'

'Did you know Braun?' Hugo approached the body. The smell of death had now become dense and cloying and would soon turn into a cacophony of unbreathable odours.

'I work with Mengele,' the Jew explained, 'but I have on occasion worked for Braun. A highly educated, very experienced person.'

Hugo put his stick against the wall and removed his coat. 'Do you have a lab coat for me, too?'

'Of course.' Rabi rushed to find a spotless one that hung at the back of the door, and brought it to him. 'Are you a doctor, Herr Fischer?'

'I'm a criminologist, but I've watched so many autopsies that I feel like a doctor.' Hugo laughed and studied him. 'I enrolled at the medical faculty this year. You're lucky that you studied, am I right?' he added, indicating the yellow wristband.

Rabi nodded. 'I'm allowed to wear my own clothes.' He showed the brown cloth trousers that emerged from the white lab coat and the well-made shoes he was wearing instead of wooden clogs. 'I get good food and have a comfortable bed. I can't complain. In exchange, I see many things I'd rather I didn't.'

'I can imagine.' Hugo thought about the phosgene experiments and felt uneasy again. A cough ruthlessly scraped his throat as he put on the lab coat. 'And now I'll watch you work,' he said. 'I'm sure I have much to learn from you.'

Rabi smiled gratefully. He seemed like a reserved person. Hugo was almost convinced that Auschwitz couldn't be the *anus mundi* described by Voigt. But another part of him sensed that this wasn't a peaceful smile but one of humility and resignation. Behind Rabi's veiled expression was the horror of a man who'd been snatched away from his home and interned purely because he was Jewish.

'Just tell me how I can help you.' Hugo focused on the body to dismiss these thoughts.

'Don't worry, mein Herr, I'll do everything.'

'You mustn't be afraid of me, you can treat me as your assistant. At least for today.'

Rabi nodded and indicated the tools near the sink. 'Then pass me the scalpel, please,' he said. Then, as he was taking the piece of rotten apple out of Braun's mouth with pincers, he asked, 'What do you think he died of? Have you got a theory?'

'I certainly have,' Hugo said. 'I think he died of cyanide poisoning.'

'Did you deduce this from the dilated pupils and light red hypostasis?'

'Not only that.' Hugo watched Rabi perform a flawless lengthwise section on the body, with the firm and determined hand of a veteran. 'One of Mengele's patients told me he smelled bitter almonds as soon as he entered the room.'

'A patient?' The anatomopathologist smiled benevolently and shook his head while cutting Braun from the sternum to the pubis and stretching the edges of the skin apart. 'You mean one of Mengele's guinea pigs. Would you pass me the saw?'

'What?'

'The saw.'

Hugo picked it up from the tray and handed it to him.

'You said "guinea pigs",' he whispered. 'Why did you say "guinea pigs"?'

Rabi pulled his shoulders in. He kept his lips so tight they'd turned white. He began to saw, and some bone dust rose in a light puff. He put down the ribs he'd removed and, with an expert gesture, took out the larynx, bronchi, lungs and, finally, the heart in one go.

'Doctor Guttman,' Hugo pleaded. He grabbed Rabi by the arm, almost making the organs slip out of his hands. 'I demand an explanation.'

Rabi was startled. Hugo could see that in the doctor's eyes there was no difference between him and an SS officer. Rabi put the organs in the sink, wiped his hands and stared at him, his eyes so small they were barely visible behind the gold frame of his glasses.

'Dr Mengele has a *zoo* of unique specimens,' he confessed reluctantly. 'Gypsies, dwarves, those who are malformed, but he's especially interested in twins, because once the war is over the Aryan population will need to be increased and every German woman will have to give birth to more children at once. He performs experiments on twins . . .'

'What kinds of experiments?'

'Mainly, he measures them. He injects some virus, tries to mix the blood of two siblings. Or else he tries to change the colour of their eyes, or surgically join their bodies to see how they behave, if they really are a single organism, as people believe. He keeps most of them in Birkenau, in the Gypsy camp, but some are in Block 10. Like Gioele.'

Rabi meekly resumed washing his hands.

The room was filled with the sound of running water

in the sink. Bewildered, Hugo stood watching him. He wanted to speak but couldn't. He struggled to believe what Rabi had just told him. He felt an impulse to make him talk more and, at the same time, to forget the whole conversation. He was only the last cog in this large mechanism, without the power to stop or jam anything. Even if he dug deeper into Rabi's story, he thought, nothing would change.

Silently, Rabi dissected the lung and heart.

He returned to the body and extracted the stomach and part of the intestine.

'You were telling me about your theory a moment ago,' he said, eager to change the subject. 'Will you continue, please?'

'Of course.' Hugo nodded despite the feeling of powerlessness that made his tongue taste bitter and numbed his good leg. He wiped sweat from the back of his neck. He tried not to think of Gioele. 'I believe Braun was forced to drink cyanide. As you pointed out, the hypostases are red. The pupils were very dilated. I think Braun was with someone he trusted. Then something happened. Maybe he was pushed, or struck with a blunt object that caused the small ecchymosis on his forehead and momentary confusion, and the killer took advantage of this to ram a phial of cyanide into his mouth. I still can't work out if it was a man or a woman. After all, I can't see any signs of struggle.'

Hugo bent over the body and opened its mouth.

'There are lesions on the oral mucosa,' he added. 'I think he was forced to bite the phial. At that point, the killer took an apple and stuffed a piece down his throat to simulate choking.'

Rabi agreed. 'What you say sounds completely possible.

109

And now I'll tell you why I too think the doctor was killed with cyanide. As you know, cyanide produces extended biochemical asphyxia and the cells instantly cease to live. The state of Braun's organs matches this condition of asphyxia: they're very congested and the thin, cherry-red blood is consistent with a lack of oxygen.'

Hugo nodded, spreading ink on Braun's fingertips in order to obtain prints. He then pressed them onto a sheet of paper, one by one.

'Please carry on,' he said.

'Braun had eaten not long before he died: his stomach was still full,' Rabi continued. 'It must have happened at around 8 p.m., but the poisoning wasn't caused by food at the refectory because he would have died on the spot. By the way, what happened to the apple?'

'Mengele made one of the prisoners eat it to see if it had been poisoned.'

'I imagine it wasn't, because your theory is correct,' Rabi muttered, bent over the corpse. He fiddled in Dr Braun's mouth with pincers and extracted from the mucosa a fragment of glass that gleamed in the lamplight. 'Somebody forced him to bite into a phial of cyanide. What do you think – shall we forego sawing through the skull and analysing the brain? We can do poor Frau Braun this favour at least.'

'All right,' Hugo replied.

He took the prints he'd found on Braun's fountain pen and studied them through a magnifying glass, comparing them to those just taken from the body: they were undoubtedly the same. Prints shaped like a peacock pattern, with lines that stemmed from one side and returned to the middle, forming a small, winding circle. Sigismund Braun had used the pen to leave a message on the pad of letter-headed paper.

Hugo approached the dead man and indicated to Rabi three scratches on the neck. 'How do you suppose he got these?' he asked.

'Those are superficial,' Rabi replied, getting organ samples ready to put in formaldehyde. 'I don't see any significant signs of self-defence. Someone probably hit him out of the blue and took advantage of his stupor to crush the phial of cyanide in his mouth. There was no struggle.'

'And what did they strike him with?'

'The skin is grazed. A well-placed blow with a hard object, small, with irregular edges.'

Rabi took the instruments to sew the body back up.

Hugo came closer and watched him work. He felt a pang of pain in his back and a sense of unease digging a hole in his stomach. He tried hard not to think about Gioele and the phosgene experiments but couldn't. To hell with Nebe and his code of silence, he thought.

'I'd like to finish talking about Mengele's guinea pigs, if you don't mind.'

Rabi gave a start and missed a suture.

'Forgive me, Herr Fischer, I shouldn't have mentioned these things to you.'

'But you did.'

'I—'

'Tell me about Gioele.' Hugo's tone brooked no refusal. He'd decided that he wanted to know. He found all things with murky, smoky outlines suffocating. He'd been born to discover secrets, to shed light and not to live in the shadows. 'He doesn't look like a guinea pig to me.'

'Gioele is a special case,' Rabi whispered. 'Mengele's

obsessed with that child. He can't understand why, in a pair of homozygous twins, siblings can be so different. In fact, how a Jew can be so different from other Jews . . .'

'So Mengele doesn't experiment on him, right?'

'Not on him, no.' Rabi picked up another piece of thread and finished suturing the Y-shaped cut on the sternum. He took the small shower hose and directed it over Braun's body, cleaning it with care. The water gathered in the drainage sump, like a pink stream. 'But he does on his brother,' he added.

'He's treating him for typhus, isn't he?'

'He doesn't have typhus.' Rabi kept his eyes down and his voice was hard. 'He's dying from Mengele's experiments.'

Hugo felt his hands tingling. It would have been much easier to stop the conversation there and then. To act as if nothing was happening, the way he'd always done since joining the Party, but he was weary of his own cowardice. 'What did he do to him?' he asked.

'He tried to change the colour of his eyes and make them pale, like Gioele's, and that made him blind. Then began the electric shocks to see if his brain responded like his brother's. In the end, they gave him blood transfusions with Gioele's blood and that of other twins, and if, as you say, you're studying medicine, you'll know all about the wicked consequences of transfusing blood of a different type. Now he's dying.'

Hugo's tongue scraped his palate. He had no saliva left. His heart pounded against his breastbone as he suddenly realized what Auschwitz represented to these doctors: a place where everything was allowed, where the guinea pigs were easily disposable human beings. That was why

112

a doctor as highly reputable as Braun had got himself transferred there. That was why Osmund Becker had raised hell to be part of his work team: the camp was an experiment centre he could never have found anywhere else.

Hugo shuddered. 'And Gioele? What will happen to him in the end?'

He searched for reassurance in Rabi's eyes, but Rabi kept looking at Braun's body as he administered the finishing touches in a professional manner. Hugo felt a surge of anger and frustration, as though what was happening was the fault of the Jew standing in front of him and not of Germans like him who'd started all this horror.

'Damn it, don't keep quiet!' he said forcefully. His voice echoed, becoming distorted in his ears, sounding like the barking of the SS men on the ramp at the station. Once again, his ears were filled with the sound of the little skull crushed by the boot.

Rabi was startled. He looked up, his eyes full of pain.

'The purpose of the study on twins is not to observe them while alive, but to analyse them through a comparative autopsy,' he replied in one breath. He looked at his blood-soiled gloves, seeming about to cry. He wiped them on his apron, leaving a vermilion stain. 'I've had to do many of them, mein Herr. Even on children who were still dying . . .'

'Alive?' As he was uttering the word, Hugo felt an abyss open under his feet. It was as though a chasm had torn through the floor and was ravenously sucking him in.

'Alive,' Rabi said, in tears.

'You're making fun of me.' Hugo rubbed his cheeks and noticed that they were hollow and rough. Dry. 'Vivisection is forbidden.'

'Animal experimentation is forbidden without a government permit,' he said, correcting him. 'Here, everything is lawful. Jews, gypsies and negroes are not considered human beings.'

Hugo felt vomit rise in his throat. Henryk had realized all this, even back on that distant day when he'd thought about escaping. 'Maybe you're exaggerating,' Hugo had told him. At the time, he couldn't have imagined just how far the Party would drag them. The economy was bad, Goebbels needed a scapegoat for his propaganda and to distract Germans from the economic problems, but nothing could have convinced Hugo that they would shortly tumble into a never-ending pit of lunacy. He stared at Rabi. A ghastly premonition sent an excruciating pain through his back, as ruthless as the fangs of an Alsatian. He felt dizzy and afraid he'd fall, and the ache in his muscles grew so severe that he found himself longing for a double dose of morphine.

'What will happen to Gioele when his brother dies?' His drowsy voice cracked. He already knew the answer.

'The doctor will give him a phenol injection straight in the heart, and I will have to perform a comparative autopsy on both twins. Mengele says that this kind of autopsy must be carried out in identical physical conditions, so the death of the boys will have to take place almost simultaneously. Mengele will save Gioele's wonderful eyes for his eyeball collection and the rest will be sent in a package to Berlin to his mentor, as urgent military material.'

Hugo shook his head.

This man with little round glasses was trying to deceive him.

Rabi studied him, eyes glistening with tears, but he was now as composed as an emperor.

'*A mol, mit yorn un doyres tsurik, iz ergets nifter gevorn a Yid,*' he said in Yiddish. '*Meyle! A Yid iz nifter gevorn. Eybik lebn ken men nit.*'

'What does that mean?'

'Once, many generations ago, somewhere or other, a Jew died. Alas! A Jew was dead. Nobody can live forever,' he whispered. 'You shouldn't be concerned, mein Herr. Gioele is only a Jew. One more, one less: what difference does it make to you Nazis?'

14

Gioele jumped slightly as the needle pierced the skin and penetrated his arm.

'I'll be quick,' Bethany said reassuringly.

Gioele always turned away when a nurse drew blood. Once the needle was in, however, curiosity would make him look at the red fluid that quickly surfaced, ran up the narrow tube and was collected in a glass phial.

He'd keep still throughout the whole procedure, then slump on the chair, exhausted, his head spinning and his legs shaking because he hated it and was scared of needles. It wasn't true, he thought, that he was scared of nothing.

The nurses, the nice ones, told him it wouldn't hurt, but you could never trust adults. They usually did the opposite of what they promised. Sometimes, it was Betsy Angel who took a blood sample, and she did everything to hurt him. That cow would miss the vein on purpose and punch several holes in him, then twist the needle until his arm was bruised and swollen. He put up with it only because he knew that the blood was needed to treat his brother. They'd often argued when they lived in Bologna and had even occasionally come to blows over sharing a game, but he had no better friend than Gabriele.

Sometimes he remembered their excursions in the Giardini Margherita, among flowers bursting with the scents of spring, or in the hills, when fireflies invaded the slopes and the moon looked like a giant eye that illuminated everything. His father had once taken them to the top of the Garisenda tower. Climbing the steps had been hard but worth it in the end: from there you could see the whole city made up of red roofs and houses, and towers that sprouted like solitary trees. Now though, the memories were fading and Gioele was afraid of forgetting them.

Another thing terrified him. As the days went by, he realized he could no longer remember what his mother and father looked like – even Gabriele, though he was identical to him. He had the dreadful feeling he'd soon be unable to recognize them. In moments like this, all he had to do was close his eyes and focus on something nice. The smell of lye when his mother did the laundry, of the ragù wafting from the kitchen, the cologne his father sprayed behind his ears after shaving. He'd then try to draw their faces, one stroke at a time. Their mouths, eyes and noses would resume their correct place and he'd remember his father's thin, angular face, his mother's soft features, and Gabriele, who was a bit like seeing himself in the mirror.

Bethany snatched him away from his thoughts about his family. 'Almost done.'

'All right,' he said.

She looked up at him to give him a reassuring smile, but immediately squinted. The hand in which she held the syringe trembled and she turned white.

Gioele thought she'd looked odd since she'd walked into the room.

Bethany was Jewish, like him, only she was French and didn't talk very much. She knew German but didn't want to speak it with him. She asked him to speak Italian instead since she'd studied it for years.

Bethany wasn't really a nurse. In Paris, she'd been a doctor – a paediatrician – and had taught medicine at the university. When she arrived at the camp, they'd taken her to work in Block 10, and so she, too, like all those who worked for the doctors, could sleep in the Stammlager, wear civilian clothes and eat in a better canteen than the one for Jewish prisoners. Gioele had heard that the Birkenau prisoners' diet consisted of slop they called *awo*. Bethany looked as though she'd eaten nothing but Birkenau *awo* for the last couple of days. Her cheeks were hollow, her forehead and chin had started protruding and her eyes were sunken.

Gioele reached out and touched her cheek.

She pulled away. 'What are you doing?'

'You feel hot,' he remarked. 'Are you ill?'

'I have a slight temperature.'

'Then you should rest.'

Bethany smiled, took out the syringe and wiped his wound with a gauze bandage she then wound tight around his elbow. She put her instruments away and labelled the phial of blood.

'Is it for my brother?' Gioele asked, stretching his neck to look.

'Yes, it's for him.'

'Are you working for Mengele now?'

'For the time being, yes, then we'll see.'

'Have you seen my brother?'

'He's fine. Don't worry.'

Bethany tidied up the worktable and turned to look at him, her hands clasped over her belly. 'I heard that German, the criminologist, came to talk to you this morning,' she whispered, shooting a glance at the door, which was ajar.

'Yes.'

'What did you tell him?'

'I showed him my drawings of the dead doctor.'

'What else?'

'That's all.'

Bethany was shifting from one leg to the other while wringing her hands over her belly, as if to soothe a sharp pain.

'Ah!' she suddenly cried out, bending in half.

Frightened, Gioele went to her. 'What's the matter?'

'It's all right, darling,' she replied. But she was struggling to breathe and her wheezing terrified him. 'I must have caught the 'flu or some other nasty bug in the camp. Don't worry. Tell me more about that German.' She stared at him in silent entreaty, leaning against the table, unable to straighten up. 'You didn't tell him about me, did you?'

Gioele remembered that night very well.

He had been roaming about, as he did almost every night when the others were already in the dormitory. He wasn't afraid, because if Mengele or another doctor caught him, all they would have done was send him back to bed. Even if it was Betsy who found him, she would have beaten him breathless, but she couldn't have killed him. As Adele said, Mengele needed him.

At some point, in the quiet corridor, he heard sighs. A phlegmy coughing fit had echoed against the walls,

119

followed by the raspy breathing of someone who wasn't feeling well. Over the sighs and the coughing, he could hear a wet kind of sound and, when he crouched to peek, Gioele recognized Bethany's dishevelled form, kissing someone.

'I love you,' she said. 'But if they discover us, we're dead.'

At the word *dead*, Gioele had run away. Bethany had seen him and, the following day, had come to speak to him. She didn't scold or attack him, like that cow Betsy, but hugged him and asked him to forget what he'd seen. To do it for her, so nothing bad would happen to her.

'No, I didn't tell him,' Gioele replied.

'Thank you.' Bethany smiled, suppressing the grimace of pain, her forehead beaded with sweat. 'And Berto? What do you know about him?'

Gioele shrugged his shoulders. 'They say he's still in prison.'

'Did the German not say anything about him?'

'No.'

'Berto's a good man. He's done nothing wrong.'

'But what if he's the one who killed Braun?'

'Berto didn't kill anyone.'

Gioele lowered his eyes and saw blood trickling between Bethany's legs. It was coming down in small drops, leaving red streaks on her calves.

'You're ill!' he exclaimed. 'You have to tell the doctors!'

She pressed her hand hard over his mouth to stop him talking. 'No, darling, it's nothing!' Then she gently removed her hand and gave him a stare that commanded silence.

'Shall I go and call Uncle Mengele?' Gioele whispered.

'It's nothing, really. I just need to get some sleep and

I'll feel better tomorrow. Trust me, I don't need those doctors. Have you forgotten that I'm also a doctor?'

He looked at her hesitantly, then nodded.

'You really are a good boy,' she said.

She ruffled his hair, picked up the phial with the blood and left, tiny drops of blood following her in a silent trail across the floor.

15

Hugo looked through the car window. Now they were close, the Birkenau watchtower loomed over them, square, menacing. Its triangular, sloping, snow-covered roof stood out against the grey sky.

They drove through the gate into the Lagerstraße that split Birkenau in two. Beyond the barbed-wire fence on either side of the main road, there was an endless number of wood and brick shacks. Hugo couldn't count them all because they extended as far as the eye could see, but there must have been thousands of them. In the distance, where you could see the white pattern that was the birch forest, the sky was bathed in clouds rising from below, some grey, others pale yellow: the piles mentioned by Tristan Voigt.

Hugo looked out of the window. A small Red Cross van clattered past them. Further ahead, he saw a group of women marching in the snow. An SS man on board a van howled through a loudspeaker to make them walk faster.

'You're in the concentration camp of Birkenau, dear ladies!' He was shouting so loudly through the speaker that Hugo could hear him even from inside the car, with the windows closed. 'Come on, give us a smile!'

The officer jumped down from the van and indicated ten or so women. An SS-Helferin ordered them to start running in a circle. The young women obeyed hesitantly. Their heads had already been shaved but you could see that they were new: they still had a strange light in their eyes, Hugo thought; their cheeks were smooth, their legs strong.

When the SS officer aimed his pistol straight at the group, Hugo ordered the driver to stop.

Confused, the young women also slowed down.

The officer fired. He struck at random the unfortunate woman who just happened to be across from the barrel of his pistol and Hugo sensed that he'd shot her without any real motive, maybe just for fun. The young woman fell like an empty sack and blood gushed onto the snow, while the others looked on in terror. The SS officer laughed, exchanging amused looks with the SS-Helferin.

Hugo was paralysed by this show of gratuitous brutality and felt as though he couldn't breathe. His temples throbbed relentlessly. He saw the frozen crystals turn bright red beneath the feet of the prisoners, who huddled together in fear as they resumed their pointless march.

He was roused by the driver restarting the engine. 'Should I take you to the Kanada, mein Herr?'

'The Kanada?' he barely managed to reply.

'The personal effects warehouse?' the driver explained.

'Yes . . .'

'They've recently moved it,' the man continued as if

123

nothing had happened. 'There are now thirty shacks and two thousand prisoners working there. It's a real industry.'

Hugo didn't reply. He just looked through the window at the huts slowly drifting by. He tried to slow down his heartbeat but found it impossible.

Beyond the barbed wire that divided each sector, he could make out other prisoners. Some were wearing the striped uniform, others ordinary clothes, while others were completely naked. He saw a woman with drooping breasts that seemed about to part from her chest. She walked slowly, with small steps, heedless of the cold. Her skin was as grey as the ashes from the crematoria and Hugo thought it looked as though it was about to slip off her entirely. She was dragging herself forward past SS officers and dogs, and nobody seemed to pay any attention to her. She was just a ghost in the middle of all that snow.

Hugo looked away and focused on the car's leather seats.

His back hadn't stopped aching since Braun's autopsy. He could feel his arm burning, like a thousand fangs sinking into his flesh, and only touching the phial of morphine could help him catch his breath. He searched for the cold bottle in his pocket. He longed to run away, to leave this place and its horrors, go back to his Berlin, far away from everything.

'Here we are,' the driver said, stopping the car. 'This is the Kanada. Shall I wait for you here, mein Herr?'

Hugo looked up and saw a series of wood and brick shacks arranged like those in the Stammlager, separated by a straight road flanked by heaps of bundles, suitcases, blankets, bicycles and prams. Everything was there. He counted thirty buildings beyond the metal fence, just as the driver had said. Chimneys from another building rose behind them. It was from them that the thick smoke emanated and, a little further, the swirling yellow cloud.

'Wait for me at the camp entrance,' Hugo replied. 'I'll be here for a while and would like to take a walk afterwards.'

The driver turned, giving the limping leg an eloquent look, but refrained from commenting.

Hugo grabbed his stick and got out of the car, heart pounding and temples droning. His first breath of cold air triggered a sudden retch that made him slump against a birch and spew his entire lunch onto the snow. The acidity of his gastric juices coated his mouth and swam up to his nostrils, along with the smell of burnt flesh that had imbued this place to the smallest speck of soil.

The air was saturated with it. It was a sickly-sweet and at the same time pungent smell.

'Heil Hitler!' a voice behind him said.

Hugo wiped his mouth, propped himself up on his stick and looked up at a tall, fit young man with jet-black hair and eyes like glass marbles peering from under his hat with the skull and crossbones. He must be Adam Schmidt, the SS officer who'd found the note.

'Heil Hitler,' Hugo mumbled in return.

'It's very hard the first few times,' the young man said jokingly, tickling the air with his fingertips. 'Then you somehow get used to it. The Kommandant said you wanted to speak to me.'

'Yes.' Hugo spat a clot of saliva on the ground and wiped his lips with a handkerchief.

'Can you tell me how you found the note about Braun?'

'Of course.' Schmidt strode with a military step towards

a heap of items next to a half-sawn tree trunk. 'It was here. The weight of the snow snapped the branches off and they crashed down, taking part of the trunk with them, so we had to saw it off and clear the area. The note was under the snow.'

'Have you mentioned this to anyone?' Hugo asked.

'No, I had orders to keep it confidential.'

'Well done. Did anyone ask questions when they saw you supervise the shovelling?'

'Not that I can remember.'

'Can you tell me where Braun's wife works?'

Schmidt indicated a hut to their left.

'Thank you for your help,' Hugo said, putting an end to the conversation and walking away.

The hut where Brunhilde Braun worked was marked with a number traced on the bricks with white paint. He went in.

Inside, the grey light of day filtered through the windows in faint beams and illuminated the long tables on which prisoners were emptying sacks and suitcases delivered at short intervals by vans. There were heaps of clothes, shoes, saucepans, prams, medicines, perfumes, banknotes, cigarettes, tinned food and cameras. Anything that could be salvaged from the prisoners' luggage. Along with the odour of burnt flesh, there was a smell of leather and cardboard in the air.

Hugo looked in the middle of the heap, not quite knowing what to look for.

There was so much stuff piled up that it would take months to sort through it all. The suitcase of the Jewish mother killed at the station must be here, in the midst of all this junk. He noticed a toy rattle, then another one, then little shoes and miniature dresses, a doll and a carved wooden top. Hugo pulled his hand away as though scalded. How many children arrived in Auschwitz?

'Hair over there,' he heard someone shout from the far end of the hut. 'Gold teeth here.'

'What a bitch.' A woman's voice hissed into his ear, making him jump. 'How she enjoys giving orders . . .'

Hugo turned and saw Rose leaning against the table. She was contemptuously referring to Braun's wife, who, riding crop in hand, was supervising the work, ploughing through the sea of female prisoners like a Valkyrie on the warpath.

'What are you doing here?' he asked, surprised.

'I could ask you the same question.' Rose winked, rubbing her hip against his thigh. 'I've come to pick myself out some perfume and clothes.'

She headed to the table most in the shade and began rummaging through the heap. She tried on a baby-blue skirt and a white silk blouse, then folded both, stuffed them into a bag and carried on looking at another table heaped with lipsticks, wigs, necklaces and perfumes. She tried a scent and half closed her eyes with pleasure, as though she couldn't smell the stench of burnt flesh wafting in from outside.

'Sigismund hated me wearing perfume,' she whispered, darting Frau Braun – who was marching between the tables – a defiant glance. 'He was allergic to it. He said it gave him headaches and irritated his skin. Now I can wear as much of it as I like. And what are you doing here?'

'I've come to speak to SS-Helferin Braun,' Hugo murmured.

'She must have killed him.' Clearly, rumours about

127

Braun's violent death had circulated. Rose grabbed two packets of cigarettes and hid them in her cleavage. 'I'm surprised she didn't kill all the other women who'd had her husband's cock inside them.'

'You shouldn't smoke so much,' Hugo retorted, pretending he hadn't heard her.

'They're not for me. They're to corrupt the kapos or an SS officer. They're always useful.' She winked and indicated a short, stocky soldier who was keeping an eye on her from a corner of the hut. She gave an amused giggle and tiptoed up to Hugo. He felt her warm, fragrant body pressing against his. She was the only beautiful living thing in this place. 'Come back and see me if you feel lonely,' she said provocatively.

Hugo watched her walk away, escorted by the SS officer, and, for a moment, all that lingered was her enticing perfume.

'You!' Frau Braun's brutal voice brought him abruptly back to reality, to this place that stank of leather and burnt flesh.

Hugo limped to the middle of the hut, focusing on the reason for his visit: this was where somebody had tried to get rid of a very inconvenient note, so whoever was involved in Dr Braun's death must have passed through here.

Frau Braun was squinting at him, her face as fierce as the muzzle of a mastiff. She must have hated him for insisting on an autopsy for her husband. Hugo put on a smug expression and walked up to her.

'Frau Braun,' he exclaimed with his best smile. 'Your husband's body is ready to go home. Once again, my condolences.'

'You've got a nerve,' she hissed. 'What are you doing here? Have you come to tell me that in person?'

'No, I've come to look for something. And to talk.'

'I've nothing to say to you. I asked you not to do the autopsy and you didn't obey me. Our relatives were waiting to say farewell to Sigismund in the Wupperhof family tomb on Wednesday.'

Hugo pictured a marble vault. Something grand, in keeping with Nazi style, complete with brass eagles and swastikas everywhere, and SS banners at the entrance.

Without another word she turned to leave, in her haste colliding with a prisoner who upset a basket of rings on the floor. The jingle of wedding bands echoed in the bustle of the hut for a long time.

'What happened to your husband's wedding ring?' Hugo asked, speaking over the noise. He looked at the gold rings scattered on the ground, removed from heaven knew whom. Taking someone's wedding band was an unspeakable act, he thought. Like severing a sacred bond and trampling on it.

'I have no idea,' she replied.

'Did he have it on the night he died?'

'I don't know. I can't remember. Now, if you don't mind . . .'

Hugo stared at her, astounded. 'Don't you even want to know the result of the autopsy?'

Brunhilde Braun froze in the middle of the room.

Hugo saw her shoulders rise and fall as she panted like a broken accordion. She nodded and turned slowly. In her pupils, which had spread into the irises, he saw a fear of discovering the truth.

'He was poisoned. With cyanide.'

Frau Braun clasped a hand over her mouth and stifled a whine. Her eyes opened wide and she wept fat tears, suddenly looking like a vulnerable little girl. She walked away, slouching, shaken by sobs, while a row of prisoners turned to look at her in disbelief. They clearly weren't used to seeing her like this.

'Don't you think that was cruel?' he heard a voice say.

Anita Kunig was staring at him, holding a riding crop. Blond hair poked out from under her cap, which she'd tugged down over her forehead in an attempt to conceal the tan birthmark that stained half her face.

'That wasn't my intention,' Hugo said in self-defence. 'Believe me.'

'Brunhilde may look tough, but she isn't.'

'I take it you know each other well . . .'

'We're good friends,' Anita Kunig replied. 'And I know her well enough to assure you that you'll get nothing out of her right now. She's too angry. You must give her time.'

'I'm only doing my job. The longer we leave it, the less likely we are to find out who killed Dr Braun. Frau Braun should be grateful to me for my work.'

'She *is* grateful to you, but death is always frightening. And when it comes so violently, then it's even more painful.' She stopped and looked at him quizzically. 'Can I help you in any way?'

Hugo nodded. 'I need to speak to someone from the Kanada.'

'For Heaven's sake, don't use the prisoners' name for it,' Anita snapped. 'This is the Effektenlager and everything you see here is a gift to Germany. It's a place of vital importance.'

Hugo leaned the entire weight of his body on his stick to let the excruciatingly painful leg rest. 'I need to speak to someone from the Effektenlager,' he said. 'If not Braun's wife, then . . .'

'You can ask me.'

'I need to know if anyone from Block 10 comes here.'

Anita Kunig smiled politely. 'Almost everyone. Nurses and doctors come here regularly to collect medicines from the prisoners. Sometimes we find interesting things, even the odd medical device.'

'Who comes, exactly? Can you give me names?'

Anita looked down at his leg, as though stalling for time. 'We have some Eukodal for the pain, if you like . . .'

'What?' Hugo said.

'I'm told you had poliomyelitis. What do you take for the pain – morphine?' She shook her head. 'Morphine's no good, it's foreign poison. Eukodal is twice, if not three times as powerful, and it'll make you euphoric and active enough to bear this place and carry out your search. Our Führer also uses it, so I think you can trust it.'

'Stop trying to dodge my question.'

Anita Kunig went to look for something among the items scattered on the table, then handed him a grey box. 'Try it,' she said, undaunted.

'I don't need it,' he insisted, his hands still clasping his stick. He didn't like the way this woman was wasting his time. 'Now answer my question: who did you see collecting medicines here? Berto Hoffman?'

'Of course,' she replied, slipping the box into the pocket of her uniform. 'Berto Hoffman often comes. So do Adele Krause, Betsy Angel and Osmund Becker.'

'And Bethany Assouline?'

131

Anita shook her head. 'No, she's Jewish, so she doesn't have that freedom of movement.'

'Do you know if Bethany and Dr Braun had a relationship?'

'No.' She pursed her lips and held his gaze to intimate that she had no intention of staining the memory of her friend or betraying Brunhilde Braun's trust.

'What about a relationship between the doctor and Betsy Angel?'

'No.'

'What kind of relationship did the Brauns have?'

'The kind a couple have after being married many years. Brunhilde missed having a child.' A sadness flitted across her eyes, and Hugo sensed that something – perhaps a painful memory – was upsetting her. 'What else do you want to know?'

Hugo rubbed his face. 'A witness told me they smelled bitter almonds here at the triage centre.' He paused for thought. 'It came from some locks of hair. Do you know anything about that?'

'Of course. It's the prisoners' hair.'

'Treated with an antiparasitic?'

'Something like that.'

Anita looked him straight in the eye. The same attitude as Tristan Voigt, the same way of concealing something by implying that there were terrible secrets in Auschwitz.

'Is there a place nearby where they burn the bodies of the prisoners?' Hugo continued. He realized too late that he'd once again dropped the Braun case to carry out another investigation: his own, the one that would earn him an angry outburst from Nebe.

Anita Kunig didn't appear surprised. She whipped the

air with her riding crop to indicate the door. The constant noise of vans arriving to unload more luggage came from outside and the malodorous smell penetrated the hut whenever the wind changed direction.

'Just out here, behind us, there are two crematoria, Four and Five,' Anita explained casually. 'Next to them, there's a clearing surrounded by a birch forest. It has pits where piles of bodies are burned. Are you asking for any particular reason?'

'Pure curiosity,' he murmured.

Hugo said goodbye to her and walked out of the hut, into the air heavy with smoke.

Once again, the retching got the better of him.

16

A plume of yellow smoke rose from behind a brick building with tall, slim chimneys.

Hugo decided to follow it.

He skirted the building and reached a small wood where a group of old people, women and children were waiting in the smoke-stained snow, under the quivering birches. It was a surreal scene of stasis. They were all waiting for something, looking around, apparently lost. The children, tired, were dozing. Every so often, someone would make enquiries of the SS officers or the Sonderkommandos in striped uniforms, but no one replied to them.

Hugo stopped to look. They all had a Star of David sewn onto their coats. He would have liked to approach and ask why they were gathered there, so far from the camp, but the SS men on duty shot him eloquent looks, so he walked on, skirting the trees.

The stench got stronger and the smoke began to sting his eyes.

He noticed another edifice made of red brick, with

sloping roofs covered in snow and transparent, glittering stalactites hanging from the tiles. Dark and menacing, the chimneys rose tens of metres high. That must be the second crematorium.

SS officers and Sonderkommandos were escorting other prisoners to the building's entrance. Hugo couldn't estimate their number. There might have been a thousand of them, and yet they all walked silently, in a single file, their heads not shaved yet, and only a few of them turned to look back, beyond the tall hedge that separated them from the rest of the camp.

An ambulance with the red cross overtook Hugo, splashing mud over his coat, and pulled up on one side of the building. A motorcycle arrived straight afterwards, revving up, lifting the muddy topsoil and driving twice around the area outside the building. Once it parked, a tall, fit man got off the saddle, imparted a couple of hasty orders and turned to stare at Hugo with curiosity.

Hugo stared back at him. Under the hat with the skull and crossbones, he could see smooth red hair and a dusting of freckles on his nose and cheeks. When he came closer, he noticed a glass eye flashing in the faint afternoon light.

'Heil Hitler!' the officer said laconically, shaking his hand. 'I'm Oberscharführer Otto Moll. How can I help you?'

'Heil Hitler! I'm Hugo Fischer, Department Five of the RSHA.'

'I know who you are.' Otto Moll opened his arms and gave a hearty laugh. 'Liebehenschel talks of nothing but you, these days.'

Hugo looked past the officer's shoulder to the spot where the Jews had vanished, devoured by the entrance to the crematorium. He looked up at the chimney, opened his hand, and impalpable flakes of ash fell into it from above.

'The crematorium's working today,' Moll said humorously.

Behind him, soldiers were unloading canisters from the ambulance. The precision of their gestures suggested it was a regular protocol. Hugo saw them position themselves on one side of the building.

'Have you discovered anything interesting in Birkenau?' the officer asked.

Hugo's eyes returned to him. He had a lopsided smile and a fierce expression that seemed to be mocking him.

'Nothing of importance for now,' he replied. His mouth was dry from the smoke and he felt unexplained terror. 'Obersturmführer Tristan Voigt told me you burn the bodies of the prisoners in outdoor pyres . . .'

'Oh, the piles.' Moll nodded and indicated behind him. 'They're just past the crematorium. Come, I'll take you to see them.'

He led the way, skirted one side of the building and stopped to examine an officer equipped with a gas mask, who was cutting the lids on the canisters. He seemed to linger on purpose so that Hugo could get a better look.

Hugo's eyes swept over the seven small, airtight windows that opened in the wall, then instinctively looked down at the canister the soldier was handling carefully. Blue-green crystals appeared, glistening in the pale sunlight.

The officer took the container, climbed a ladder and tipped the crystals into the window, then closed it diligently before continuing with the others. When he put the canister on the ground, the label became visible.

'Zyklon B?' Hugo heard his own voice crack and echo in his ears.

Otto Moll sneered smugly in a way that made Hugo's hands itch. If it hadn't been for the pistol in Moll's holster, ready to blow his brains out, or the risk to his entire career, Hugo would have pushed him against the wall and struck him in the face with his stick to wipe that sneer off.

'Come, I'll take you to the piles,' the Oberscharführer said. He had the self-satisfied voice of someone showing off their home city and its wonders to a tourist.

Hugo couldn't take his eyes off the Zyklon B label. The skull and crossbones printed over the inscription *Giftgas* seemed to be staring at him with a sardonic smile. That was the odour Gioele had smelled on the locks of hair collected at Kanada. It was the smell of bitter almonds in this fumigant made from hydrogen cyanide. A shudder travelled through his body, like when he had a high temperature as a child. He recalled the laughter echoing in the RSHA corridors when a Gestapo officer said how prisoners in Chełmno had been executed with gas from the lorries.

'So, do you want to see this pile or not?' Otto Moll asked, showing his teeth in a brilliant, predatory smile.

Hugo practically sleepwalked after him. His head felt heavy, confused.

All those Jews had gone into the crematorium and the SS officer had poured Zyklon B through the window. He thought he heard again the officer in Berlin laughing, telling them about Chełmno, and Nebe listening and nodding, drinking coffee substitute, knocking his teeth together loudly, the way he did whenever people talked of things he already knew about but wanted to keep concealed. Hugo felt his guts being wrenched in a terrible

137

awareness. His hands began to shake: a symptom of morphine withdrawal. He wished he could take a step back and forget everything while the drug slid slowly up his vein, carrying him to a faraway place.

Instead, he took a step forward.

He followed Otto Moll to an area where the yellow cloud was so thick it made his eyes water. He coughed as smoke penetrated his lungs, and wept – unable to stop himself because his eyes were on fire and his heart was screaming.

'It happens the first few times,' Moll said. 'The smoke's irritating. Then you get used to it.'

Then you get used to it.

Hugo felt the heat from the flames in his face. In front of him, in a clearing just outside the birch forest, the bodies were burning in a huge pit, raising to the sky blazing tongues that formed the nauseating cloud he'd seen from a distance. He saw the bodies crackling like logs, sputtering like chestnuts on embers and frying whenever a Sonderkommando collected the fat flowing into the side holes and poured it over the pile.

There were more bodies lying on the sides of the pit, looking asleep.

The Sonderkommandos were cutting their hair. Some were pulling out gold teeth with dental pincers and throwing them on a sheet that mirrored the glow of the blaze like a forbidden, obscene treasure. A little further on was a lorry loaded with dozens and dozens of corpses waiting to be burned, heaped in such unnatural positions that Hugo struggled to make them out as human beings.

'My God,' he murmured.

'Ah, God's taken a holiday away from here!' Otto Moll

replied caustically. 'Do pick up a little soil to take home as a memento.'

'What?'

Hugo stared at him, dumbfounded. He thought his leg was going to give way and that he was about to tumble to the ground like an empty sack. He propped himself firmly on his stick. All around, the snow had melted in the heat, turning to mud. He felt rooted in this swamp, unable to take even one step forward.

He rubbed his burning eyes and bit his smoke-filmed tongue.

He searched his pocket for cigarettes and encountered the coldness of the morphine phial and the syringe case. He lit himself a cigarette, but it didn't produce the desired effect, so he spat it out.

Otto Moll's fat laugh caught up with him like a kick in the back. 'I'm not laughing at you, Herr Fischer! But watching the reactions of someone seeing this shit for the first time is always exhilarating!'

And another laugh echoed in Hugo's ears like distorted barking.

'Are you all right now?' the officer asked. 'Do you require anything else?'

Hugo coughed and spat a thick clump of saliva that tasted of burnt meat. He clenched his teeth and focused on the only thing he needed to investigate, the sole reason for his being here. Damn Auschwitz and Nebe, who'd sent him all the way here knowing what he'd find, and damn Hitler. He tried to collect his thoughts and push away the images of the Jews walking into the crematorium, of the skull teasing him from the Zyklon B label and of the bodies crackling in the pile.

'Have you ever seen anyone from Block 10 at the Ka-Effektenlager?' he stammered.

Moll looked up at the sky. 'Of course,' he replied. 'The nurses also come here to the piles. I think they come to take the medicines hidden in the pockets of the bodies before they get to the warehouse, to avoid fighting over them with the doctors in Birkenau or the dispensary or a kapo.'

'Have you ever seen Adele Krause?'

'Adele.' Moll gave a wolf whistle. 'The German nurse. Very attractive woman, with that red hair and big green eyes . . . Yes, I often see her around here and I must say she's always a sight for sore eyes.'

'Betsy Angel?'

'How can anyone forget her!'

'Any male nurses?'

'Berto Hoffman. I think that's the name of the man now in the death block, right? And then there's often a doctor, a handsome young man – looks like an actor. I think he's Braun's assistant.'

'Osmund Becker.'

'That's right, Osmund Becker. I remember him because he has the same gap in his teeth as Mengele.' Moll tapped his own teeth. 'Women go crazy about it, you know?'

'In other words, everybody came here.'

The officer smiled but his amused expression soon turned into a savage mask. He strode past him towards a Sonderkommando who was arranging a body behind them.

'What did you put in your mouth?' Moll barked. He grabbed the Jew by the scruff of his neck and lifted him off the ground. 'I may only have one eye, but I'm not blind and I can smell shits like you from a mile away!'

The man shook his head like a frightened bird, his eyes staring from the gaunt face, worn out by the Polish winter and the heat of the flames.

'Open your mouth!' the Oberscharführer ordered.

The Jew slowly parted his lips. Moll grabbed his mouth and stuck two fingers inside, pushing until the man retched, and extracted a diamond that sparkled in the light of the pyre.

'Always trying to be clever, these filthy bastards.' Moll turned the diamond between his fingers with contempt. 'As soon as they can, they steal something. No respect even for the dead!'

'Please, mein Herr!' The prisoner was crouching at his feet, shaking. 'It was a mistake, mein Herr!'

'It was a mistake, mein Herr!' Moll parroted, then burst into a coarse laugh, his hand on the butt of his pistol. 'Once,' he continued, turning to Hugo, 'a Jew hid four top-quality diamonds up her vagina. I mean, why do you need this stuff when you're about to die?'

The prisoner was still trembling.

Hugo felt his throat tighten and his lungs demand air. Moll took his hand away from his weapon and clicked his fingers to get the attention of the other Sonderkommandos.

'Throw him on the pile,' he ordered.

The men looked at him, confused, and no one stirred. Hugo turned cold.

'Throw him on the pile,' the officer repeated with another bark. 'Or I'll pick five of you pieces of shit and you'll be hanged like dogs after I've cut your dicks off and stuffed them down your throats! Do you understand?'

The Sonderkommandos quickly grabbed their companion. The prisoner screamed and struggled like a man possessed, scratching the air to free himself. He slipped out of their hands, managed to kick one of them, but was soon captured again in a lethal vice and dragged to the edge of the pyre.

The prisoners swung his body until it gathered momentum, then Hugo saw the Jew fly into the fire like a bird with broken wings. He watched him glide onto the burning bodies, and then the flames enveloped him. He wriggled like a burning torch, rolling over the boiling corpses and screaming in the crackling fire. One of his companions looked on, trembling the whole time, but as soon as Moll turned to him, he resumed pulling gold teeth from the bodies.

'I'm sorry, Herr Fischer,' Moll announced with a cherubic smile. 'But sometimes there's no other way to educate them.'

17

Hugo hid behind a Kanada hut, in a sheltered spot next to a mound of luggage and blankets.

He quickly screwed on the syringe, nearly dropping it in the snow a few times.

His hands were shaking and he was sweating.

He filled the syringe with morphine, stuck the needle into the crook of his elbow without fastening the strap to find the vein, and pushed the piston. He felt his muscles stiffen and waited for the wave of warmth to relax them. The Wattenmeer tide. Slow and powerful.

Then, exhausted, he slumped against the wooden beams and cocked his head to look at the sky darkened by smoke. He could still hear the flames crackling, the bodies bursting, the Jew screaming while burning alive, his companion trembling in silence. Otto Moll laughing.

In Wattenmeer he'd been a child and the sound of the backwash had filled him with joy. He thought he could hear it again now, slow and rhythmical. Then came the sound of Zyklon B dropping through the window. A crystalline *sssh*, like sand running through your fingers. The SS man had poured it after the Jews had gone into the belly of the crematorium. He thought he could hear their screams as they were locked in a room, crammed together. They were treating them for lice. That's what they were doing, just that, he told himself.

Hugo was shaking. He thought of Gioele, of the phenol injection Josef Mengele would administer to him as soon as his brother was dead, and about the sound his heart would make when it burst.

A hollow thud. *Tu-tum*.

In his exploding temples, the *sssh* of Zyklon B drowned out the *tu-tum* of Gioele's heart in a terrible, asphyxiating melody.

Hugo rested his gaze on a threadbare suitcase sprouting from a heap of things next to him. Someone had written their name and address on it in paint, in case their luggage went missing. Next to it, he saw a pair of broken spectacles and a razor blade sticking out. At that moment, he understood where it had all begun: with small, ordinary things, the banality of everyday acts, the unawareness of danger.

It had begun as soon as he'd read about Kurfürstendamm in the newspaper, when a group of Nazis had randomly attacked anyone who looked Jewish and smashed shop windows with stones. No one had taken this act seriously, no one had expressed public outrage, it was an isolated, almost insignificant event everyone had underestimated, which, precisely because it was downplayed, had put down the roots of the insanity to come. Two years later, the economic crisis worsened, the number of unemployed increased disproportionately and there were countless homeless people. Hugo saw the shops of friends and relatives close down, bankrupted one after the other, and Adolf Hitler's face raging from the city's advertising stands and election campaign billboards, promising Germany's rebirth.

At the election parade in 1933, Berlin was covered in red flags with swastikas, while thousands of people made the Brandenburg Gate and Unter den Linden glow with a trail of torches. The following day, the *Berliner Volks-Zeitung* announced the new government and Hugo read the article while still in his dressing gown and nightclothes, sipping his coffee and remarking to his father that hard times were over and that Germany would rise from the depression again. He still remembered the overwhelming enthusiasm and adrenaline that his father, a fierce opponent of Hitler's party, quickly dampened. Like everybody else, Hugo had already forgotten the stone-throwing in Kurfürstendamm.

That was where it had all begun, he understood it clearly now. On the day when the Party was allowed to take that small step unopposed, or perhaps, a month after the new government had taken office, when the *Berliner Volks-Zeitung* reported the suspension of a few basic rights for the well-being and protection of the country and the people. Communists were hunted down and nobody was surprised. Some grimaced during the book burning in Opernplatz and found the call to boycott Jewish shops bizarre, but they certainly didn't feel concern. Nightclubs closed down, one by one, to respect public decorum, and the first to be affected were meeting places for homosexuals. Then came the swing clubs, which Hugo often frequented. And even an episode of extreme violence in which he'd been personally involved failed to convince him that something was about to come to a head: Hitler wanted brutal, intrepid and cruel youth, capable of making the world tremble, and perhaps he was right, perhaps Germany really needed that, and not young people who danced to swing. When Hugo had fallen ill, he'd felt a profound sense of shame about being unable to be a part of that new generation of predators.

The Party's next step went so far it created an unbridgeable gap between reason and madness. By now, the machine was so well oiled with the illusion of an Aryan race, administered in small doses of propaganda, that no one was surprised by the laws hastily passed in Nuremberg, or by the pogrom advertised on the city's billboards. Nobody was shocked when gypsies were arrested and taken to the Marzahn camp in order to rid the city of them for the Olympic Games, or when yellow stars had to be sewn onto the clothes of Jews or when they were confined to ghettos. The leap had been taken, the flags were too red and alluring to stop and tell good from evil, and fear too powerful to oppose.

Looking at the Kanada mounds, made up of daily items and little things, it became clear to Hugo that this infernal machine had been built year after year with tiny cogs, passing unobserved, and was now irremovable. Everything drifted so slowly and sharply before his eyes that he was surprised he hadn't noticed it sooner.

'What have we done . . . ?' he murmured.

He caught his breath. His thoughts grew sluggish and the morphine embraced him in a soporific warmth that made everything feel less stifling. By the time he saw Adele Krause's face over him, it was too late.

'Herr Fischer . . .'

She was in front of him, looking at him through the red locks escaping from her cap, wrapped in a coat that revealed the hem of her uniform, clutching a basket filled with medicines, syringes and stethoscopes. As though in a dream, Hugo glimpsed a Leica camera and a pair of dental pincers covered with a white handkerchief.

Adele looked at him with her green eyes.

He found himself thinking that birches must be that colour in the spring.

'Fräulein Krause,' he managed to utter, embarrassed. He unrolled his sleeve and tried getting back up but couldn't.

'It must be very painful.' Adele picked up the syringe from the ground and handed it to him. 'In Irsee, I saw many children with poliomyelitis.'

'And to think that I hoped to become a war hero,' Hugo said, laughing, embarrassed.

'And you don't think surviving a disease is heroic?' Adele smiled. Her cheeks were red from the cold, her lips chapped but plump. 'Don't worry. I won't tell anyone what I've seen.'

'Thank you,' he murmured, still in a daze.

'Can you manage to stand up?'

'Yes,' he lied.

'Good. I must dash to Block 10. I've been recruited by Mengele's group, now Braun isn't here anymore, and I don't want to be late on my first day.'

'Go, go, I can manage.'

Adele walked away but kept turning back, smiling at him. Her fresh appearance was at odds with all the greyness around.

'See you soon, Herr Fischer!' she shouted from a distance.

Hugo saw her trip in the snow and drop her basket. He tried to get up and run to help her, but felt immobilized, inept. He'd tried to help a young woman once before, so long ago it seemed a different lifetime, and hadn't succeeded. He felt just like that day, useless and complicit with murderers he was incapable of standing up to for fear of losing everything.

She waved at him.

She was all right. She picked up her things, gave an embarrassed laugh and carried on walking.

'Damn it . . .' Hugo bit his tongue and punched the frozen snow.

She must think him pathetic.

He rubbed his face hard in order to recover and felt the bristly hairs of his beard pressing against his skin, piercing it. He wondered if, once the war was over and all this shit a distant memory, he'd be able to look at himself in the mirror again.

He grabbed a handful of snow and swallowed it. It seemed to make him feel better.

He managed to stagger back up and shook his drenched coat.

He ventured down the same road as Adele, dragging himself along with his stick. He'd told his driver that he'd wanted a stroll and was already sorry. He was filled with anxiety at the very thought of tackling the road and walking between the prisoners' huts. He didn't want to see anything anymore. All he wanted was a hot shower, a good meal and sleep. He wanted to forget everything and wake up in the morning feeling the way you do after a horrible nightmare, when you realize it wasn't real.

Hugo lengthened his stride. He hadn't covered more

148

than a couple of metres when he noticed something shining in the ash-soiled snow, on the spot where Adele had tripped. He shifted a small mound of fallen snow with his stick and saw the pincers – the kind the Sonderkommandos used for pulling the Jews' gold teeth. The same ones he'd seen fleetingly in Adele's basket.

He picked them up and examined them. He noticed a tiny, rolled-up note caught inside. He removed it carefully and unrolled it. It was no larger than a fingernail and the writing was so tiny he had to move to a sunnier spot to be able to read it:

UNION EIGHTEEN

The inscription absorbed the pale rays of the sun and the letters remained silent, nothing but ink. Hugo put the note in the inside pocket of his coat and threw the pincers into a bush in the frozen snow.

'Hell!' he said.

He'd had enough of coded messages.

18

Gioele leaned over the side of the swimming pool. A thin layer of ice had formed on the surface and crackled every time he tossed a stone or scratched it with a twig.

When he'd arrived at the camp, a month earlier, he'd seen other prisoners bathing in it. Even though the weather in Poland had turned cold, the SS officers had fun throwing something to the bottom which the prisoners, in particular those who could swim, had to fetch. The best one at retrieving things was Jan, the Polish swimmer.

Now, the pool was silent.

On the edge, the snow had crystallized and was glistening in the fading, late-afternoon light. Ahead, Gioele could make out the fencing, dark as smoke, the street lights coming on one by one and, beyond the barbed wire, the white birches bending in the icy wind. Behind him, he could sense the breath of the camp blocks, as austere and orderly as the Germans' faces.

There was someone behind him.

He could hear the ice cracking under their uneven steps: one was heavier, the other lighter.

He turned and saw Hugo Fischer advancing with that strange walk of his, firmly preceded by his stick. He wondered how he'd hurt his leg: if it had happened in the war or if he'd been born this way. Once, in the Bologna ghetto, a child had been born whose legs and arms never grew.

'The SS officers told me you were here,' the man said from a distance.

His face was ashen and there were rings under his eyes. His pupils looked like two pinheads disappearing in the middle of a metal lake as pale as moonlight. He approached and stared at the swimming pool, rubbed his jaw, then loosened the knot in the tie protruding from his coat.

Gioele wrinkled his nose.

'What's the matter?' the man asked defensively.

'Nothing. You smell bad.'

'What do I smell of?'

'Of something burning.'

Hugo Fischer grabbed the collar of his coat and smelled it with revulsion. 'I'll have to take it to the laundry,' he muttered. 'There is one in the camp, isn't there?'

'Of course there is.'

'Can you take me there?'

'Yes.'

Gioele set off slowly to keep in step with Hugo's limp. He looked at his tall silhouette against the crimson sun plunging behind the horizon. He was staring straight ahead, apparently worried. Gioele reached out and put

151

his hand in Hugo's to calm him, strolling with him the way he had with his father in Piazza Maggiore.

Hugo Fischer stopped for a second, surprised by the contact, but didn't reject it.

'Did you find my parents?' Gioele asked.

'No, but I've instructed an officer to look for them,' he replied. 'I'll do everything I can to find them, I promise.'

Gioele felt his heart warming. He wanted to give him something in return, but had nothing in his pockets, not even a lump of sugar. He thought of Bethany and felt like a thief betraying her trust, but he liked this German who made his heart feel light. He wanted to help him in the struggle that caused those dreadful dark rings under his eyes and those pinhead pupils.

'There's something you should know.' Gioele looked down at the frozen gravel to feel less guilty. 'Some time ago I told you I saw people at night doing adult things. And I also told you I hadn't seen anyone's face, but it's not true. I did see one of them: it was Bethany.'

Hugo froze. Judging by his expression, this was an important piece of information.

'Was she with Dr Braun?'

'I don't know.' Gioele shrugged his shoulders. 'I couldn't see the man. It was very dark, the light through the blind was on her, but not him. But I did hear them talking.'

'And what were they saying?'

Once again, Gioele shrugged, trying to remember the exact words. 'Bethany was saying "I love you, but if they discover us, we're dead." But he was quiet. I couldn't even tell who he was by his voice. But he was coughing a lot and breathing so strangely I got frightened.'

Hugo leaned towards him until their faces were close. He

smiled with that row of strong white teeth, and that was enough for Gioele to shake off any scruple about betraying Bethany to a Nazi. Because Hugo wasn't just any Nazi. He had to be a much better Nazi, he was sure of that.

'Thank you for telling me,' Hugo said. 'Bethany was having a dangerous relationship. Because when adults say that kind of thing, they're generally not joking. She and her lover were having a forbidden affair.'

'Aryan Germans aren't allowed to love Jews, is that right?'

'That's right.'

'Why not?'

Hugo sighed and looked up at the sky catching fire beyond the clouds. The snow on the roofs was ablaze. 'It's a difficult subject.'

'Is it to do with race?' Gioele kicked a pebble and it rolled into the pale shadows on the ground in front of them. 'Betsy Angel says that Aryans mustn't mix with Jews because we're a bastard race. Herr Fischer, what does a real Aryan have to look like?'

'Blond like Hitler, slim like Göring and tall like Goebbels. That's what he must look like.'

Gioele stared at him, confused. Except for Hitler, he had no idea who they were. But he knew that Hitler wasn't at all blond.

'It's an old joke,' Hugo muttered, shaking his head.

Gioele thought about Dr Braun again. His father had once told him about an English detective with a hat and pipe. Gioele put the twig he'd just used for scratching the ice in the pool into his mouth and pretended to chew on the mouthpiece of a pipe.

'Bethany was meeting a real Aryan at night,' he declared, acting as though he, too, was a detective.

'Exactly. Yesterday, you also told me there was a nice smell on the body. Could you be more specific?'

'It was a pleasant smell. Perfume.'

'Braun didn't wear perfume because he was allergic to it. I'll check with his wife, but let's say that was true: what does it mean?'

Gioele took the twig between his fingers and pretended to exhale smoke. The vapour, aided by this play-acting, dispersed in the cold air.

'It means he didn't put on the perfume deliberately,' he replied, 'but that someone he hugged was wearing a lot of it.'

'Very good.' Hugo smiled and ruffled the boy's hair.

His hand was large and coarse, just like his father's. Gioele felt his nose and eyes sting, and he nearly started to cry. Hugo also seemed about to cry, because he was looking at him with a miserable expression and, even when he smiled, he appeared to be wracked by something.

'There's something else that's important, Herr Fischer,' Gioele added, trying to bring him relief. 'Bethany's sick. I don't know what's wrong with her, but she's bleeding. Do you remember the drops of blood in Braun's office? Maybe *she* left them . . .'

Hugo studied him at length, this time. 'There are people's lives at stake,' he said. 'There were no traces of blood in the office when I arrived there. How can I trust you?'

'I'm not lying to you,' the boy protested bitterly, clenching his fists and stamping the ground. 'There was blood. The attendants cleaned it off.'

'Try to understand me . . .'

'Is it because I'm Jewish?'

Hugo Fischer looked at him, mouth open, as though that word had slapped him across the face.

'It's because you're a child,' he replied hesitantly.

Gioele sniffed. He was certain of what he'd seen that night.

Hugo resumed walking, his hand firmly guiding his stick. 'I'll take into account the fact that there may have been drops of blood on the floor,' he said after a protracted silence. 'Can you tell me anything else about Braun's nurses – do they get on well or do they argue? What was their relationship with the doctor like?'

'Betsy Angel's a cow,' Gioele hissed. 'She hates Jews and would happily kill me if she could. Adele's kind. Betsy accuses her of being a friend of the Jews and says now Braun's gone, she'll get into big trouble if she carries on being so nice to us.'

'Are you saying they don't get on?'

'They hate each other. Betsy's jealous because Adele had already been working with Braun for a long time. He never told her off. Adele can't stand Betsy either, because Betsy used to meet Braun at night.'

'Did Braun do adult things with Betsy, too?'

'That's what I've heard.'

'Frau Braun couldn't have been happy about it.'

'Adults don't like sharing things, is that right?'

'Not always. Is there anything else you can tell me? Sounds like you have ears everywhere.'

'Adele asked me if I'd found anything strange in the doctor's office, but I didn't find anything except him.' Gioele looked down to better conceal his lie. He would help the German, but he would never give up his little treasure. A small gold medallion like the one he'd found in Braun's office could be worth a lot of money after the war was over.

'Did she look like she knew what this *something* might be?'

'No. Maybe she was just curious . . .'

They walked in silence in the twilight for a while. Gioele was still holding the twig like a pipe, puffing steam into the heavily humid air. He thought that someday he might like to be a detective.

'Herr Fischer,' he asked, suddenly curious. 'Why did you decide to become a criminologist?'

'Good question.' He rubbed his nose, red from the cold. 'I was in a Berlin nightclub. They were playing swing. Do you know what that is?'

Gioele shook his head.

'It's a kind of music that gets into every part of your body. It made me dance, too, though I wasn't sick yet. It was a lovely nightclub, there was all the drink you wanted and stunning girls.'

'Girls . . . Eek . . .'

'You'll think differently in a few years' time.' Hugo laughed but quickly turned serious again. His eyes were gloomy and moist. Gioele got the feeling he was looking at him with fear. 'One night, there was a raid by the Hitler Youth, because swing is American and dancing to it is forbidden,' he continued in a suddenly harsh voice. 'My friends managed to run away, but I didn't. I don't think I've ever been beaten up so badly. They struck me with whatever they could lay their hands on. There was a girl lying next to me. She was terrified because one of her attackers had pulled out a pistol. She asked me to help her but there was nothing I could do except lie there on the floor.'

Hugo paused and mimed a pistol with his fingers. He aimed it at the ground and pretended to pull the trigger. Gioele shrank into his shoulders as though the shot had really been fired and the bang had echoed through the Stammlager, setting the birds perched on the birches in flight.

'That young Nazi aimed and shot the girl without a second thought,' Hugo murmured. 'The shot made my ears ring and I fainted. I came to in the hospital. A couple of days later, much was written about her death: that the crazy crowd in the nightclub had trampled her and crushed her skull, that it was what the depraved young people who danced to swing in clubs on a Saturday night did. I knew that a good detective would have examined the crime scene, questioned me – the only eyewitness – studied the trajectory of the blood splashes and looked for the bullet casing. But no one cared how it really happened . . .'

'Did you tell the police how it happened?'

'I had to lie. I backed the Nazis' version.'

Gioele stared. He felt the ground give under his feet.

Hugo Fischer, the Nazi who didn't seem like other Nazis, was just like all the others. Sudden anger caught his breath and his guts were wrenched at the thought of having sold him Bethany's secret.

'Why did you do it?' he asked.

'There are things you'll understand when you're older.'

'But you lied!'

'And that's precisely why I decided to become a crim-inologist. I owed something to that girl.'

Gioele clenched his fists. He stared at the German and wondered how he could have been so stupid as to trust him. And yet he knew what Germans were like. He saw it every day in this terrible place he'd been dragged to. They were cruel, liars, and they hated Jews.

'Wait for me here,' Hugo commanded.

Gioele noticed they'd reached the officers' lodgings.

Hugo disappeared into the block, and Gioele was left loitering in the snow that was turning his calves and exposed knees purple. He jumped on a mound of snow and fell. The snow went under his jacket and slid down his neck, tickling him, but he didn't giggle. He couldn't get what the German had done as a young man out of his mind. He hadn't told anybody the truth about how the girl had died in the dance hall and so had become an accomplice to her death just to save himself. How could Gioele possibly continue to trust him?

When Hugo came back, Gioele's attention was entirely caught by his coat. He was now wearing a black leather one, too much like the SS officers', the same red armband with the swastika and a dark hat. He was carrying his old clothes folded under his arm.

'So, where's the laundry?' he asked.

Gioele pointed at the street that led to Block 10.

They set off in silence. Dressed like this, Hugo Fischer really was like the other Nazis in the camp, even though under his coat he wasn't wearing the grey uniform with the skull, but a jacket and tie. He inspired the same fear, made him equally angry, and this time Gioele made sure he didn't hold his hand.

'You Jews don't celebrate Christmas, do you?' Hugo asked when they were halfway there. He lit a cigarette using a metal lighter with the Nazi eagle embossed above the swastika.

Gioele shook his head. 'No.' He remembered the cold

winter evenings when his mother would light the log in the fireplace and his father the candles in the nine-branch candelabra, one for every day of the holiday. 'But we celebrate something similar at the same time of year. It's called Hanukkah, the festival of lights.'

At the last Hanukkah, his parents had given him a four-faceted top and some pocket money for having studied the Torah. Those moments now seemed distant and elusive. A little light lost in the Auschwitz cold.

'Next year you'll celebrate with your parents,' Hugo said to comfort him, though he didn't appear very sure of it either. His eyes were moist and sad. Another lie.

They walked into the laundry in dejected silence and were hit by a wave of warm steam from the disinfecting machines and a smell of detergent and lye that reminded Gioele of the ash concoction his mother used for washing sheets and towels.

He followed Hugo and watched him put his clothes on the wooden table and discuss delivery times with the Polish prisoner. He stared in astonishment at the washing tubs, the taut lines from which SS uniforms were hanging to dry, the steamrollers that looked like metal monsters and the hanger with the uniforms that were already dry and labelled. He went closer and read the names of people he knew.

'What are you doing?' Hugo asked behind him.

'This one was Dr Braun's.' Gioele indicated the grey uniform decorated with the skull and crossbones that had always frightened him. Next to it hung Uncle Mengele's uniform; he knew its every detail, from the runes on the collar to the insignia of rank.

'This one's Clauberg's and this one Voigt's.' Hugo looked at the labels pinned to the collars, which stated names and the date the clothes were handed in to be cleaned. Both Clauberg's and Voigt's had been brought in a couple of days ago. 'Is this the smell you noticed on Braun?'

Gioele sniffed the sleeve and shook his head. 'This is the smell of lye. What I smelled on Braun was perfume, the kind people put on their skin. I'm sure of it.'

Hugo pondered this, his gaze on Clauberg's insignia.

By the time they left the laundry, the sky had grown dark. The clang of the bell vibrated through the air and music by the orchestra that accompanied the return of the workers wafted between the buildings. The melody caressed the snow skimmed by the searchlights, slid through the tree-lined streets, among the blocks, then flitted away freely in the evening light.

'They're back,' Gioele said with a gasp. 'It's the roll call, I have to go!'

He sprinted across the snow towards the Appellplatz, which was swarming with prisoners. You could never tell how long the roll call would last, and if the SS officer on duty felt like letting them stand for hours in the cold and the snow, nobody could object. But, every evening, Uncle Mengele would come to pick up him and the other twins before the bell rang again.

That wasn't necessary tonight though, since the roll call was over very quickly. Maybe because it was Christmas Eve and the guard couldn't wait to get rid of them.

As they were being counted, Gioele looked up at the stars and was sure he saw a shooting one, as sparkling as the flame on the nine-branch candelabra.

He made a wish.

To go home.

19

Hugo went to his room, the whole day's exhaustion on his shoulders. The pain radiated into his lower back again and his numb arm caused him to swear through gritted teeth.

Not much could relieve the pain except morphine. He'd given all his cognac to the SS officers in the brothel and had only three cigarettes left. Once these ran out, he'd have to get someone to find him another packet.

He put the leather coat on the bed and went to the desk, the camp searchlights slicing like cold shadows through the coarse wood and illuminating a rectangular box that hadn't been there earlier – popped out from heaven knew where. He stroked the grey label and read the red letters, rubbing them with the fingertips of his healthy hand: Eukodal.

'Consider this a Christmas present,' he read out loud.

It had started to snow again and the flakes were crashing against the windowpane. He imagined Berlin with festive decorations, like before the war, with dressed trees,

Christmas markets on the banks of the Spree and the air filled with the fragrance of mulled wine.

He pictured himself in front of the fireplace at his home, with the rotary candle holder going round and round, and an Advent wreath on the dining room wall.

The chill in the room brought Hugo starkly back to reality.

He sniffed the note and felt its texture, then opened the drawer and compared it with the one found at the Kanada. They were alike, only one had been typed and the other handwritten in an elegant, precise hand. Anita Kunig's, evidently.

He stood looking at the box and the cylinder-shaped tablets for what felt like infinity. He knew he'd become addicted to all this stuff. He'd started on Pervitin when almost the entire German population was using it. It had allowed him to stay awake for days on end while writing his criminology manual and given him an energy he would never experience again. He hadn't been surprised when these tablets were administered to the army: no doubt it was purely thanks to this methamphetamine that German soldiers had been able to beat Poland and France to the punch, marching night and day with an energy and speed the enemy could not match.

Then the pain of the illness had come and Pervitin had no longer been enough.

Doctors had suggested adding morphine. He'd once tried to stop and ended up in the university lavatory, teeth chattering and breaking into a cold sweat in the month of August. It was revolting. So he'd realized that stopping would be much worse.

Hugo looked at the little box, as grey as Auschwitz ashes.

Anita Kunig was offering him the chance of a carefree, pain-free Christmas Eve. Tomorrow, he'd have the strength and lucidity to go to Solahütte, where he'd been invited for Christmas dinner at what had been described as a pleasant retreat for SS officers, located by a lake and surrounded by mountains. There, he'd be able to talk to everyone he wanted to question.

Hugo opened the box and took out a tablet.

It was the drug even the Führer used, Anita Kunig had said.

However irksome he found her, he was indebted and grateful. He placed the Eukodal on his tongue, swallowed it and felt it graze his tonsils as it travelled down his throat.

It was like turning the camp lights out one by one.

His temples sizzled and he was filled with so much rage he could have gone to the brothel on the spot, to Rose's room, and made love to her for hours. But no, it wasn't her he wanted. The image of Adele bullied its way to him – Adele and her copper-coloured, soft-as-a-cloud hair, her piercing green eyes, her laugh and shrewd expression that were so at odds with the camp's sadness.

Hugo was overwhelmed with excitement, but that was immediately dampened by the drug-induced, slowly intensifying angst. He collapsed on the bed and stared at the chipped ceiling, where all he saw was Gioele's face and his heart stopping on a beat.

Tu-tum.

Next year you'll celebrate with your parents. He'd lied to him.

Tu-tum.

Auschwitz, 25 December 1943

The dawn slowly flowed into the room and woke him up.

Hugo sat up on the bed, unable to recall even falling asleep. It had been a long time since he'd gone to sleep so quickly, without first tossing and turning, unable to close his eyes. He rubbed his back. There was no pain. The Eukodal had worked.

He got up, still full of energy, unused to this total anaesthesia. It was like being back to how he'd been before his illness.

He washed and shaved carefully, then went out.

Outside, there was a festive atmosphere, but his heart was like a desolate, withered heath. Music filled the camp and the Appellplatz was empty: even the prisoners had been granted a break. Where the mobile gallows usually stood, he saw a small choir of children singing at the foot of a decorated Christmas tree, their voices making the cold morning air more bearable. He recognized Gioele among them.

Hugo walked past the choir, his stomach churning, unable to forget Rabi's words or the blazing piles in Birkenau or the canisters emptied of fumigant. He walked past the last blocks, gripping his stick, and through the gate that looked black against the clear, luminous sky. He'd arranged to meet Tristan Voigt outside the camp, at the SS garage, where he was already waiting for Hugo next to a van.

'Happy Christmas, Herr Fischer,' Voigt said.

'Happy Christmas to you.' Hugo pointed his stick at the sky. It was of an almost blinding blue, extending as far as the eye could see, making the frozen snow sparkle. 'What a glorious day.'

Voigt invited him in with a slap to the green top of the vehicle. 'Don't get used to it. The weather here in Poland is unpredictable and can change in an instant.'

Just like my illness, Hugo thought.

He climbed in. The driver started the engine and the van rumbled off. They drove down the icy road, leaving behind the camp's sad profile and the grim inscription that now sounded like what it was: a practical joke. Voigt looked straight ahead, jaw clenched in barely detectable anxiety. Hugo wondered if he had a family and if the festivities were making him miss them. He couldn't help thinking about Berlin and his own father, alone at home, while outside the air-raid sirens sounded their frightening wail.

'I've heard you helped capture Otto Hampel and Elise Lemme,' Voigt said, after Hugo had accepted the prospect of a silent journey spent looking at the glaring, snowy Polish countryside.

'Yes.' Now deeply ashamed of that episode, Hugo would have preferred to forget it and talk of something else. 'I helped with the psychological profile of the wanted man. A simple man, tormented by the loss of a relative on the French front . . .' he recited.

'A man who scattered two hundred and seventy-seven postcards against the Führer in the streets of Berlin,' Voigt said. 'No mean feat.'

'Two hundred and eighty-five,' Hugo said. 'Eighteen post-cards were never handed to the police or publicly reported.'

'Eighteen rebels.' Voigt adjusted a button on his coat that had missed the hole. 'Talking of battles, have you heard about the Russian front?'

'I haven't heard the radio. To be honest, I've not heard it for days.'

165

'The Red Army staged a surprise attack.' Voigt pulled an angry face. 'A Christmas present from Stalin. The 13th and 14th army corps were defeated. And to think that this is where it all began.' He tapped on the window, then wiped a round porthole through which you could see the snow-clad Polish forest. 'The Blitzkrieg, fierce and lethal, that made everyone quake. And now we're up to our eyes in a war of attrition . . .'

Hugo sighed. 'I feel sorry for the soldiers at the front.'

Voigt turned and gave him an embittered smile that did nothing to lift the atmosphere. 'Enough talk of war. Tell me about your investigation. How is it going?'

'To be honest' – Hugo looked out of the window at the clouds beginning to stain the horizon – 'it's slow, but today I'm counting on speaking to the people closest to Dr Braun. People don't like being questioned – have you noticed?'

'I know.'

'But I have Christmas on my side. They'll all be more relaxed and willing to chat, and perhaps forget I'm a criminologist. Berto Hoffman won't be there, but I hope to speak to him again in the next few days – unless the guards make him unfit for questioning again . . .'

'They've guaranteed that nobody will lay a hand on him,' Voigt said. 'And I sent a nurse to take a look at him. His bronchitis has got worse and could turn into something more serious.'

'He has bronchitis?'

'It was diagnosed two weeks ago, but Berto seems to be a very hard worker, so he ignored the early symptoms.'

'I'd say that's the least of his worries now.'

'I think so, too.'

Hugo fell silent again and thought about the note

scribbled by Braun – he couldn't have written it after ingesting the cyanide because the poison acted too quickly. He'd had enough time to realize someone would force him to bite into the phial, so by writing the note, he'd shown impressive shrewdness and lucidity even as he was about to die. The murderer had torn the message out, heedless of the paper beneath it, clearly too agitated to notice it, or perhaps believing the message was too obscure to arouse fear.

Hugo looked at the steamed-up window, tempted to write 'Doll O A B' in the condensation.

Names came to his mind, which he'd turned over in his mouth time and again without detecting their taste: Osmund, Adele, Anita; Betsy, Bethany, Brunhilde. Every one of these initials could be significant.

'You're deep in thought,' Voigt's cold voice interrupted his train of thought.

'I'm just trying to piece things together. It's not easy to clear your mind, especially here.'

'Have you already come up with the murderer's profile?'

Hugo nodded. 'In the beginning I thought it was a man, simply because it takes strength to keep someone of Braun's build still and crush a phial of cyanide in his mouth. But now I'm not ruling out the possibility that it might have been a woman who forced him by pointing a pistol at him – that would explain the absence of a struggle. But the bruising puzzles me. Could a woman have struck Braun without him overpowering her?'

'There could have been two killers,' Voigt remarked.

'Possibly. In any case, the person I'm looking for knew the victim well. They didn't catch him unawares but talked with him for a while. They were familiar with his office

167

and the medical room. They knew there was a basket of apples on a shelf and that one could be used to simulate choking. It's someone cunning but they made a couple of errors, which means they were emotionally involved, possibly connected to the doctor in a romantic way. It's not a complete profile yet. I have to rely on a child for many of the details, which has never happened to me before and is embarrassing because I have to take what he says with a pinch of salt . . .'

'That Jew again,' Voigt snarled. 'A potentially innocent man's life is at stake, a man now in the clutches of death!'

'I know,' Hugo replied defensively. 'But that child knows many things.'

The vehicle jolted, hurling them face to face, eye to eye. Hugo felt the officer's calm, deadly breath and momentarily imagined it as the warm breath of a wolf stealthily emerging from the forest to hunt and maul its prey.

'You won't find your answers in a Jew,' Voigt muttered. 'Jews have only one role here, and that's to vanish from the face of the earth. They're picked up from the train convoy and chosen. Those able to work are interned. The others we line up on the right and take to the Sanatorium. The gas chambers, Herr Fischer. Did you understand that during your tours of Birkenau or not?'

Hugo's eyes opened wide.

Another jolt pushed them apart.

'They're locked up in rooms with showers,' Voigt added coldly. 'We let them believe they're there to wash off the dirt of the journey. Mostly old people, women, children and the odd cripple. A petty officer opens a canister of Zyklon B and pours it in through a window. I've done it myself. It really doesn't take long for Zyklon B to become gas. We're able to kill a thousand in one go. By the time we open the doors, they're all dead and if anyone miraculously survives, we finish them off with a bullet in the head. From there they go directly to the crematoria ovens.'

While Voigt talked, Hugo was only aware of the jolting van.

He couldn't move anything – not even a muscle. A stabbing pain in his leg made him realize he was still alive and, for the first time ever, he thanked his pain.

Auschwitz had a bad reputation in Berlin. It was a detention camp, after all, and people sometimes died in detention camps. Occasionally, things got out of hand and typhus epidemics spread all too easily. But what Voigt was describing was different from a detention camp: what was being carried out here was extermination.

Hugo heard the fierce *sssh* of the Zyklon in his ears again. He'd understood what was happening the very moment Otto Moll had accompanied him to the piles, when he'd seen the officer's hands pouring the contents of the canisters through the crematorium window. Hearing it from Tristan Voigt's lips, however, was like a wave of iced water in his face. He'd learned that, for as long as there was doubt, there was also hope: *doubt* that one day his lungs would stop, *doubt* that his illness could get worse, *doubt* that one day he would no longer be able to walk. It could happen – or not. Certainty, however, was a terrible thing.

Now, Hugo had the certainty of how things in Auschwitz really were.

'I'm telling you this to make you understand just how little a Jew is worth here,' Voigt continued, slow and painful, like a red-hot blade in his flesh. 'You must protect your

169

career and mine. You mustn't tell anyone you believe what that child's telling you, because if you do, no one will believe you even if you do discover the culprit, and Hoffman will be executed all the same. You must find a non-Jewish prisoner and have them tell you the same things as that child. That will be truly useful evidence.'

'Do you have children?' Hugo asked like an automaton. He almost couldn't imagine that possibility, not knowing how a man could look his own child in the eye after seeing hell. A tear flowed out and he wiped it immediately.

'I did have one.' Voigt looked down. 'He was beautiful, a very special child. No one realized just how special . . .'

'Did he die?'

'Pneumonia,' he whispered, a shadow drifting over his ashen eyes.

The van was driving through a mountainous landscape with sharp, narrow bends, the road unfurling between dense beeches. Bathed in this lunar whiteness, the two men could only keep silent.

All that remained in the vehicle was the rumbling of the engine and a clatter whenever they drove through a dip.

'Here are the documents you asked me for.' Voigt proffered some papers, suddenly breaking the cloying silence.

'What are they?' Hugo quickly leafed through them, still dazed. His tongue hurt after the recent exchange and his head felt heavy.

'I've been to the Kommandantur. It's where they keep the files and documents on the prisoners. Aronne Errera is still alive. He's at the quarantine camp. Barrack 10, to be exact. Only don't tell the boy. I've no idea what condition he's in.'

'And his wife?' Hugo's heart was in turmoil.

170

Voigt shook his head and pointed at the 'S.B.' next to the woman's name. 'Special Treatment,' he translated. 'Frau Errera was gassed on arrival in the camp.'

Hugo stared into Voigt's eyes and felt as though he was falling. He now understood that the officer had slammed the truth in his face partly to prepare him for that abbreviation.

'S.B. – Sonderbehandlung. Special Treatment.'

The man who a moment earlier had pounced on him like a ferocious animal now seemed genuinely saddened by the fact that after travelling for days in a small, dirty train carriage without food or water, Gioele's mother had been dispatched to the gas chamber for slaughter. Hugo pictured her intent on reassuring Gioele and Gabriele, whispering lullabies on frosty nights, promising that all would be well.

'They take the place of God,' Franz had said in the brothel about the triage doctors. 'They go there drunk.' Now, Hugo understood.

'Don't tell the boy,' Voigt added.

'Of course not.'

Hugo looked through the window and saw the Solahütte lodge. Made of carved timber, it jutted out over the lake, in the middle of a white landscape. The sun was making the icy bank of the lake sparkle, outlining a small bridge and lighting a terrace overlooking this enchanted hollow. There were women and children lying in deckchairs, their legs wrapped in woollen blankets, holding cups that gave off swirls of steam. They were smiling and Hugo felt a wave of anger.

In hell, too, it was Christmas Day.

20

The bellows of the accordion expanded and contracted in a Christmas carol.

Hugo couldn't remember the lyrics, but the children came to his aid, jumping off the deckchairs to form a small crowd around the officer who was playing. 'O Tannenbaum, o Tannenbaum,' they sang in chorus, holding hands, 'Wie treu sind deine Blätter!'

Hugo couldn't smile.

He could see a majestic fir tree at the far end of the terrace, so dark green it seemed artificial. It gave off a scent of resin that blended with that of ginger biscuits and cinnamon. Everything was perfect. There was no ash in Solahütte.

'Our criminologist!' He was still on the steps when Liebehenschel's voice surprised him from the French window on the terrace. He had a cigar in his mouth, his hair was pomaded to one side, his eyes even more protruding and staring than normal. He was with Mengele and Clauberg, the gynaecologist, and there was another man next to him, not very tall, elegant-looking, with hair thinning at the temples and a face that was still young and pleasant.

Hugo came forward, carefully propping himself on his stick to avoid being knocked down by children in short trousers running from one end of the terrace to the other. On the bridge, a group of SS officers were singing in chorus with SS-Helferinnen, their cheeks all flushed from the cold and the fun. For a moment, the smell of burnt flesh seemed far, far away, and Voigt's story practically impossible.

'Heil Hitler,' he said with little ardour as he approached the group of officers gathered around Liebehenschel.

'Heil Hitler!' the Kommandant replied, picking up a champagne flute and handing it to him. 'Dom Pérignon '36. It's from the first grape harvest, back in '21. A rarity these days.'

'Thank you.' Hugo raised the flute and drank. The bubbles pricked his palate, almost making his eyes water, and he felt the urge to cry floods of tears, as he did when a child. He sensed how these tears were seeking any excuse to burst out and free him from all the pain and anger inside him.

'Let me introduce Eduard Wirths,' the Kommandant said, referring to the elegant man next to him. 'Chief doctor in Auschwitz.'

'A pleasure to meet you.'

'The pleasure's mine,' Wirths replied. His broad forehead, well-proportioned features and straight nose gave him a reassuring look, but by now Hugo had learned not to trust appearances. 'Liebehenschel won't stop singing your praises,' he added.

'Liebehenschel is too kind,' Hugo said.

'Any news on the Braun case?' Clauberg broke in, intrigued. 'The Kommandant may be singing your praises but, apparently, there's not been an ounce of progress. A case should be solved in three days at most – isn't that what they say?'

He'd spoken with a cigar in his teeth, mumbling and tactlessly butting into their conversation.

'The investigation continues.' Hugo took a sip to conceal his annoyance. The Dom Pérignon was chilled to perfection, with a strong yet unfathomable flavour, like a fragrance he couldn't make out. Like Braun's.

He studied Clauberg, pondering his next step. If it was true he and Braun had been friends, he must know many things about the doctor.

'What kind of man was Braun?' he asked.

Clauberg inhaled the smoke in large gulps and returned it in fragrant clouds. 'Sigismund and I were born in the same town,' he replied, adjusting the round glasses that had slid practically down to his nostrils. 'We went to the same schools. When we were ten, he courted the most beautiful girl in the town – I was madly in love with her and the scoundrel knew it. I only forgave him because he ended up marrying her.'

Clauberg burst into a coarse laugh that eventually infected Liebehenschel.

'What kind of man was he?' Hugo insisted. Clauberg was so short, Hugo had to drop his head down to look at him. 'Besides being the sort who steals his friend's girlfriend and then marries her, I mean.'

Clauberg burst into another laugh. Perhaps he'd already had an ample amount to drink. Mengele gave a faint smile that masked a grimace, evidently annoyed by this behaviour, and Hugo remembered what Tristan Voigt had told him in the chapel of rest: that Clauberg only got on with Braun. The other doctors barely tolerated him and considered him arrogant.

'Sigismund was an excellent doctor,' Clauberg snorted as soon as he'd caught his breath, watering his words with a copious helping of champagne. 'He wouldn't have been here otherwise. The Reich sent its best doctors to the camps so they could experiment. Here we have what's missing in a university or an ordinary research centre; even those bastards the Americans would give anything to come here. I mean, what they give you in a research centre is rats and rabbits. Here, you can have Jewish rats and rabbits, if you see what I mean!'

Another nasal laugh.

Hugo looked around, revolted. There was no smell of burnt flesh here. You couldn't hear flames crackling or see prisoners with lean faces, skin sagging like threadbare cloth over their bones, or corpses piled high on the back of a lorry. The waiters were all healthy Polish prisoners. The SS officers were singing, one of them was playing the accordion, a few were dancing.

Human rats, Hugo uttered in his throat, pushing his voice back.

'I'm sure Braun was good at his work,' he said, stifling his anger, 'and had many opportunities here. You're right when you say that no other place in the world offers researchers so much. In some ways, though, it must be like any other research centre. I know from experience that silly jealousies and petty resentments often arise among colleagues. I'll bet Auschwitz is no exception to the rule. What can you tell me about his assistants? There's that young man—'

'Becker,' Wirths said helpfully.

'Osmund Becker,' Clauberg echoed.

Liebehenschel was still following the conversation, riveted, examining every word for a clue in the hope of finding the solution before everyone else.

'Osmund Becker's a novice,' Clauberg explained, suppressing a belch. 'He's got a long way to go before he reaches Sigismund's level, but he's got determination and an eagerness to learn on his side.'

'What does he do?'

'He's a geneticist. He's studying hereditary diseases. Glitches in what should be a perfect process, if you see what I mean. Think what an achievement it would be if we could erase the possibility of passing on a flawed gene. Multiple sclerosis, for instance, could be caused by genetic degeneration, right?'

'What?'

Hugo's heart skipped a beat and an electric discharge struck a specific spot in the middle of his back.

Multiple sclerosis.

Nobody could have told him. He clutched his stick and prayed that the nystagmus in his eyes wouldn't give him away or that his brain wouldn't pick that very moment to play a nasty trick on him by making all his muscles tremble like a man possessed.

Clauberg squinted and smirked. 'Are you sure you had poliomyelitis?'

Hugo's instinct was to hit him with his stick and silence him once and for all.

'You don't walk like a horse,' he insisted. 'Your limp's

different. I'll bet you use the stick more from fear of falling in public, when you get dizzy and your leg doesn't obey your command, than out of real necessity. I've noticed your eye sometimes quivers too.'

Hugo laughed. He looked at Liebehenschel, who caught his eye and also laughed. Mengele, too, joined in, giving Clauberg a dirty look. He must have felt visceral contempt for him.

'You're the first person who's suggested this diagnosis,' Hugo lied brazenly. He could feel his knuckles turn white over the handle of his stick. 'I can assure you I had poliomyelitis. Maybe I should get young Osmund to check me – what do you say?'

Clauberg snickered. A loud, irritating giggle that ran under Hugo's skin like a scratch on the wall. 'Of course you had poliomyelitis! Besides, I'd hope that anyone with an illness like multiple sclerosis would have the common sense to request euthanasia or, at the very least, sterilization. Do you all remember Heidemarie Hatheyer in Liebeneiner's film?'

'A superb performance,' Wirths said. 'A talented actress.'

'I think the scene where she asks to be killed with morphine is one of the most moving in the history of German cinema,' Clauberg insisted. 'I've often shown that clip to my students to illustrate the importance of mass sterilization in subjects that carry genetic diseases. Nobody would want to live with the burden of a degenerative illness, and we doctors have a duty to offer the option of a dignified death rather than prolong a life not worth living. Liebeneiner's film outlines this issue perfectly.'

'Let's go back to Osmund Becker, please.' Hugo loosened his tie slightly and tried to store as much air as he could in his lungs. His tongue felt coarse and his temples burnt hot.

'Let's go back to him.' Clauberg's lips thinned in a smile and he raised his eyebrows impudently.

Hugo remembered that he had before him a man who'd killed a young woman in cold blood because she'd refused to follow him to the bedroom. A cynical, ruthless man, quick-tempered and arrogant, one he should give a wide berth to from now on.

'What exactly do you want to know?' he asked.

'Did Becker and Braun get on? Was there any jealousy between them?'

'Osmund has two problems.' Clauberg lifted two fingers. 'First, he thinks more about skirts than about work. Don't get me wrong, he's a good doctor and he actually asked to be sent here, but I don't think he expected to find so many women to distract him.'

He indicated the laughing female auxiliaries. They were beaming this morning. Even in their grey uniforms, they no longer looked like the sad guards of a concentration camp and the plain ones also seemed oddly charming.

'And this caused friction with Braun?' Hugo enquired.

'Some. Maybe they'd got their eye on the same woman.' Clauberg burst into another unpleasant, high-pitched laugh. 'His second problem is arrogance.'

'Nasty beast, arrogance,' Mengele said with a barbed expression. Clauberg seemed not to pick up on the hint, or chose to pretend he hadn't.

'Osmund is sure of himself and a social climber,' he continued. 'He hides behind the image of a pupil, but there's a flame in his eyes I immediately recognized.'

'Did Braun think so, too?'

Clauberg nodded. 'He had to silence him more than once, make it clear where he stood in the pecking order. I think there was a lot of competition between them. You're right about that, Herr Fischer: Auschwitz has all the drawbacks of any other research centre, where academics compete to be the first to obtain a result, so they can please the Reich and its Führer.'

'It's normal for a student, sooner or later, to want to overtake his teacher,' Wirths said, downplaying it. 'It's human nature.'

'True,' Mengele said.

'And did you get on well with Braun?' Hugo asked Clauberg.

'You want to know if I forgave him for marrying Brunhilde?' He rubbed his practically bald head. His eyes smiled from behind the round glasses. 'For God's sake! Of course I did! He's the best friend I ever had. I don't get on with many of the doctors here. No offence, Josef,' he added, putting a hand on Mengele's shoulder, 'but with Sigismund, there was a lot of esteem and affection, as well as an excellent working relationship – something I don't have with the other doctors.'

'Did you see him the night of the murder?'

'The last time I saw him was at the officers' mess. We worked till sunset.' Clauberg glanced at his pocket watch. 'Until 3.40 p.m., to be exact. After that, we each went to our lodgings while waiting for dinner. We met again at the mess at 6 p.m.'

'Did Braun live in the camp lodgings?'

Wirths intervened. 'No. Braun had a small farmhouse that had been seized from a Polish family, about a kilometre away from the camp.'

'A fully refurbished rural house,' Clauberg said. 'With a splendid swimming pool in the middle of a few hectares of well cared-for garden, where we sometimes had parties. Happy times.'

Hugo studied the doctors, their impeccable SS uniforms, the champagne flutes they were holding so casually. How could they party by a pool when they saw the stinking smoke rising from the camp?

'Do you think he went home between finishing work and dinner?' he continued.

'I couldn't tell you,' Clauberg replied.

'Did he look upset in any way?'

'Not in the least. He was in high spirits, as usual. Even more so.' Clauberg spoke of Braun with the light-hearted sadness people use when talking about friends who've just died. Of one thing Hugo was certain: his affection for Braun seemed genuine.

'What do you mean by "even more so"?'

'Maybe he was meeting an old female friend after dinner, but I'm not sure.'

'Who?'

Clauberg mimed a key locking his lips, meaning that in no way would he sully his friend's memory.

At that moment, out of the corner of his eye, Hugo saw Adele Kraus arrive. Betsy Angel was behind her, and many SS officers had already gone to meet her with flutes of champagne and biscuit trays they'd removed from the waiters. There was no doubt she didn't go unnoticed, and Braun, too, must have enjoyed her graces.

Hugo caught Adele's eye. Betsy may well have been a 'doll', but Adele was a flame in the middle of the white snow. She greeted him and he smiled. The image of the

180

note stuck to the dental pincers came back with a vengeance, demanding an answer.

'Can anyone tell me what "Union" means?' he asked point-blank. He downed the last drops of the Dom Pérignon and held them between his tongue and his palate.

Liebehenschel frowned. 'Union?'

'The other day, an SS officer was talking about this "Union".'

'The Union-Werke? The bullet fuse factory?'

'Of course.' Hugo shook his head and huffed. 'The talk was actually about ammunitions. I nodded and pretended to know what it was about. I don't like to appear stupid . . .'

'Who does?' Clauberg laughed coarsely.

'And now, if you'll excuse me, I'm going to have a chat with Braun's nurses.'

'Go and enjoy yourself.' Clauberg winked at him in a roguish manner.

Hugo firmly headed towards Adele. Why was there a note about an ammunitions factory stuck to the pincers? And who was it for? He caught her eye, but an officer swept her away before he could reach her.

Hugo found himself in front of Betsy.

'You seem disappointed to see me,' she said, looking at Adele and the SS officer walking down the path that led to the frozen lake. 'You'd prefer somebody else's company, perhaps?'

'Yours will do nicely,' Hugo replied, beaming a polite smile.

21

The children of the Auschwitz staff members had all gathered at the foot of the tall Christmas tree to sing a carol.

They looked like angels, with their small, pale faces and smart clothes. They attended school in the city or at the SS garrisons, lived in farmhouses a few steps away from the crematoria, maybe took long swims in the river Soła in the summer, and in the morning their parents took them to the camp kennel to pat the Alsatians. The smell of burnt flesh probably wafted in with a vengeance when the wind allowed it, but nothing in their eyes suggested they knew where their mums and dads had brought them to live.

Hugo tried to sing, spurred on by Betsy Angel, who had taken his arm, attracting everyone's looks and comments, but he couldn't recall the lyrics.

The carol ended and, at last, Liebehenschel picked up a candle and initiated the celebrations by lighting the rest of the Christmas tree lights. One by one, the candles sizzled, giving off a smell of wax from the wicks and illuminating the wonder-filled faces of the children.

'Would you like a drink?' Betsy chirped, dragging him to the veranda, where refreshments had been laid out.

Hugo's leg made him stumble and he had to cling to the handrail to keep up with her. She picked up two glasses of wine and handed one to him.

'I know you couldn't wait to interrogate me,' she said provocatively. 'And I couldn't wait to talk to you.'

'You're the kind who gets straight to the point,' he said ironically.

'I keep preliminaries for other occasions . . .'

Betsy had a sly expression. The doll-like look was just a cover. Gioele had called her a cow, so she must have a significant amount of cynicism, as well as hysteria and cruelty, to have earned that reputation.

Hugo tried to break the ice. 'What kind of man was Braun?'

'A good and very experienced doctor,' she replied.

'So many people have said.'

Hugo sipped his wine and moved to a corner of the veranda, away from the crowd and the bustle. A prisoner was playing the piano in the dining room, her hands moving delicately over the keys. Her thin fingers hinted at the privations she clearly suffered, but that didn't stop her from filling the lodge with heartfelt music, passionate as a slow tide that ends up swamping everything.

'Don't you feel like dancing?' Betsy asked.

Hugo looked at her in a daze. He'd been an enthusiastic dancer once upon a time, but now the mere idea of dancing and drawing everyone's attention to his leg annoyed him.

'I'm sorry,' he replied, 'but I'm very tired and my leg is aching.'

'I understand,' she said with a sigh.

The Eukodal effect had worn off. It wasn't yet noon and he already felt all broken up by neuralgia. Tiredness was sneaking up on him like a sly worm he couldn't stop from burrowing in to his body. These days he lived waiting for the moment when his symptoms disappeared, making way for a long break when pain would be a faded memory. All he had left then was his numb leg, an indelible sign that the disease was always with him despite the phases of attack and remission. Just like the Wattenmeer tide. That childhood place, Hugo thought, kept returning like a constant in his life.

'Let's get back to Dr Braun,' Betsy said, rousing him.

'Of course.' Hugo licked his lips. 'What time did you work until on the night he died?'

Betsy reclined on the cushions of a small couch and crossed her legs. 'Until sunset,' she replied, confirming what Clauberg had stated. 'It was almost four o'clock. He went to the officers' mess, and I stayed and had dinner in the block.'

'With Bethany Assouline?'

'For God's sake!' Betsy put her hand in front of her red-painted lips. 'What do you take me for, Herr Fischer? Bethany's a Jew . . .'

'I beg your pardon,' he said. 'I'm still struggling to match names and faces. With Adele Krause, then?'

'No, I don't get on with her. I was alone.'

'Wasn't Osmund Becker there?'

'No. He seldom eats with us.'

'What about Berto Hoffman?'

'Berto was busy with some work at the Birkenau experiment station.'

'Tell me about him and Adele.'

184

'I don't get on with either of them, if that's what you want to know.' Betsy didn't beat about the bush. 'They'd been working together since Irsee. When Braun came to Auschwitz, he insisted on bringing his work team with him, and it wasn't easy for me to integrate. It's hard to become part of a tight-knit circle, it's a bit like always being in the wrong place or a step behind the others.'

Hugo looked at her, wondering if that was why she'd had an affair with the doctor: to break into that closed circle and secure a privileged position.

'Osmund thinks the same as I do,' she added. 'I think he, more than anyone else, understands how I felt. It was like being strangers in a family where all the other members know one another all too well.'

'Have you any idea where Osmund Becker had dinner that evening?'

'No.'

'What's he like?'

'Clever; he'll go far.'

'And Adele Krause?'

'Adele.' Betsy grimaced. 'Braun was too soft with her.'

'What do you mean?'

'Adele is out of place here, as much as I was in their work group. She wasn't ready to come to Auschwitz. Sigismund must have given her a good sales pitch. She's always been far too kind to our guinea pigs, but he turned a blind eye and never reported her to a superior, maybe because he felt guilty towards her. I call her "friend of the Jews", and that makes her angry,' she said with a snigger.

Hugo stared at the shiny edge of the glass. Adele had in her basket a pair of dental pincers with a message – pincers used for removing gold teeth from dead bodies, he'd seen that at the piles with his own eyes. Was the message for the Sonderkommandos?

'And is she really a friend of the Jews?' he asked.

'I don't like to malign people,' Betsy whispered, glancing around, 'but I have my doubts about whether the green triangles were really being sold by Berto Hoffman. It could have been Adele who hid them in his mattress. It would be just like her to do something like that.'

'That's a serious accusation. Do you have proof?'

'No,' she grumbled. She pouted before returning to the offensive. 'One day, she and Braun had an argument. Adele was furious about the Jews' special treatment.'

'I think the nature of the "special treatment" could easily upset a person.' Hugo felt his voice becoming hoarse. 'Perhaps Adele was troubled by what was happening in the camp and felt obliged to tell her mentor.'

'The elimination of Jews is a sacred duty,' Betsy replied. Her eyes were aglow with a fire Hugo had already seen in many others, a blind faith in the Reich that had always frightened him. It wasn't just about sympathizers or non-sympathizers, but about seeing Hitler as Germany's Messiah. 'Did you know that during the Great War, our Führer was saved by a mysterious voice?'

'So I've heard . . .'

'A voice told him to leave his shelter,' she continued doggedly. 'He obeyed and a moment later a grenade fell on the shelter. Everyone died except him. After the Beer Hall Putsch he tried to commit suicide, but Sepp Dietrich's wife stopped him with a martial arts move: she says she was prompted by a mysterious force. The Führer is enlightened and only a madman would doubt his mission to free the world from the infestation of Jews.'

'What are you getting at?'

'If Adele doesn't understand the importance of Auschwitz, she's mad. And a mad person can carry out terrible acts to support their cause.'

'So can a lover,' Hugo said with a lopsided smile. 'Were you and Braun intimate?'

Betsy closed her lips in a hard, blood-red line and opened her eyes wide. Her flushed cheeks betrayed her. 'No,' she replied, quivering with rage. 'I don't know how something like that could cross your mind.'

'I know that the doctor had a weakness for women—'

'Not that his wife is a saint,' Betsy snapped back but fell silent as soon as she glimpsed Frau Braun making an entrance onto the veranda, dressed in the auxiliary uniform that made her look as angular and icy as ever.

Hugo could ask no more questions. Brunhilde Braun was walking up to him with a firm, military step. Suddenly, her face relaxed into a faint smile that lifted her cheek-bones, red from the cold, and Hugo was astounded.

'Heil Hitler!' she exclaimed, strangely gentle. 'And happy Christmas, Herr Fischer.'

Hugo studied her for an extended moment, the way wolves study their rivals before a skirmish, smelling the air, assessing every movement.

'Happy Christmas to you,' he finally replied.

'Fräulein Angel, do you mind if *I* steal a man from you for once?' Her voice was filled with a quiet sarcasm in which Hugo sensed old animosities. 'I'd like to speak with Detective Fischer alone.'

22

'Let's take a stroll,' Frau Braun said authoritatively, not as an invitation but an order. Maybe she was too accustomed to issuing them and no longer knew how else to interact with other people.

They left the lodge and walked down the winter-grey path.

The lake shore glistened with ice crystals. The sparse tufts of grass, where the snow had been shovelled, now yielded, defeated, under their feet. The mist smelled of ash and burnt wood, hinting at the odour of dead things and nothing of the fragrance of clean water gushing out in the mountains in the spring.

They walked in silence for a long time.

The hardened snow crunched under their steps with a faint lament that was then lost in the fog along the escarpment, the barely visible birches standing like guardians against the milky expanse.

'I apologize for my hostile attitude before,' Frau Braun said. 'I attacked you for no reason the other day. I didn't understand that you're here to help Sigismund and not to offend his memory. Perhaps I was too upset.'

Hugo smiled, propping himself firmly on his stick so as not to slip on the icy bank.

'Your reaction was perfectly normal,' he said reassuringly. 'I'm used to it.'

'I just didn't want my husband's body to be defaced . . .'

'I know. Your friend, Anita Kunig, said I was cruel towards you. Perhaps she's right, I should have responded to your grief with more tact. But the autopsy was necessary, believe me . . .'

Frau Braun smiled, moved. 'Anita's always worried about me.'

'A good sort, isn't she? One that doesn't bend.'

'Life has already bent her once, that's why she's become so tough.'

With a look, Hugo urged her to continue. Frau Braun needed to feel comfortable, make peace with death, merge with this solitary, sad landscape before facing her own fears.

'She lost a child,' she said, her breath dispersing in the misty air and dissolving like a prayer to the sky, which had clouded over.

In Poland, the weather can suddenly change, Voigt had said.

Like life, Hugo thought.

'How did the child die?' he asked.

'He had health problems. His name was Bastian – he was a gorgeous child.'

'Did you know him?'

'No. Anita showed me a picture. She's always talking about him.'

Hugo paused on the bank and his gaze swept over this

place that seemed suspended in nothingness. No time, no space. No ash.

'It was in December, four years ago,' Frau Braun went on. 'She still carries him in her heart. They say you never get over the grief of losing a child. It changes but never goes away. When Mengele showed us his Jew, Anita felt ill. That boy looks so much like Bastian . . .'

'Do you mean Gioele Errera?'

'I don't know his name. He's the boy with those striking eyes. I only know that the resemblance is heartbreaking, trust me, and since that day Anita's changed; she's sadder, it must have been like seeing a ghost.'

Ghosts, again. Hugo sighed and his gaze wandered to the white sheet of ice over the lake. He was always shaken by the painful stories people concealed. Now even Anita Kunig seemed less tough. Water beneath the ice.

'Some people wear armour,' he remarked. 'If you try and tear it off them you discover things you'd never have suspected. A past of suffering, an unavowable secret that made them into what they are, for better or worse.'

'Exactly,' Frau Braun replied. 'What's yours?'

Hugo didn't feel like lying, not in this place. It wouldn't have been fair. 'I have an illness I don't like to talk about,' he said, surprised by his own words. 'And there's an episode in my past that keeps tormenting me. There was a girl I could have saved, but didn't because when it comes down to it I'm a coward and my whole life's been conditioned by that. What about you?'

'I couldn't have the child I wanted, and my husband cheated on me.'

Her voice quivered. She'd dropped her armour with a loud clang.

They resumed walking, slowly, more complicit, suspended in the subtle mist that promised to become sleet.

'Sigismund had other women,' Frau Braun began again. 'He'd say that Hitler encouraged polygamy to give Germany new children.'

'Did he cheat on you here in the camp?'

'Yes, but I never blamed him. I loved him in my own way, and the Führer's words are true and right. My husband's work was dreadful and exhausting, so it was natural he should allow himself diversions. Only I didn't think he'd go that far . . .'

'What happened?'

Frau Braun turned abruptly and stared at him with eyes of ice once again. 'You'll discover it for yourself anyway, I'm sure of it, and then my reputation and Sigismund's will be compromised. I'll tell you the truth, but you must promise me you'll use it only in order to find my husband's killer, and not to expose us to public ridicule.'

'You have my word.'

'Sigismund slept with the Jewish nurse.' Her voice trembled and her cheeks flushed with shame.

This confirmed all the rumours Hugo had gathered. Sigismund Braun had had many affairs, and his wife had been aware of all of them, but his last one had crossed the line of decency, at least according to Germany's racial laws, and could have landed him in jail.

'Did you have an argument when you found out?'

'No. I swallowed that terrible grief. It was the umpteenth stab wound I had to endure so as not to soil our family's reputation.'

'Did nobody notice except you?'

'Clauberg. But he's a trusted friend.'

191

'Did Braun take off his wedding ring because of your argument?'

'No.' She shook her head, clearly bewildered. 'He was still wearing it in the morning, when he left.'

'The evening of the murder, before dining at the officers' mess, did he come home?'

She shrugged her shoulders and shook her head. It was obviously hard for her to admit that her husband wouldn't come home until late at night, after satisfying his urges.

They turned and walked back to the Solahütte lodge.

You could barely make out the sun now above the dark, increasingly thick clouds, and Hugo hoped they wouldn't be caught in another snowfall.

'When did you hear about his death?' he asked.

'The morning after he was found, when Anita came to pick me up and tell me the news. It was awful.'

'Do you have any idea who could have harmed him?'

'No.' She smoothed the folds of her coat and her face hardened. 'Of all the people who work here, I don't know anyone capable of something like that.'

Hugo swallowed the frosty mountain air in a single gulp. Brunhilde didn't seem to consider the fact that, in Auschwitz, everybody was a killer in their own way. Including him, with his silence.

'I understand,' he said. 'One final question, then I'll leave you alone. Did Braun use any particular fragrance?'

'No.' Brunhilde gave a laugh filled with sadness. 'It made him itch and gave him migraines. He couldn't stand the stuff.'

Hugo gave a faint smile. He propped his whole weight on the stick while enjoying, one more time, the nostalgic sight of these mountains.

23

The room was bathed in a luminous white. Candles flickered on the table, drawing circles of light on the expensive
linen tablecloth, porcelain and silverware. Cheerful music
glided from the piano, the touch on the keys flawless. The
Christmas decorations gave off a scent of resin that blended
with the smell of spices in the food. The Polish prisoners
paraded at every course, well-groomed in their clean white
uniforms, displaying overfilled trays in a dance that had
probably been rehearsed and re-rehearsed countless times.
Everything was impeccable in Solahütte.

Hugo sat next to Osmund Becker. Adele was at the
other end of the table, talking, laughing, carefree, and he
couldn't take his eyes off her. There was something fresh
about her that clashed with all that grey, with the secrets
of Auschwitz and its terrible murders. In her eyes, however,
a tempest was raging, and Hugo couldn't help thinking
about the message concealed in the dental pincers.

'Meeting Braun was a stroke of luck.' Osmund Becker's
voice summoned him back. The young man smiled broadly,

revealing the gap between his front teeth. He plunged a forkful of potato into his mouth and chewed noisily. 'Seeing him at work was a great source of inspiration for me.'

'What made you decide to become a doctor?' Hugo cut into a piece of duck – so tender that pressing the tip of his knife was enough to fray it – chewed it, then took a sip of red wine before dabbing his lips with the napkin. His gaze returned fleetingly to Adele.

Osmund twirled his fork in the air. 'I had a sister,' he said, licking his teeth. 'Charlotte. She was beautiful and kind, and she enjoyed writing. She was very intelligent. A role model for me.'

'Go on,' Hugo said.

'Charlotte married a man from Munich.' Osmund tried the duck and half closed his eyes. He had delicate features, smooth, perfectly shaved cheeks and dark hair cut with care. He must have made the nurses swoon. 'He couldn't bear Berliners. You're from Berlin, aren't you? We Berliners are all fire and passion. He undermined my sister's independence. She got pregnant and became meeker and more willing to give up her social life. He was happy, and so was she. The problem is, she gave birth to a freak of nature.'

Hugo looked at him quizzically.

'A phocomelic child,' Osmund explained.

'How did she take it?'

'With a leap from the attic window.' Osmund's eyes filled with sadness. 'I enrolled at the faculty of medicine because I wanted to spare another woman ending up like Charlotte.'

'I'm sorry . . .'

Osmund smiled and continued eating. 'So I have my

reasons for doing research here in Auschwitz. Braun, on the other hand, worked here only to defend the Aryan race. Of course, I don't mean to imply it's a less noble cause . . . Do you know that in Irsee he was part of a special programme?'

'What kind of programme?'

'I don't know exactly. Adele and Berto could tell you more about it.'

'I imagine they got on very well with him.'

Osmund placed his knife and fork across each other, wiped his mouth and grabbed an apple from the centre-piece, then polished it with his napkin. The red peel reflected the white lights in the room.

'I don't know,' he said, pensively. He looked up at Adele, who was having fun chatting with the other nurses. 'You would think so, but I had the feeling that Berto and Adele didn't much like him. Maybe they hadn't been duly briefed on what they'd find here. And, as you must have realized, this place isn't for everyone.'

Osmund bit into the apple with a loud crunch.

So the trio formed by Braun, Adele and Berto hadn't been the closed, inaccessible circle Betsy thought. Osmund had spotted friction, perhaps some subtle resentment on the part of Braun's colleagues for dragging them here, the *anus mundi*. And how could you blame them?

'Where were you on the evening of the murder?' Hugo asked.

Osmund bit off another chunk of apple and stared at him for a long time. 'I was in my room,' he finally replied.

'You didn't dine in the block?'

'I didn't dine at all,' he said. 'I fast once a week. I always keep apples in our office and often eat just those.' He looked at him, lifting the bitten apple. 'An apple a day keeps the doctor away, doesn't it?'

Hugo let the tasteless remark rest at the bottom of his stomach. He was about to respond when he felt a warm hand on his shoulder.

'I hope I'm not disturbing you.' Adele was sipping hot, mulled wine and looking at him from behind the steam swirling from the cup.

24

Through the window, a dark shadow was climbing quickly up the slope of the mountain.

'Did I interrupt something?' Adele asked.

'Not at all,' Hugo replied, looking outside. 'I'd already finished interrogating him.'

'Is that what you're doing?' she laughed. 'Interrogating us?'

'It's my job.'

Hugo wondered if she'd realized the pincers had fallen out of her basket. Maybe she'd returned to look for them and figured he'd picked them up.

'Thank you for the other day,' he said tentatively, to gauge her reaction.

'What for?' She gave a faint, polite smile and he saw that he'd made her as taut as the string of a violin.

'For not going around telling people that Hugo Fischer uses morphine.'

She laughed, not even bothering to put a hand over her

mouth the way the other women did. There was no need to and, he thought, it would be a pity to.

'You're most welcome,' she whispered. 'You're not an addict. You need it.'

The pianist had stopped playing, giving way to the orchestra. Hugo recognized the light, then louder vibration of the cymbals, then the rhythm picked up and every instrument joined in that perfect music with vigour and expertise. It wasn't as vibrant and fluid as swing or jazz, of course. Swing and jazz tasted of smoke, sweat and whisky sipped in a thick, liquid half-light, while this was only Aryan music.

Adele tapped her foot in time with the music. 'How do you find it here in Auschwitz?'

Hugo licked his lips. He took out his last two cigarettes and offered her one.

'I'd be lying if I said I liked it,' he admitted without shame, clicking open the cap of the lighter. The eagle and swastika on the front gleamed in the light of the blue flame, showing in no uncertain terms the great contradiction that was his life. 'Why, do *you* like it?'

Adele looked around, her tapered fingers clutching the cigarette, the filter resting lightly on her naked lips.

'No,' she murmured once she realized no one was listening to them. 'I hate this place. I hated Irsee, too, but I've always done my job well.'

'What were you doing in Irsee?'

Lost in her own reflection in the windowpane, Adele did not answer.

Hugo turned his gaze to study himself in the glass and didn't like what he saw. His eyes were as grey as the SS officers' uniforms; he was a coward, a careerist who'd

198

sacrificed his morals to his profession while balancing on the tightrope of what you could and couldn't say, what you could and couldn't do. He hid behind the Nazi symbols he wore, like shields. 'You're a disgrace,' his mother would have said, had she still been alive.

'Berto's in the clutches of death because of a stupid joke,' Adele said, snatching him away from his conscience.

Hugo took a long drag on his cigarette and looked outside. The nimbus clouds were ashen, heavy with snow, and didn't herald anything good. Behind them, people were dancing, laughing while the music glided softly over everything.

He felt Adele shudder. She clearly had a lot to say. Only, she had to trust him, to be sure that what she confessed wouldn't get her into trouble.

'I prefer swing,' Hugo muttered.

She turned to him, surprised. 'Really?' she said, looking around to make sure no one could hear them.

These days, admitting to liking swing – or worse, jazz – was tantamount to declaring war on Germany and on all Aryan culture.

'And how!' Hugo blew a silver cloud that dissolved against the window. 'I was one of those young men who went dancing in Berlin nightclubs when the Hitler Youth staged raids. But please don't tell anybody.'

'*Swing Heil!*' Adele sniggered softly, parodying the Nazi salute the way *swing-boys* did back then. She looked around nervously.

'So.' Hugo took a long drag that scratched his throat. 'What was it Dr Braun did in Irsee?'

She became serious again, extinguished her cigarette, only half-smoked, and crossed her arms over her chest, as though to protect herself from something that could strike her at any moment.

'Braun was part of Aktion T4, the euthanasia programme,' she said with a weak sigh. 'To start with, I didn't realize what was happening. Braun had received an official communication from Berlin and looked euphoric: history was being made there and it was an honour to take part in such an important programme. His orders were to create a special section for children with genetic illnesses and physical or mental disabilities. We didn't find anything strange about it, at first.'

Adele paused and caught her breath.

'Afterwards,' she continued, 'the order came to take all the children indicated by the medical commission to the hospital. They were taken from their families with the excuse of keeping them under observation for a couple of weeks.' Her voice cracked. 'At the end, euthanasia would be implemented.'

'It's all clear now.' Hugo crushed his cigarette in the ashtray. 'Berto Hoffman believed that Braun's death was just Divine punishment for the suffering he'd inflicted on those children. That the "ghosts" of the past had done their job. Right?'

Adele nodded. 'Yes. He couldn't have known the joke would cost him so dearly.'

'Do you think Berto had something to do with Braun's death?'

'Berto's a good man.'

'And those green triangles?'

'I don't know about those . . .'

Hugo took his stick in both hands and looked at the mountain and lake. At this altitude, the ice was thick and spread over the entire surface of the water. It was a hard sheet, which, when the sun was high during the day, must have been blindingly white, but now it was a dull grey, almost metallic colour. It was impossible to tell what lay at the bottom.

He recalled Berto Hoffman's puffy face and swollen, bruised eyelids. Hugo had been unable to look into his eyes and didn't even know what colour they were. What he did know was that Berto had been forced to work on a programme he found repellent at first, then moved to a place that was hell. His conscience had driven him to a minor act of rebellion, that of the green cloth triangles. And what about Adele's pincers? Was she also performing her silent act of rebellion against the monstrous machine that was Auschwitz? A pang, like a painful dart, pierced through his lower back and travelled up to his neck.

'Do you want to dance?' Adele asked.

'What?' Surprised and embarrassed, Hugo looked at his stick.

'Let's go.' Adele gently took him by the arm. 'I'm tired of talking about death and killers. You, too, try and relax a little. It's Christmas.'

Unable to resist, Hugo followed her, realizing that this woman had a strange power over him and, for a moment, felt lost.

They reached the centre of the room, where other couples were dancing, among children running up and down, enjoying themselves. He hoped nobody would collide with them.

'Can you hear the music?' Adele asked, amused.

Hugo could feel it in every fibre of his body. He enjoyed dancing, but the stick had become a bothersome appendage

201

that always made him fear an embarrassing fall. He wished he could be rid of it now, but lacked the courage.

I always lack courage, he thought accusingly.

He considered that, if he weren't a coward, he could have screamed at these people that while they were dancing and laughing, a few kilometres away Jews were being slaughtered like animals. That a child worth as much as them would die as soon as his brother did. That Dr Sigismund Braun had been taken by his *ghosts* and that was fine, because he'd been a total bastard inside the camp and out and deserved the end he got, and that he, Hugo, should return to Berlin without taking any further interest in the case.

But he didn't. It was easier to keep quiet, as usual.

Adele put her warm hands around his neck. Hugo thought he could hear the crazy rhythm of swing, crystal glasses tinkling in a room crammed with people, then shuddered as the quick strides of the Hitler Youth bursting into the dance hall echoed in his ears.

One had come up behind him, that day, just as Hugo was heading for the exit through the crowd. 'Where do you think you're running to?' he'd yelled, before grabbing him by the collar and throwing him to the ground. Hugo had seen others arrive. Three, four, five – he'd had trouble counting them. They'd beaten him so hard, he could barely breathe.

That's when the girl had fallen next to him and Hugo had seen her eyes open wide in terror, begging him to help her. Protect her. Do something for her.

He felt as though once again he was sliding to the floor under the fierce blows, and he held on tight to Adele and his stick. The orchestra drums thundered. A shot echoed in his ears, cruel and lethal, and Adele's eyes became the blood-filled eyes of the murdered girl.

'I'm sorry,' he panted, disengaging himself from her embrace. He limped to the cloakroom and frantically looked for his coat, put it on, stuffed his hands in his pockets to feel the cold phial of morphine, and headed out of the lodge.

'Herr Fischer!' he heard behind him.

He didn't stop.

He walked up the slope, following the wooden fence of the path, inhaling the icy afternoon air, filling his lungs to expel the pain and the memories, feeling ashamed of himself.

He hated Auschwitz. This place would ruin him for ever. It would suck him up and grind him down if he didn't flee as soon as possible, leaving everything behind him. But what would he tell Nebe? It would be like admitting he'd been wrong to send Hugo on such a delicate case, and Department V would think his work for them wasn't important after all. That he wasn't the best criminologist to trust but just a cripple who couldn't do his job. They'd get rid of him in a minute. 'Lightning riddance,' his father had once joked, referring to how easily Nazi Germany shed weak links.

Hugo stopped on a high point, a small spur of rock overhanging a natural terrace. He slumped to the ground with all his weight, his back against a fir tree that stood there silently.

He'd betrayed the girl who had died next to him.

He'd told the newspapers the version the Nazis wanted to hear, pressured by his lecturer. 'Do you want to finish your studies or don't you?' he'd said to Hugo. He'd been a coward to the very end.

203

'Fischer!' a woman's voice shouted from what sounded like the depths of the lake, ringing in his ears like an echo.

He gave a start when he saw Adele's green eyes instead of those, filled with blood, of the girl from his memories.

'What's wrong with you?' she said, panting, worried, studying him with irises that now seemed like ponds. 'Is your leg hurting?'

This woman was creeping into his weak points. It was the second time she'd caught him in a situation he was deeply ashamed of, and this filled him with dull anger. He tightened his lips. He didn't want to tell her about his illness, he didn't want to be pitied like a deformed being, like one of the children in the Irsee euthanasia programme.

Adele rummaged in his pockets without asking permission.

'What are you doing?' he grumbled, sweating.

'Keep calm,' she said flatly. She snapped the pinhead off the phial, took the syringe out of its iron case and filled it. 'You must sterilize the needle with boiling water every time: do you do that?' she said, pushing the piston to expel the remaining air.

He clenched his teeth. 'Of course I do.'

'Good.' Adele made him slip off his coat and rolled up his sleeve, then tied the cord around his arm with a quick, expert gesture, searched for the blue line of the vein on the surface of the muscle and injected the morphine.

The wave of warmth swept over him instantly, soothing his tremor along with his anger.

Wattenmeer. The tide. His father.

Hugo looked at the barely visible dark sky between the tree branches and slumped against the trunk of the fir. He looked down at the red band with the swastika, which was now lying in the snow.

'You mustn't be ashamed,' she said encouragingly. 'I don't know why German men are so afraid of illness. If God created these ailments, then there's nothing to be ashamed of. On the contrary, I've always admired people who face life with their head high. I've seen more courage in the eyes of children killed in Irsee than in the sons of Auschwitz officers.'

Hugo sighed. 'I didn't have poliomyelitis,' he mumbled. 'What then?'

'I have a degenerative illness. Multiple sclerosis. There are moments when I'm fine and can act like a normal person, but the relapses are hell.'

'Are you in the relapse phase now?' she asked.

Hugo laughed. 'Is it that obvious?' He felt a wreck. 'According to Clauberg, I should prefer death to this unworthy life.'

'Such nonsense,' she said with a huff, patting his hand. 'Braun certainly picked a really bad time to die.'

'I've been telling myself that for days.' Hugo laughed heartily, free from restraint. 'Fucking bad timing!'

Adele sat next to him and they laughed together. Hugo realized his coat and trousers were soaked, and she that her skirt had got dirty, and they laughed even more.

They were close. Hugo could feel the warmth of her body, the faint smell of her hair and the cologne on her neck. She wasn't wearing any make-up and yet she was beautiful, with cheeks and nose red from the cold and eyes sparkling with fun. He leaned over to kiss her.

They were interrupted by a sound.

It came from down below, from the terrace that extended

beneath the embrace of the rock and the foliage. Adele pulled away, embarrassed, and he took the opportunity to compose himself.

'Look,' she said quickly.

She pointed at Frau Braun. She wasn't alone. She was talking to someone.

Hugo opened a gap in the foliage and recognized the tall, athletic figure of Osmund Becker. He couldn't hear what they were saying but observing the scene was enough: Frau Braun was crying; Becker was stroking her cheek, then pulled her towards him gently and kissed her.

'I can't believe it,' Adele whispered, crouching at his side. 'I should have realized sooner!'

'Were there signs?'

'Osmund often didn't dine in the block . . .'

'He went to the Braun farmhouse.'

'Yes, I think so.' Adele nodded and her short, voluminous hair stirred like an untamed flame. 'And a week ago, I was with Betsy, we went into Braun's office and these two were there. Alone. For a moment, I thought they looked uneasy. Does that make Osmund a murderer?'

Hugo shook his head. 'No, not necessarily.' A few snow-flakes had started to fall. Below them, the lovers had crystallized in a long embrace charged with love and suffering. 'It's not enough, but it gives them both a motive. And only two things are important in an enquiry: clues and a strong motive.'

25

Auschwitz, 26 December 1943

They must have pulled out all the stops in the anatomy room, Hugo thought.

The sectioned bodies had already been taken to the crematorium and all that was left on the tables was a pink rivulet that stained the ceramic and ran down the drain. On the shiny steel trolleys, there was a row of jars with formaldehyde containing swaying organs.

'Heterochromia,' Josef Mengele said behind him, indicating a pair of eyes in a smaller jar.

Hugo stared at the eyeballs floating in the liquid, illuminated by a surgical lamp.

'Today, we analysed four pairs of children,' Mengele continued, 'all with irises that had different shades of colour.'

Hugo clenched his jaw. He caught Rabi's contrite look as he washed the tools, and thought again about Gioele's wonderful eyes.

'I'm looking for a nurse,' he said, returning to Mengele. 'Now that Braun's research has been suspended, she works for you.'

Mengele immediately moved to a desk and picked up a stack of papers, took out a chart, wrote something on it and bent down to look at some slides. 'Dr Epstein sent me these from Birkenau,' he muttered, ignoring Hugo's request. 'Tissue samples from Gypsy children with noma: dry gangrene of the face. They're almost all affected by it. Do you know what that means? That race degeneration in gypsies is now at the most advanced stage. A consequence of hereditary syphilis.'

'Herr Doktor,' Hugo said.

'Yes?'

'I said I'm looking for a nurse.'

'Which nurse?'

'Bethany Assouline. Where can I find her?'

'At the camp infirmary, Block 20,' he replied. 'She's been unwell.'

'Can I speak to her?'

'I think so. She's not contagious.' He finished examining the slides, then put them in a box bound for Berlin. 'She should have gone to the Ka-Be, the camp hospital in Birkenau, but somebody insisted she stay here . . .'

'Who?'

'Officer Tristan Voigt.'

Hugo gave a start and must have looked more surprised than he should have, because Mengele shook his head.

'I honestly don't know why he did.' He opened his arms and dropped them against his hips with a thud, then put his hands into the pockets of his lab coat. 'Maybe this Jew has distinguished herself in her work. Usually, it's

Wirths who mediates between us and the Jewish medical staff, but this time it was Voigt.'

Hugo stared at the handle of his stick for a prolonged moment. Voigt never ceased to surprise him. One moment, he expressed unprecedented ferocity, and the next he indulged in acts of humanity, acts that could cost him his reputation: like interceding on behalf of Bethany or searching for the Erreras's file.

'I must see to these now.' Mengele tapped on the boxes for Berlin.

He left, leaving Hugo in the room with the Jewish doctors, who were finishing their jobs. Two Polish attendants had already started cleaning the operating table and there was now a smell of detergent in addition to formaldehyde in the air.

Rabi approached meekly. 'Herr Fischer, I must speak to you.'

They went down into the courtyard. It was snowing heavily and the prisoners were smoothing the road with a heavy roller.

Hugo lit a cigarette. Liebehenschel had got him some. As soon as he'd heard Hugo had none he'd gone out of his way to send him a packet, as well as an iron cigarette case with the initials of a Jew from whom it had been confiscated. Hugo had put it in the drawer and left it there.

'Do you smoke?' he asked Rabi.

The man shook his head, then appeared to change his mind, took a cigarette and put it between his lips. Hugo opened the lighter; the paper sizzled and slowly ate away at the tobacco.

'Herr Fischer,' Rabi said, his nose and eyes red from the cold and worry. 'Mengele wants to kill Gioele.'

The smoke stuck in Hugo's throat. He looked down at the small, frail man, but couldn't say anything.

'His brother is at death's door.' Rabi's voice dissipated in the muffled silence of the snow. 'Mengele doesn't want him to die from natural causes. He wants both twins to die from the same cause, at the same time. Identical conditions for a perfect autopsy. Remember?'

'What does he want to do?'

'A phenol injection to both.'

'When?'

'I don't know. Either today or tomorrow. He hasn't told me. But soon.'

Hugo filled his lungs with smoke. They seemed to contract, as if in a spasm. Why was Rabi telling him this? Why was he torturing him like this, just now when he most needed to be lucid? His career depended on the Braun case. The Braun case depended on his peace of mind. You couldn't investigate a case if you were emotionally upset – that was one of the golden rules. There was no room for feelings: they always ended up ruining everything, forcing you to lower your defences and leading you to commit a potentially fatal error.

'I'm sorry,' he said at last, his voice cold and hard. 'There's nothing I can do for Gioele.'

'But, Herr Fischer . . .' Rabi protested.

Hugo didn't let him finish. He stamped angrily on the cigarette butt, which died instantly in the snow. 'I have no power here. My hands are tied, like yours. What do you expect me to do? I cannot interfere in Mengele's studies. Now do you really want to make yourself useful?'

Rabi shrugged his shoulders, disappointed and disorientated. 'Yes,' he replied.

'Then come with me to the camp infirmary.'

26

Bethany Assouline's body sank into the cot as if in a shroud. Her pale chest, beaded with sweat, rose, trembling in time to a hesitant breath, suggesting a stillness close to death. She reminded Hugo of his mother in the final days of her agony, after her skiing accident.

Rabi touched her clammy forehead and grimaced. She must have been burning up.

'She has a high fever,' he said. His glasses had steamed up, his comb-over was dishevelled on one side and his cheekbones stuck out under his flushed skin. Hugo was moved by this man who went out of his way for others, not thinking of what would happen to him a few months from now.

'Wake her,' he murmured.

Rabi held a bottle of smelling salts under her nose and Bethany shuddered out of her slumber. Her teeth chattered tersely, rhythmically, and she began to shiver, evidently feeling very cold. The scalding iron stove was at the other end of the room and didn't give off enough heat.

'Water,' she whispered.

Rabi gave her some cold tea under the authoritative but compassionate eyes of a stout nurse waiting next to a window, against the light.

'Can you hear me?' Hugo whispered.

Bethany swallowed the tea, wetted her parched lips and nodded.

'What's wrong with you?' he asked. 'Why are you here?'

'There's nothing wrong with her,' the nurse answered instead of her. She was overweight, with large breasts and wide hips. A mass of dark, curly hair framed her face and a decided mouth gave her the appearance of a mastiff ready to bite. 'She's just got a problem with her ovaries.'

'What kind of problem?'

'An infection.'

Hugo realized that she wasn't allowed to talk about it. He ignored her and returned to Bethany, who was staring at him with dark, weary eyes that reflected the sterile light of the bulb on the ceiling.

'I must ask you a few questions about Dr Sigismund Braun,' he said.

Outside, the snow was falling slowly, hitting the windowpanes before landing on an expanse of dazzling white that muffled everything. This wasn't the right moment – or place – to question a sick person and he would have preferred to leave her to her slumber and the silence of the frozen flakes, but there was no rest in hell.

'I know you had a relationship with the victim,' he continued implacably.

Bethany found the energy to blush with shame, a faint, rosy shade covering the deadly pallor on her cheeks.

'Please,' she whispered. 'I don't want to talk about it.'

213

Hugo was immovable. 'I need you to tell me everything you know.'

The clock on the wall was ticking ruthlessly, reminding him that the more time passed, the more the probability of his solving the case approached zero. Going back to Berlin defeated was a possibility he couldn't contemplate.

'Did you have a relationship with Braun?' he insisted.

'He forced me.' It was a long moan that ended in subdued weeping.

Rabi's lips tightened into a narrow, furrowed line, and he squeezed her hand.

'How?'

'Mein Herr!' the nurse thundered, her bulk heading towards them. She projected a large shadow over Bethany that seemed to devour her.

'I must hear it from her own lips,' Hugo protested. 'I promise I'll leave her alone afterwards. How did Sigismund Braun force you?'

'*Les fantômes*,' Bethany mumbled, staring at the window and the snow beyond it. 'The ghosts. The ghosts at night were Clauberg's women crying.'

'Carry on,' Hugo urged her, a terrible premonition slithering under his skin, making his hair stand on end like he'd had an electric shock.

'The men come to take them at night.' Her voice had the regular rhythm of a dirge. She wasn't talking to him. She was talking to the snow falling outside the window. 'They take them in the night, in silence.'

Rabi gave her a fatherly pat.

There was no need for explanations. Among the hundreds of guinea pigs in Block 10, there were many attractive young women. Hugo had seen them fleetingly

214

in the half-light of the corridors or through the gaps in the open doors.

'Clauberg encourages it,' Rabi allowed himself to say with a courage that made even the mastiff nurse turn pale. 'This way he can check if his sterilization experiments work. The official procedure stipulates that a group of men should donate their sperm, which is then injected into the guinea pigs, but every now and then they allow a few kapos to have fun the old-fashioned, traditional way. The crying and screaming you hear at night is that of the prisoners, not "ghosts".'

Hugo clenched his fists, a boulder crushing his chest.

'Braun forced you to have relations with him?' he insisted.

'He told me he'd send me to Birkenau if I didn't.' Bethany's gaze shifted to the ceiling, and she asked for more tea and drank it. In just a few days, her face had become a skull covered by emaciated skin, peppered in stains.

She spoke with her eyes shut tight, as if she were afraid to see either the images again or the accusatory looks from those present.

One evening, Braun had asked her to stay behind in the autopsy room. They were alone and that had frightened her. He'd noticed and ridiculed her for it, then placed himself between her and the door, as though she could possibly consider running away from an SS officer. She had noticed the way he looked at her: with a blend of desire and rejection. He considered her an inferior being, a prank of nature, and yet he wanted her. So he'd told her, while pushing her face down on the cold tiles of the anatomy table and lifting her skirt.

Bethany opened her mouth in a sob. She was tired.

'I'm sorry,' Hugo muttered, upset. 'Did you harbour resentment towards Braun?'

'I harbour resentment towards every doctor in Auschwitz,' Bethany hissed in one breath. 'Towards every filthy German like you.'

Rabi gave a start and glanced at Hugo. The nurse also turned around, slowly, like a mummy. Both were afraid of his reaction, of an angry gesture that never came. How could Hugo be offended by these words after all he'd seen and heard in the camp? Germany was soiling herself with a sin she would someday have to account for, and for which he had to ask forgiveness now, before this tormented, humiliated woman.

'Were you a nurse before you were deported?' he asked.

'A doctor.' She smiled sadly and, for the first time since they'd arrived at the infirmary, she looked him straight in the eye. 'I was a paediatrician. I wrote books. I studied German and Italian. If anybody had told me how barbaric a level we'd reach, I wouldn't have believed them.'

Hugo felt his blood curdle.

A stab of pain made Bethany's face twist. She lifted her pelvis and wrung her hands on her belly. Hugo remembered the blood trickling down her calf the day he'd first seen her.

'Do you know what they make us swear, when we become doctors?' she panted. She took a steadying breath and recited the promise: 'To any home I go, I will enter to bring relief to the sick, and will abstain from giving any deliberate offence or doing harm, from any act of corruption on the bodies of women and men, be they free or slaves. As for me, who keeps this oath and does not

216

break it, may I enjoy life and my art, and be honoured by all men for ever. May the opposite befall me, should I break it and forswear myself . . .'

Bethany clung to what little strength and passion were left in her body and propped herself up on her elbows to raise her chest.

'Do you think these doctors are respecting their oath?' she hissed through her teeth. 'What kind of doctors are they? What kind of men?'

Hugo licked his teeth, then his lips, unable to say anything. He wished he could lift this woman and carry her out of the camp, into the immense Polish countryside white with snow, and lay her down on the whiteness to show how her how beautiful the landscape was. He would have stroked her and been at her side until death, with snowflakes falling slow and impalpable, far away from all this horror.

Instead, he could do nothing.

This wasn't the time for being compassionate, let alone yielding to grief. This was the time to think. If Bethany was telling the truth, then Braun had blackmailed her into having relations with him. It had therefore not been with him that she'd shared secret displays of affection. The impossible love that must be kept concealed on pain of death – who did Bethany share that with?

He looked around.

The infirmary was clean and the smell of disinfectant covered the stench of urine in the bedpans, and of illness that altered the odour of the body, corrupting it. Everything was as dignified as possible. If Bethany had been thrown into the Birkenau Ka-Be, she would have died of starvation or been led to the crematorium. Tristan Voigt had undoubtedly prolonged her life. Was he the man she was in love with?

'Besides Braun, did you have relations with other SS officers?' he asked point-blank.

Bethany closed her eyes, defeated. Hugo figured she must hate him as much as she hated the doctors. Talking had taken an indescribable toll on her body and he was paying her back with more questions.

'No,' she said on an outbreath. 'I'm not that kind of woman.'

'Then do you feel affection for someone else here in the camp?'

'There's no room for feelings in Auschwitz.'

'Where were you the evening of the murder?'

'You think I killed Braun, don't you?' she snarled.

'I've just asked you a question. The same I've asked everybody.'

'I was in bed. I wasn't feeling well.'

Bethany instinctively touched her belly and Hugo finally realized what was happening: something had grown inside her. She'd got pregnant and Braun must not have taken it well. He'd probably forced her to have an abortion.

'Do you know Dr Clauberg, the gynaecologist?' he asked.

'Of course,' she sighed, exhausted. Her eyelids kept closing, crushed by an unsustainable load.

'Did he ever "treat" you?'

Bethany opened her mouth in a shiver. Her fever was rising and draining the blood from her cheeks and lips. After just a few days, nothing was left of the beauty – albeit emaciated – he'd been so struck by in the chapel of rest.

'I think that's enough,' the nurse said, moving away

from her position. She grabbed a drip-feed pole and pushed it, creaking, to the cot. With an abrupt gesture, she invited them to leave.

Rabi stood up, his thin body swaying under his lab coat and greatcoat. He adjusted his glasses on top of his nose and, dejected, headed towards the exit.

Hugo followed him. He glanced at Bethany one last time and pictured her beautiful and calm, standing on a cliff in Normandy, looking at the green expanses that plummeted towards the white, sandy beaches of the ocean, a brackish wind whipping her hair. That's how he wanted to dream about her: free and full of life.

Once they were outside, Hugo clicked the lighter open and cupped his hand over the flame to light a cigarette. He offered one to Rabi.

'What do you think?' he asked.

'I don't think anything,' Rabi replied.

'Bethany had a good reason to want Braun dead . . .'

'That's true.'

'The doctor was discovered with his lab coat on, but he wasn't working. It could have been an attack on his betrayal of the Hippocratic oath—'

'Bethany has been barely able to stand up for weeks,' Rabi protested.

'You're right. She couldn't have done it on her own, but there's nothing to say the murderer didn't have an accomplice. It's something I've considered from the start.'

A van with a red cross parked next to them. The exhaust spat thick black smoke. Rabi and Hugo kept quiet, finishing their cigarettes, until a line of prisoners by now more dead than alive was ushered out of the infirmary and loaded gruffly on the back of the van.

Hugo licked his lips, which tasted of bitter tobacco. 'Where are they taking them?'

'Birkenau. What's the point of keeping them here? They're doomed now.'

Rabi was looking at him, disappointed. Perhaps, during the autopsy, he'd hoped to have found an ally, or at least a German who would open his eyes to the horror being perpetuated in the camp. Hugo felt a surge of self-loathing. He couldn't save Gioele's life – or do anything to dismantle this monstrous machine.

'Thanks for your help,' he concluded.

'Doing my duty,' Rabi replied.

Hugo threw the cigarette butt, which glowed bright like a dying comet before going out on the ground. He walked on the compact snow, even though flakes kept falling fast and soon the prisoners would have to work on removing it again. He was surprised by how peaceful this place could be, even though all you had to do was turn and see the barbed-wire fence, black and menacing, to dispel the lie.

27

'You revolting little worm! Where did you steal it from?' Betsy Angel had grabbed him by the hair, yanking it.

Gioele wished he could do something, but he couldn't free himself from her grip. One more tug and his hair would all stay in her hand. She was using her free hand to prise open his fist, and soon Gioele had no choice but to unclench it and give up the medallion.

Betsy pushed him to the floor and held the medallion to the lamp. It glowed with a soft, golden light.

'Little thief,' she hissed. She dropped the medallion in the pocket of her apron, then removed the case from a pillow and twisted it in her hands. 'Now pull down your trousers.'

'No!'

'Do as you're told, you Jewish pig!'

Gioele's hands and legs shook. He thought of what Adele always said: Betsy couldn't hurt him, he was one of Mengele's 'guinea pigs'. She could hit him, but not kill him. So he summoned up his courage and unfastened his

221

short trousers, lowered them, then his pants, and bent over the cot. He closed his eyes and lips tight.

The first lash landed hard on his right buttock, its crack drowning out every other sound. The second caught both buttocks and he let out a long moan. The third made his skin burn so much, he started to cry, salty tears flooding his mouth.

'Fräulein Angel!' a voice behind them boomed.

Gioele heard the fourth lash interrupted in mid-air.

Someone had walked into the dormitory. Gioele turned slightly and saw a pair of wet shoes, the hem of grey, damp trousers and the edge of a dark leather coat.

'What are you doing?' Hugo Fischer demanded.

Gioele felt his breath come back to his throat and his tears pressing hard as the tension was released. He'd got really frightened, this time.

'Put that pillowcase down immediately,' Hugo commanded.

He was towering over that cow Betsy with his entire body. Gioele sighed with relief. He'd been wrong to judge him after hearing about the girl killed in the dance hall, because the man in front of him now was his friend and not like the other Nazis. The thought sent a dart of hope through his heart.

'Herr Fischer.' Betsy composed herself and threw the pillowcase in a corner of the bed. 'This little Jewish worm stole something . . .'

'What?'

Betsy hesitated, then took the medallion out of her apron pocket. She placed it in the palm of her hand and showed it to him. The soft lines with which the goldsmith had fashioned the letter B glimmered. It was valuable. A diamond was set on one side and a date engraved on the other: 4 December 1931. Hugo picked it up and weighed it in his hand.

'Where did you find it?' he asked the boy with a cold look.

'In Braun's office.' Gioele cast his eyes down, sorry and ashamed. He pulled up his pants and trousers.

'Filthy thief!' Betsy said. She grabbed him by the hair again and forced him down on the chair. 'You're nothing but chimney fuel!'

'Fräulein.' Hugo Fischer's voice quivered like a rope stretched in the air, ready to whip Betsy. 'Is this medallion yours?'

'What?' Betsy let go of Gioele and stared before replying. 'No, it's not mine. Of course it's not.'

'Then you may go. I'm sure the doctors need you, I've seen much activity on the first floor.'

'But—'

'I'll take care of the boy.'

Betsy Angel opened her mouth but couldn't come up with a response. Her face was so red with anger that Gioele felt like laughing, though he didn't dare. She walked out with a shudder that made her every step quiver, and closed the door behind her.

Hugo sighed. 'Now tell me.' He took a chair and sat opposite him, clearly angry. Gioele could tell by his mouth, tightened in a sharp line, and his forehead, split in two by a furrow. 'When did you find this?'

'After Braun died,' Gioele confessed. 'It was under the Christmas tree. I dropped a pencil, it rolled all the way there and I found it.'

'Why didn't you tell me?'

'I thought I could keep it. When we get out of here, my

family and I won't have anything. The Germans took everything away from us. I thought it would come in useful.' Gioele looked down. He felt guilty for stealing and lying. He wasn't someone who stole. He'd never done it. He told lies, but stealing – never.

He didn't have the courage to lift his eyes to Hugo, who would now be sure to look at him as if he were a thief or a scoundrel.

The man grabbed him by the shoulder and Gioele held his breath.

It was one thing if Betsy hit him. But if it was a man of Hugo's size, then he could really get hurt. Instead of striking him, however, Hugo hugged him. Nothing like this had ever happened to Gioele in Auschwitz and he burst into tears at the warm, intimate contact. He hadn't been wrong about Hugo.

'You're not angry with me?' he whispered.

Hugo pushed him away and Gioele looked straight into his eyes. They were inexplicably moist, as though he, too, was on the brink of tears.

Hugo sighed. 'Only a little, because I know you would never have told me about the medallion if that nurse hadn't discovered it. But I'm grateful you kept it because it could be useful to us.'

'How?'

'Use your brain and your intuition, Gioele.'

The boy smiled. They were playing at being detectives again. 'If the medallion doesn't belong to Braun, then it's the murderer's!' he ventured.

'Exactly. The office is cleaned from top to bottom every evening at five, so only Sigismund Braun or his attacker could have lost the medallion.'

'What are you going to do now?'

'First I'm going to show it to Frau Braun, to make sure it isn't her husband's. I can't take fingerprints from it because both you and Betsy have handled it, but if it isn't Braun's, then I'm sure it will still be useful somehow.'

Gioele shuddered with satisfaction from top to toe.

'Did you manage to find my parents?' he asked. Someone like Hugo Fischer couldn't have forgotten his promise, and Gioele had provided so many useful elements for his investigation, he couldn't not reward him.

The man's face darkened. 'Not yet, but today I'll go to look for your father personally.'

'Thank you!' Gioele flung his arms around his neck and hugged him, his heart beating fast in his chest.

Never mind the medallion, he thought, if he could have his family back.

28

Hugo looked out of the van. He saw the black profile of Birkenau against the snow. It was gloomy, and on the watchtower you could see the guards ready to shoulder their machine guns.

The driver went straight up the main road, among SS officers on bicycles and motorbikes. There was even one on horseback. They overtook a slow van puffing black smoke from the exhaust. Hugo noticed a white stain in the back that looked like a dangling arm and when the vehicle was forced to stop he also made out a head. Dead bodies. He'd never seen so many. They were folded on top of one another, naked, skeletal, with eyes and mouths wide open, like rag dolls.

The driver sped up, overtook the van and continued to the triage warehouse. As soon as he got off, Hugo was greeted by the same sickly-sweet smell as the first time, and his tongue immediately felt furry.

This time, he held back his retching.

He opened his hand and snowflakes fell into his palm,

some melting, others turning into grey mush that smelled of ash.

'They're grilling, aren't they, Daddy?' a voice rang.

Hugo turned and saw a little girl with blond pigtails quivering in the air. She was bundled in a red coat, with black, glossy boots. In one hand, she was clutching the lead of an Alsatian and in the other the hand of her father, who was wearing an SS officer's uniform. There was a sign with her name and surname around her neck. A German surname. Hugo figured it was a way of keeping the children of the SS officers safe, away from accidents in gas chambers.

The child smiled innocently. She placed a hand on her stomach and rubbed the woollen fabric of her coat. 'They're cooking meat. I'm so hungry.'

The father smiled and patted her head.

She tugged on the lead and the dog resumed walking in step with her.

A devastating hollow in his chest, Hugo watched them disappear behind the Kanada huts and remained motionless, immersed in a stifling, surreal kind of lethargy, until the two figures became just dots across the road.

'Herr Fischer!' Frau Braun's voice roused him from his stupor. She was marching up to him, but smiling. 'Any news?'

'Frau Braun,' he mumbled.

He went up to her and they entered the hut, ploughing through the sea of female prisoners at work. They looked like tireless ants, with grey scarves over their heads and eyes downcast. None of them spoke.

'So?' she asked.

Hugo took the medallion from his pocket and showed it to her. 'Do you recognize this?'

She frowned. 'Should I?'

'It was in your husband's office, on the floor. Are you sure it wasn't his?'

'It's neither mine nor my husband's, I'm sure of it.'

Hugo studied her. Her face was relaxed, clear: she wasn't lying. If the medallion wasn't Braun's, then it was the killer's, he thought. He just had to find out who it belonged to.

'Do you have any other news?' Frau Braun murmured, trembling.

'Trust me,' Hugo said to comfort her. 'I'll get to the bottom of this business. This afternoon I'll also question Osmund Becker.'

The woman became as stiff as a pole and wrung her riding crop. Hugo sensed her tension: she was afraid of being discovered.

'Do you know Osmund well?' he asked.

'Not very,' she said defensively.

He clasped the medallion and recalled the lovers' embrace, the tenderness of their effusions under the snow that slowly fell in Solahütte.

'Is everything all right?' someone behind them asked. Anita Kunig had approached and was staring at Hugo suspiciously. The faint light that filtered through the windows glided over the stain on her face and emphasized the expressive lines on her forehead, making her look like a she-wolf ready to attack.

'Everything's all right,' Frau Braun reassured her.

Hugo opened his hand and showed her the medallion, too. 'I came here because I found this in Dr Braun's office. Do you recognize it?'

She looked at the medallion for a long instant. Hugo

thought he saw the stain on her face come alive and throb on the white, taut skin.

'Never seen it before,' she finally replied.

'Don't you even remember noticing anyone wearing it?'

'No,' she replied resolutely. 'I don't think so, although many nurses have their blouses buttoned all the way up to their necks.'

'Thank you.'

Hugo put his hat back on and left the hut, leaving the two women next to each other. He paused in the doorway, lit a cigarette and stood looking at the sky, moist with snow. Beyond the huts, the crematoria were working at full speed, and he realized that Moll was right: you did get used to this ghastly smell.

He finished smoking in silence, confident only that the medallion didn't belong to Braun. Frau Braun had seemed sincere: she'd never seen the medallion.

Hugo gave the medallion one last look before putting it back in his pocket, then took out his diary and read the note he'd scribbled: *'Hut 10.'*

29

The Quarantänelager, as Voigt had called it, was separated from the other camps and from Birkenau's main road by an electric barbed-wire fence between the dirty snow and a dark canal with frozen banks.

The Lagerführer of this camp was waiting for him at the entrance. He was a tall, robust man with reddish hair, a face chapped from the cold and small dark eyes that stood out like pieces of charcoal from under his beret.

'Tristan Voigt has ordered me to give you a hand,' he said, inviting Hugo to follow him. 'Hut 10, right?'

'Yes.' Hugo nodded and pushed his stick into the snow.

'It's with regard to the investigation into the dead doctor, isn't it?'

Hugo nodded.

The Lagerführer shook his head. 'Nasty business.'

They continued along the icy road flanked by wooden huts. The odd human form peered at them from the doorsteps.

'Be careful not to get too close to the prisoners,' the SS

man said. He gave a surly look around. 'They're riddled with parasites.'

'What's this camp for?' Hugo asked. It was obvious from the daytime crowd that these people weren't destined for work, but weren't in quarantine either.

The SS officer gave a raucous laugh, counting the huts between words. 'We teach these dregs how things work around here. We give them the camp rules. They have to learn to obey and submit totally. It's an entrance exam for the "high numbers".'

'High numbers?'

'*Die Großnummer*. Those with the highest numbers. The latest arrivals.' The SS officer indicated his own arm, referring to the prisoners' tattoos. 'Whoever passes quarantine is ready for work. Whoever gets ill stays here.'

When they reached hut 9, there was a sudden racket. A young boy ran out of the hut, tripped and fell face down in the snow and mud, his mouth opening in a silent scream. A short, burly man with a face disfigured by a long scar that split his lips in two stood over him, brandishing a rubber crop which sliced through the air with a hiss.

'I'll catch you, anyway!' he shouted. 'What are you expecting to do – run against the fence? You want to die electrocuted, you fucking Jew? Come here and suck my cock – come on!'

'Help!' the boy implored.

Hugo gave a start. The boy was looking at him with the same expression as the girl in the dance hall had.

'What's going on, Gereon?' the SS officer boomed.

The short, burly prisoner suddenly stopped, removed his beret with canine devotion and stood to attention. He was wearing a blue military jacket with the armband, and there was a green triangle on his tunic. Hugo realized he was a German kapo, a real criminal, as Voigt had explained.

Other prisoners came out behind him, like a flock of little birds. They were so skinny that you could count their ribs under their large, low-cut clothes.

'This little parasite hid bread in the latrines,' Gereon growled. 'An entire loaf!'

'Where did he get it? Did someone hand it to him from outside?'

'He won't tell me. And if he doesn't tell me I must punish him.' Gereon grabbed the boy by the neck and squeezed hard. 'So,' he hissed. 'Are you going to tell the Lagerführer where the fuck you got that bread? Did someone pass it to you through the fence? Who was it?'

The boy kept shaking his head, refusing to speak.

'Maybe he doesn't understand German,' Hugo said.

The SS officer gave him a dirty look.

Hugo felt his temples boil. He was nobody here. He couldn't order the SS officer to spare the boy's life, or stop the kapo. He was a drop in the midst of an immense ocean of excrement.

'Kill him,' the Lagerführer commanded. He picked up a stone shiny from the snow and threw it in the air then caught it firmly in his hand to assess its weight. He examined the prisoners who were staring at the scene, frightened, and laughed. 'What is it Jews do? It's even written in their sacred scriptures. Take a stone each and teach this thief a nice lesson.'

He handed the stone to the kapo and motioned for Hugo to follow him to hut 10. Hugo trod uncertainly on his unsteady leg. The acute phase of his illness was subsiding, but he still thought he felt pain biting him all over. The boy's screams echoed in his ears together with the sound of the stones falling one by one. It was a hollow sound, like the stones he would throw into the Spree as a child. Then the boy didn't scream anymore and the final stone fell.

Hugo stopped himself from turning.

'The kapos have to do this,' the SS officer said. 'We don't want any insurrections and if these parasites know that every wrong action is followed by punishment, they behave properly. That's what the quarantine is for.'

Hugo felt tears stinging the corners of his eyes but tried to push them back.

'They did try to rebel once,' the Lagerführer said. 'But they don't have any weapons. If they had weapons or explosives, we'd be in real trouble.'

Hugo felt a shock straighten his neck. The SS officer's words had troubled him and triggered something in his unconscious. He tried to work out what it was, but all he was left with was the sense of just having heard something important, like an answer he'd been seeking for a long time.

'Here we are,' the SS officer said, rousing him.

Hugo followed him into the hut. It was a large rectangle with wooden bunk beds so close together there was hardly any room to move. There was a dreadful stench and Hugo had to shield his nose with the sleeve of his coat to stop himself from vomiting. Dozens and dozens of emaciated people huddled on the straw beds, piled up on top of one another, looking at them from the shadows like animals.

The SS officer made his way and called out a number. No one replied.

He repeated the number and a prisoner stepped forward fearfully, meekly removing his hat. His face was covered in acne, his hair shaved, and you could see the stained skin of his skull. He had no more teeth and looked nothing like Gioele.

The Jew muttered something in Greek and indicated a man lying on one of the beds.

Hugo took a step forward.

The man lay staring at the beams of the bed above his. He was shaved and his grey skin clung to his body like thin papier mâché. You could count his ribs under his tunic and a growth protruded through his bare belly. His expression was blank, his mouth agape, his hands open at the sides of his hips. Hugo had never seen thinner fingers. He read on the inside of his forearm the number the SS officer had called out.

Hugo bent over the stranger.

'Signor Errera?' he asked in horror.

The man did not reply but kept staring at the beams with a vacuous expression, then suddenly shuddered, and a pestilent stench filled the air. A dark puddle of diarrhoea spread beneath him and ran over the blankets and the straw.

'*Muselmänner,*' the officer said with disgust. 'That's what the prisoners call them when they're already half dead.'

Hugo felt anger rise in his guts. 'Why isn't he in the infirmary?'

'What's the point of sending him there? This is crematorium fodder. They're leaving him to be consumed by illness, then they'll come and harvest him with the van and take him to the piles.'

Hugo felt powerless. He bent down once again and searched the withered face for Gioele's nose, thin lips and pale eyes. He couldn't tell the child that his daddy, tall and strong, who carried him on his shoulders, no longer existed.

30

Hugo leaned against the wall of Block 10, smoking a cigarette.

He couldn't get Signor Errera's ravaged face out of his mind – nor the Lagerführer's words: if the Jews had weapons or explosives, they'd be in real trouble.

The sentence had stuck to him, damp and troubling.

He now knew why.

There were weapons and explosives in abundance at the Union: the prisoners were escorted to the factory every morning before dawn and came back at night. How much explosive would a group of Sonderkommandos need to stage a proper revolt? Eighteen grams?

He lit another cigarette and watched the sun die behind the Auschwitz blocks. A dark, dirty, sad light trickled over the buildings. Even the snow had lost all its appeal and Hugo stood like that until the door to the block opened with a dull sound.

'Herr Fischer.' It was Adele's voice. 'Tristan Voigt said you wished to speak to me.'

Hugo looked her up and down. She was wearing her coat unbuttoned over her nurse's uniform and her fresh, make-up-free face was like that of a little girl. He couldn't picture her in an act of rebellion – not by any stretch of the imagination: the only way he could see her was as the vibrant, beautiful woman she'd been in Solahütte, when he'd been about to kiss her. She must have thought the same thing, because she dropped her eyes and blushed.

'I need someone who knows the camp well,' he said. 'I need to know where one can get a phial of cyanide.'

'Oh,' she replied, seeming almost disappointed, buttoning up her coat. 'They should have some at the chemist's dispensary, I suppose. Will you give me a cigarette?'

'Of course.'

Hugo lit one for her. For a moment, as they shielded the flame from the lighter, they came close again and smiled. Had they not been in the middle of hell, he would have taken her to the nightclubs still standing in Berlin and kissed her, surrounded by music, the taste of Jägermeister on their lips. But not only were they in hell, they were in its lowest circle.

'How are you today?' she asked.

'I'm well.' Hugo wriggled two fingers, no longer numb.

'I'm glad.' Adele gave a smile that warmed him even in the middle of that cold, and headed down the road, smoking slowly, holding the collar of her coat tight around her neck with the other hand, shielding herself from the freezing air. She'd lifted the collar, but he could still see her translucent neck under the blanket of copper-coloured waves. She was talking, telling him about the holidays she'd gone on in Bavaria when she was a child, and Hugo found it absurd that he had met a woman like her in a death camp.

'Here we are.' Adele indicated the three-storey red-brick building in front of them.

She led him through the ground floor to a small room with a cloying smell of cigarettes. She slapped her hand on a metal table full of index cards that shook with a faint ticking. A man at the end of the room turned to look, closed the filing cabinet abruptly and came over.

'This is Sikorski,' Adele said. 'He runs the dispensary.'

Hugo gave the room another look. Sitting at a table under the window, a short, stocky man was writing a list of the medicines strewn in front of him, labelling them with care before placing them in an iron box. Two women, on the other side of the room, were restlessly typing and still hadn't looked up from their papers.

Sikorski adjusted the glasses on his nose and smiled. 'How can I help you?'

'I'd like to know if in the past few weeks anybody's asked for a phial of cyanide,' Hugo replied.

The two women stopped typing and turned to look.

'Cyanide?' Sikorski raised his grizzled eyebrows.

He picked up a register, licked his fingertips and leafed through it. His index finger scrolled down all the columns on the paper as he squinted through his thick lenses. After several minutes of checks, he smacked his lips and shrugged his shoulders.

'There's nothing here,' he declared. 'The SS officers requested large doses of Evipan and Gardenal in the past month, but no cyanide.'

'You note everything, don't you?' Hugo asked.

'Of course. It's my job. I note every drug that leaves this building, let alone a poison. If anyone had asked me for cyanide, it would be written here.'

'And is there any way someone could have got it without going through the dispensary?'

'*Klepsi-klepsi!*' one of the women exclaimed.

'What?' Hugo looked at her, puzzled.

Sikorski, however, darted her a dirty look. 'Piroska!' he yelled. 'How many times do I have to tell you not to speak *Lagersprache*!'

'*Lagersprache*?' Hugo was even more confused.

'It's the camp language,' Adele explained, stepping beside him. 'Too many languages are spoken here, so you end up mixing them all and creating new ones.'

'And what did she say?'

'*Klepsi-klepsi*,' Sikorski repeated. 'Theft. The cyanide could have been stolen at the Jews' ramp, from suitcases or else from the Kanada. Someone might have stolen it in exchange for a favour. Besides, here at the dispensary we only get the Kanada scraps, isn't that why the doctors from Block 10 send you to Birkenau in person, Adele?'

Adele shrugged her shoulders and blushed. Hugo sensed that this was a source of significant tension among the doctors, who were trying to grab whatever they needed before anybody else.

'Is it possible to see if you still have some?' he asked.

'Come with me.' Sikorski made a hasty gesture and headed for the stairs. On the first floor, they walked past a room with beds and patients and he half closed the door so as not to disturb them. 'This is the Aryan staff infirmary,' he whispered.

He carried on up more stairs.

The dusty attic with its sloping ceiling served as a warehouse. There was a very strong smell of must, cardboard and old things. Shelves covered each wall and every kind of medicine was stacked on them. Sikorski opened a metal filing cabinet and looked for a card.

'Here it is,' he said, leafing through the files until he came to the letter C. 'Cyanide.'

He searched through the numbered shelving units, rummaged in a box, took out phials that glimmered in the dusty light through the skylights, then handed them to him. Hugo took them in the palm of his hand and studied them one by one.

'Three phials,' Sikorski exclaimed with displeasure. 'The file says four, but in the register of outgoing drugs there's no sign of a fourth.'

'Could someone have stolen it?' Hugo asked.

The pharmacist shrugged his shoulders, confused. 'Usually, the dispensary is very well monitored. We try to make sure there's no waste or theft, precisely because we get the leftovers from the Kanada. Maybe it's a clerical error: every now and then Piroska and Eva make a mistake with the figures, it can happen . . .'

Hugo gave him back the phials and placed both his hands on the handle of his stick, to think. Any nurse or doctor from Block 10 could go to the Kanada undisturbed to take drugs. Only Bethany couldn't go to Birkenau freely. Maybe she had found a way of sneaking into the dispensary.

'Do you have a record of admitted patients?' he asked.

'Of course,' Sikorski replied.

They left the attic. Adele walked behind him in silence while Sikorski whistled as he walked down the stairs. He stopped at the first floor and took a register from a cupboard, sat comfortably behind a metal table and leafed through it.

239

'What am I looking for?' he asked. 'Recent admissions?'

'Check if Bethany Assouline was admitted here . . .'

Sikorski checked the pages one by one and shook his head. 'No, she's never been here. She's Jewish, if memory serves. This is an infirmary for Aryan personnel, not for prisoners.'

'I know,' he murmured. 'Then read out the names of all those admitted over the past few weeks.'

'All of them?'

'All of them.'

Sikorski put his index finger on the sheet and began listing.

Hugo listened to the volley of names of SS officers who'd been admitted for influenza, gastroenteritis, the odd case of typhus, a tooth abscess. At one point he tensed up and had to lean more firmly on his stick.

'Go back,' he ordered.

'Franz Himmer.'

'The one after that.'

'Berto Hoffman.'

Adele and Hugo exchanged a look of surprise.

'What was he admitted for?' Hugo enquired.

'Two weeks ago, for an onset of bronchitis,' Sikorski read out.

Hugo remembered Gioele's story. By night, Bethany concealed her love from prying eyes. Gioele hadn't heard his voice but only coughing and a rattle that had scared him. Voigt, too, had confirmed that Berto's health had deteriorated and Hugo himself had heard him coughing and breathing noisily when they had questioned him.

Berto was Bethany's lover. He was the German she was in love with.

'Thank you very much, that's all I need,' Hugo concluded.

As he walked away, leaving the warmth of the dispensary behind him, he remembered Berto's bruised face. Voigt, the ruthless SS officer capable of rare acts of humanity, knew everything, that was why he'd insisted that Bethany be taken to the Auschwitz prisoners' infirmary and not to Birkenau: he owed Berto – whom he hadn't managed to save from beating or almost certain death – a favour.

'Do you think Berto's guilty?' Adele asked, breathless, catching up with him.

He'd almost forgotten about her, overwhelmed by a whirlwind of thoughts.

'I have to think,' he replied.

They walked in silence in the sun setting behind the blocks. The sky, ablaze above, seemed to want to swallow them. Hugo could sense all Adele's tension as she kept up with him and watched him nervously. She clearly feared for her friend's life.

They were skirting the kitchens when the camp orchestra gathered outside the roll-call square to make the prisoners returning exhausted from work march in time to the music – prisoners who were nothing but dark, hunched forms walking clumsily in the snow. One of them fell down. A kapo was immediately onto him. He gave him a kick in the back and forced him to get up by grabbing him by the scruff of the neck. In the scuffle, the prisoner lost one of his clogs and now stood with a bare foot in the snow, teeth chattering from the cold. Hugo couldn't help thinking about Gioele's father, about his tormented body, and felt powerless once again.

'So?' Adele asked. 'I've known Berto for a long time and he's no killer.'

241

Hugo searched his pocket, took out the medallion and showed it to her.

'Do you recognize it?'

Adele had insisted on knowing if Gioele had found anything special in the doctor's office. Now Hugo could feel the medallion burning in the palm of his hand as the umpteenth piece of evidence against Berto.

'No.' Adele shook her head. 'Where did you get it?'

'Gioele found it in Braun's office. Is it Berto's?'

'No.'

'Then it's Bethany's,' he said.

Adele shook her head. 'Impossible. They would have removed it from her when she arrived in the camp.'

'She could have found a way of hiding it.'

'Even if that were the case, you forget that Bethany is Jewish.'

'So?'

'If she wore a medallion with her initial, it would be written in the Hebrew alphabet, don't you think? It would have the symbol of the letter *Bet.*'

Hugo clasped the medallion before putting it away. This young woman was cunning and bright. She could have given several Berlin criminals a run for their money.

'But if a German had given Bethany the medallion,' he suggested, 'wouldn't he have used a letter from the Latin alphabet? Have Berto and Bethany known each other since before Auschwitz?'

'Not as far as I know. Bethany arrived last summer. Why do you ask?'

'There's a date engraved on the back of the medallion: 4 December 1931. It's a date to remember. An important moment. A lovers' rendezvous, perhaps? A wedding?'

'Are you implying that Berto and Bethany may have been lovers since 1931?'

'I'm only putting forward theories . . .'

'Has it occurred to you that this medallion may not belong to the killer at all, but to an attendant or a nurse?'

'Yes, it's a possibility I must also take into account.'

'Have you asked Braun's wife?'

'She says she knows nothing about it. It's neither hers nor her husband's.'

Hugo let out a sigh and headed towards the officers' mess. Adele sniffed and huddled in her coat. At one point, he heard her stop on the road.

'Will you have dinner with me?' she asked.

Hugo couldn't stifle his smile. This proposal was unexpected and gave him a joy he didn't believe he could feel after all he'd seen in the camp.

'Bethany is in the infirmary,' Adele said, trying to justify herself. 'Berto's in prison. As usual, Osmund won't be there, and Betsy avoids me like the plague. All this conversation has made me very sad and—'

'All right,' he said. 'With pleasure.'

31

Adele walked into the room with a trolley and two trays. The wheels squeaked, filling the silence.

'The food isn't as good as at the officers' mess,' she said apologetically, putting both trays on the table. 'But it's edible.'

'It smells nice.' Hugo uncovered the bowl of soup, waited for Adele to sit down, then tried a spoonful. 'Where do you think Osmund Becker is now?'

'With Brunhilde Braun,' she answered confidently, sipping her soup. 'Or else he's celebrating.'

'Celebrating what?'

'His promotion.'

Hugo loosened his tie and leaned back against the chair, stretching his good leg to make himself more comfortable, and looked at Adele, motioning her to continue.

'Which motive is stronger: passion or money?' she asked, biting into a piece of bread she'd just soaked in the soup. She chewed it, then picked up the crumbs from the tray. 'This afternoon, Osmund announced that we'll be going back to work on our old projects. Same group, same methods: he'll be leading the research. He's just received a letter from Reichsführer Himmler in person, authorizing him to continue Braun's studies on genetic diseases.'

Hugo put his spoon down, crossed his hands on the metal table and looked first at Adele, then at the window with its closed shutters.

'Braun's killer was emotionally involved,' he said. 'A cold, self-serving motive wouldn't have led him to make the mistakes he made.'

'Osmund also has a love motive,' she replied, contradicting him. 'He's having an affair with Braun's wife.'

'It's true that he actually does have two motives.' Hugo ran his fingers over his face. That morning, he hadn't been able to shave and all the demons inside him were pushing furiously against his skin.

'Something wrong, Herr Fischer?'

'Your attempts at diverting my suspicions away from Berto are truly commendable,' he replied in all honesty, 'but Bethany's suffered too much because of Braun. If the woman I loved had to go through what Bethany went through, I, too, would taint myself with such a dreadful crime . . .'

'Only there's something else that worries you,' she said.

'Are you interrogating me?'

'No. Just offering you a friend to talk to.'

Hugo sighed heavily. 'I found Gioele's father.' He felt his eyes tighten, his forehead furrow and his teeth gnash from the tension that never left him. He was no longer hungry and pushed the tray with the soup away from him. 'He's dying,' he added.

'I'm sorry,' she said earnestly.

'They told me they're waiting for him to die, from neglect. He's no longer even worth a human death. They're waiting for him to do it all by himself, for disease and starvation to consume him. Then, they'll proceed to the "harvest" – that's what they said. They'll load him onto a cart and take him to the piles. How can I say something like that to Gioele?'

'Tell him you couldn't find him,' Adele said, her chest heaving under her nurse's uniform, shaken by perceptible anxiety.

Hugo shuddered. 'Why don't any of the Jews rebel?'

Adele stared at him with eyes like two flames in the room's half-light. Hugo felt the impulse to ask her who the pincers were intended for.

'I know that at the Union factory, one can find explosives,' he began, meaning to gauge her reaction. 'They could use it to attempt a revolt. All they'd need would be – what can I say? – *eighteen* grams of explosive?'

Adele jumped, stung to the quick.

The chair scraped noisily against the floor as she got up from the table.

'Jews don't have that spirit of initiative,' she muttered, getting a hold of herself.

She went to a cabinet, opened it and fumbled for something. Hugo realized that she was doing it to stall for time and grew certain that, just like Berto Hoffman, she was silently revolting against the terrible Auschwitz machine.

'They'd never rebel because they're inferior creatures,' she added. 'They're subhumans incapable of defending their own freedom, and those incapable of defending their freedom don't deserve to live.'

Hugo stretched both legs under the table and stared at

her. Adele was reciting the part of the perfect Nazi, but a shadow of fear in her eyes made her pupils widen, like an oil slick. She was afraid of being discovered.

'It's called mass psychology,' he said. 'People turn into a flock of sheep and no one wants to take the first step. It could happen to us Aryans, too, in the same circumstances.'

She did not reply and just took out a bottle of spirits, carefully concealed behind various boxes, unscrewed the top and filled two glasses.

Hugo decided not to torment her further. If she and Berto Hoffman really were two traitors, it wasn't up to him to discover it. He had turned a blind eye so many times when the Nazis had struck hard that he could do it now that a German was rebelling against a place as horrible and demoralizing as Auschwitz.

'Don't tell anybody,' she said, returning to the table. 'We nurses keep this bottle of whisky for especially stressful moments, but it's better if that doesn't get around.'

'My lips are sealed,' Hugo replied, referring to the Union rather than to the little glass of amber liquid now sparkling in his hands.

Adele swigged the whisky. Hugo raised his glass in a toast, drained it in a single gulp and felt the alcohol burn his throat then glide, warm, down his oesophagus. The feeling made him sigh with joy.

Hugo was about to ask for some more when a shadow appeared in the corridor, through the half-open door. He could hear a murmur in the lobby, and he recognized a woman's voice.

He stood up, driven more by instinct than curiosity.

Adele started to open her mouth, but he gestured at her

to keep quiet. He kept to the wall as far as the partly open door, no more than a chink through which you could just about glimpse the floor tiles and the shadow on the wall.

'He asked about the wedding ring . . .' a woman moaned.

In the mass of dark shadows, Hugo recognized Frau Braun's blond hair and proud bearing and opened the door a little more. Facing her, leaning against the wall in a film star pose, Osmund Becker was shaking his head.

'What are you worried about?' he said angrily. 'You've become paranoid.'

'I don't want them to find out about us . . .'

'The wedding ring's in the pool, no one will find it.'

'I know, but . . .'

'And even if they do find it, what then? It wouldn't mean a thing.'

Osmund reached out to caress her face, but she pulled away and looked around warily. She must have noticed the light coming from Adele's room, because she gestured at Osmund to leave.

'Damn!' Adele murmured, still flat against the wall to avoid being seen. 'I told you these two have a perfect motive . . .'

'I must find that wedding ring,' Hugo said, nodding.

'I told you Berto's innocent.' Adele had a triumphant glow in her eyes.

'Do you have any Pervitin?' he replied.

32

The pool used for collecting water was dark and looked more like a gaping mouth than a swimming pool. The prisoners had to break the ice every day, so it would be usable in case of need, and chunks of ice floated on the murky surface like solitary wreckage.

Hugo looked at it for a long time. Next to him, Adele was shivering from the cold.

'Do you really think the ring is in there?' she asked, confused.

'It's the pool nearest Block 10,' he insisted. 'If they took the ring off the body, they'll have thrown it here.'

Adele gave him a Pervitin tablet. 'It's not a good idea,' she protested. 'You won't find anything in the dark. Get one of the guards to search for it tomorrow.'

'Tomorrow is always too late.'

Hugo swallowed the tablet, waited by the pool for it to take effect and within a couple of minutes noticed euphoria starting to sweep over him – he was a hunter ready to accept the murderer's challenge. It was the same drug that his fellow Germans were using on the Russian front in order not to feel cold, not to sleep, not be hungry or afraid. In Auschwitz they were testing it on prisoners to study the resistance to cold induced by methamphetamines.

'It's dangerous in your condition.' Adele's voice sounded muffled to him. Beautiful but distant.

Hugo figured that, in his condition, he couldn't afford to waste any more time. He stripped down to his vest and underpants. He took the small net used for dredging the pool and sat on the edge, which had been dusted with salt. He slid into the water and the cold was nothing but a volley of pin stabs that he soon stopped feeling at all. He could die, what with being in the cold and the Pervitin circulating through him. His brain would no longer be sending any signals, a bit like in the case of his scars, and his body could no longer defend itself. He'd heard of soldiers who'd undressed in the high snow of the Russian steppes and frozen to death without noticing.

He moved slowly, leaning on the edge to avoid slipping, then threw in the little net. He took it out to check, then plunged it in again, then out again, but it came back empty every time. He felt nervousness tense all the muscles in his face and his heart rate increase.

'Herr Fischer, I beg you!' Adele's voice was a moan. 'Come out of there!'

'Not yet!' he protested.

He carried on, beating every corner of the pool, dull anger rising in his gut. There was nothing there.

'Damn it!' he cried, exasperated.

Adele gave a start and shrank into her shoulders, then ran to him, supported him as he came out, and helped him get dressed again. Hugo put his coat back on and shook his wet hair with disappointment. He noticed that his hands were so frozen, he couldn't even clasp his stick, his fingers livid, and yet they didn't hurt. He was almost sweating from the heat.

'It's not here,' he hissed. 'How many other pools are there, between here and Birkenau?'

'You want to check them all?' she snapped. 'You can also try the river Soła, if you like, but I promise it's a lot nicer in the summer.'

'You heard them, too,' Hugo replied. 'Braun's wedding ring is in a pool.'

'Maybe it's in the one at his house.'

Hugo opened his eyes wide and felt stupid for not thinking of that possibility sooner. Even Clauberg had said it: Braun had a beautiful swimming pool among hectares of land. That's where they held parties despite the smell of burning flesh and the ash falling on the water.

'You are not going into Braun's swimming pool.' Adele grabbed him by the collar of his coat and shook her head. 'You'll send a swimmer. I know a very good one, a prisoner. Prisoners do this, not Germans. You need to stay alive, Herr Fischer. Otherwise, who'll continue the investigation?'

Hugo laughed, euphoric from the Pervitin. 'You! You're really very capable!'

The Braun farmhouse stood on the junction with the road that led from Auschwitz train station to the Stammlager. It was surrounded by a tall, thick hedge through which you could see nothing except the sloping slate roof and the smoking chimney.

Jan, the Polish swimmer, was sitting next to Hugo in the back of the Kübelwagen.

251

He wasn't speaking.

He was tall and slim, but his broad shoulders revealed his past as a professional swimmer, while his shaved head emphasized a perfectly round skull, exposing his protruding ears.

He was silent because he didn't speak German.

He'd put up no resistance when they'd gone to pick him up, even though he didn't understand where they were taking him. An SS officer had told Hugo that he'd arrived in August and ever since, whether it was warm or cold, he'd entertained the camp's officers by going to fetch from the swimming pools whatever they threw in. A true prodigy with quick, darting muscles, the officer had added. Hugo could see little muscle under his tunic, however; by now hunger had eaten away at all of it.

'Here we are,' he said.

Jan remained impassive.

The Kübelwagen drove in and parked at the foot of a large weeping willow leaning over the snow like a wistful embrace. It was old, centennial perhaps, had seen the Great War and heaven knew what else, and towered over the entire courtyard alone. An Alsatian tied near the garage was barking and snapping at the air, announcing their arrival.

Hugo got out and let his eyes sweep first over the snow-covered roof of the farmhouse, which sheltered a slate porch, then over a hut from which protruded the gleaming front of a motorbike, and finally the swimming pool amid statues and a lawn coated with soft snow.

A short, stocky man came out of the front door, wearing a striped uniform and the purple triangle of the Jehovah's Witnesses.

'Heil Hitler!' he said awkwardly.

'Heil Hitler,' Hugo replied dismissively. 'Is Frau Braun at home?'

'What's going on?' She'd appeared on the doorstep and was putting a coat over her civilian clothes. She quickly fastened it and came out. 'I'm having dinner and my food will get cold on the table.'

Hugo squinted. 'I have to look for something,' he said peremptorily.

'In the house?'

'In the garden.'

He got the impression he wasn't welcome inside the farmhouse. He gestured at Jan and led him to the frozen edge of the pool. The young man stripped, but stood as still as a rod, looking around. The searchlights shone on his damp, pale skin.

'So?' Hugo asked, irritated. He remembered that Jan didn't speak German and was used to diving only to fetch things the soldiers threw. 'You!' he shouted at the Jehovah's Witness. 'Where are you from?'

The man trotted towards him and indicated a letter on his tunic. 'Polish,' he muttered.

'Then tell this man that he must dive in and look for anything that's at the bottom of the pool.'

'In the pool?'

'Yes.'

'But it's frozen . . .'

Dispirited, Hugo looked at the expanse of water on which chunks of snow-covered ice were floating. The dog, enraged, kept barking at him from the hut. Hugo's ears were hissing and he was overexcited by the Pervitin.

'I know. It's frozen. But he's used to the cold.' He gave

the young man a tap on his chest and found it less firm and muscular than he was hoping. 'He'll be fine.'

'He'll freeze to death.'

'Enough!' Frau Braun stepped forward, her hair tousled from the agitation. 'Tell me what's going on!'

'I'll show you straight away.' Hugo gestured at the Jehovah's Witness, who asked the swimmer to bend down so that he could speak in his ear.

'You arrive at my house without permission,' she said. 'You can't—'

'It's for the investigation,' he replied.

'Stop that young man now!' Her voice was now shrill and unpleasant, and Hugo could clearly sense her fear.

'Too late!' he said serenely.

He watched Jan dive in. The young man disappeared under the water, concentric circles expanding on the surface in his wake. Every now and then, as he swam on the bottom of the pool, the pieces of ice wobbled side to side, like solitary boats in the middle of the sea.

'I hope that afterwards, you'll have the heart to let him warm up by the fireplace and give him something to eat,' Hugo said. Unfortunately for Frau Braun, his body was still so saturated with Pervitin that he said whatever came to his mind, without restraint.

Frau Braun gave a start.

At that very moment, Jan surfaced, shaking like a leaf, teeth chattering so loudly they echoed in his bones. He came out of the pool holding something shiny between his fingers.

Hugo took the item, moved to the area illuminated by the headlights and held his breath. He felt a stabbing pain in his stomach and a wrench in his guts, but paid little attention to it. He held up the ring to read the engraving on the inside and felt a smile spread over his face.

'It's your husband's wedding band,' he said, looking at Frau Braun.

Her eyes were open wide and her pupils so dilated that the irises seemed like lakes of tar.

Hugo put the ring in his pocket. He felt another sharp pang in his stomach and a burning sensation that constricted the breath in his throat for a moment. This time, it was so strong that he couldn't ignore it. 'Get the young man dry now,' he commanded. 'And feed him.'

'What?' she gasped.

'It's an order from an Aryan,' he enjoyed retorting. Frau Braun realized it wasn't a good idea to argue. She was clever enough to understand that she was in an awkward position. She signalled at her servant, who collected Jan's clothes and took him to the servants' kitchen.

'How did the ring end up down there?' Hugo asked when they were alone, in the trodden snow mixed with mud. 'Did you throw it there? Were you angry with your husband for cheating on you?'

Frau Braun shivered in her coat. 'No! I had no idea it was there!'

'Don't lie. I heard you talking to Osmund Becker, this evening . . .'

She stared, lost. She'd grown pale and her lips were trembling: she could no longer barricade herself behind lies.

A window squeaked in the house, startling her. Hugo glimpsed a shadow behind the curtains, which closed again quickly.

'Osmund's here, isn't he?' he asked.

Another shudder went through her. 'How dare you insinuate such a thing?' Her face was red from the cold, her hair ruffled, her eyes glistening. She looked on the brink of collapse.

'Tell me how the ring ended up in there,' Hugo commanded. 'Or you'll both be in a lot of trouble. You're suspected of murder . . .'

Frau Braun burst into tears and slumped on the ground, rubbing her face hard, as though trying to tear it off.

'Sigismund found us in bed together,' she moaned. 'He was beside himself, I'd never seen him like that. And yet he'd cheated on me so many times!' She was slurring her words, snarling angrily. 'That day, I followed him to the garden and asked him to forgive me as I had forgiven him, but he looked at me with such hatred and contempt that I thought I'd die. He took off his wedding ring, threw it into the swimming pool and said we could carry on pretending to be a committed couple to keep up appearances, but that things would change for ever. I stopped seeing Osmund, then Sigismund died and I felt so lonely . . .'

'Why were you so worried I'd find it?' Hugo crouched to look her in the eye better.

'When you asked me about the ring, I was scared my relationship with Osmund would be discovered. If the other doctors found out . . . I couldn't bear the shame. I chose to say he was still wearing it on his finger the evening he was killed, so you'd think it had been removed by the murderer.'

'I understand.'

Hugo propped himself on his stick to get back up and put out his hand to help her up, too, feeling all the fragility of this woman who seemed made of steel, but wasn't.

33

Hugo slammed Braun's wedding band on Liebehenschel's desk.

The glass of cognac that usually kept the Kommandant company before he went to bed trembled.

'Becker?' he said, incredulous. 'Osmund Becker and Frau Braun?'

Hugo looked at him for a while before managing a reply. He was in a cold sweat. The pain in his stomach, which had been no more than irksome at the Brauns' house, had now grown into a fierce vice, as if a blade kept plunging relentlessly into his belly.

'Nobody must know for now,' he finally said.

'You may rely on my discretion.'

'There's also this.' Hugo put the gold medallion on the desk. 'I found it while searching Braun's office, under the Christmas tree. Have you ever seen anyone wearing it?'

The Kommandant turned the medallion in his hand. 'No,' he replied. 'I don't think I've ever seen it. There's a valuable diamond in it, so I would have noticed it around the neck of an auxiliary, and a prisoner is most unlikely to succeed in hiding such an item. It's not Braun's or his wife's?'

'No. At least that's what she'll have me believe.'

'Let me see if I understand this: are you openly accusing Brunhilde Braun and Osmund Becker of murder?'

'I never accuse anyone "openly" until I'm certain. I'm only saying that I've narrowed down the list of suspects.'

'So Berto Hoffman is innocent?'

'Hoffman fits the profile of the killer like a glove and could have had access to phials of cyanide. He's also a suspect.'

'And what profile would that be?'

'That of an educated man who'd long been harbouring resentment towards Sigismund Braun, and got involved in a love affair that clouded his judgement.'

'Becker and Frau Braun are lovers,' Liebehenschel said. 'But who would Hoffman have fallen in love with?'

'Allow me to keep this a secret.'

'For the benefit of the investigation?'

'Yes, absolutely,' Hugo lied. He had no intention of feeding Bethany to him. 'I wouldn't conceal anything from you if it weren't for the good of the enquiry.'

Liebehenschel gave him a look that was at once disappointed and excited. 'Carry on with your search,' he concluded. 'I want to send you back to Department V with a crown of laurels on your head, not a kick in the backside. That's not my style, as you'll no doubt have realized by now.'

The Kommandant gave a hearty laugh. Hugo couldn't, though. The possibility of returning defeated was an obsession that kept him awake at night. The stabbing pain in his stomach took his breath away again, a feeling of hot and cold made him shiver and he grimaced. He saw a double image of Liebehenschel for a moment. He couldn't recall this reaction among the listed side effects of Pervitin.

'In any case do be careful,' the Kommandant added sternly. 'Whoever murdered Braun could be capable of anything to get away with it. Get a prisoner to taste your food before you eat it . . .'

'I'm not the Führer.' Hugo gave a faint laugh, but an impulse to vomit made him close his mouth and keep quiet.

He felt the urge to run out of the office. The potato soup was rising from his stomach.

Hugo flung his entire dinner onto the snow. He slumped against the wall, muscles quivering and teeth chattering so hard he was afraid he'd wake everybody up.

He was sweating and cold at the same time.

He was jolted by another tremor and vomited again. The best he could do afterwards was grab a handful of snow and stuff it into his mouth to rinse away the acidic taste on his tongue. He looked at the ground, at the viscous puddle soiling the snow, and Adele's face pushed its way into his mind. He could see her opening the cabinet, taking out the whisky and slipping some rubbish or other into his glass. Poison.

Get a prisoner to taste your food before you eat it.

'Bitch!' Hugo swore.

More retching dragged up his stomach, squeezed his oesophagus so hard that he vomited with a curse that was lost in the evening shadows. He spat and rammed more snow into his mouth. There was a stabbing pain in one of his molars, and he realized he would die here, slumped in his own vomit. He pictured Liebehenschel's contrite face the following day, and the shocked expressions of Voigt and the doctors. Nebe tapping his teeth together furiously. And his father, alone among the bombs that lit up the Berlin sky, with no more son or wife.

Hugo tried to take a step. Around him, the camp was deserted. The blocks stood in a row, red bricks and windows watching him with apparent disapproval. The outline of the fencing extended all around, and the barbed wire suddenly made him feel trapped.

'Herr Fischer!'

That voice again. It had echoed among the birches, travelling through the snow-laden branches and the wind.

Hugo turned. Adele stood still in the light raining down from the searchlights, just a couple of steps away from the thick, gummy shade where he was huddling. Her face was deformed by a chiaroscuro effect. He thought he saw a frightening sneer on it.

'Step forward,' he commanded.

She approached. Hugo grabbed her coat, catching her by surprise, and pulled her into the narrow recess between the two buildings. Adele didn't even have time to scream. He dropped his stick and clamped a hand over her mouth, pressing on it with all the strength he had left.

His head was spinning.

Everything was blurry, covered with a thick layer of ashes that smelled of charcoaled bodies. All he could see, besides his hand firmly over her lips, were Adele's eyes, alight like fires in the night. They stared at him in terror. She whined, trying to say something, but didn't struggle: she was still, like a frightened little bird.

'What did you put into the whisky?' he hissed.

She shook her head. Her red locks, which smelled of the sea, trembled around her face.

'You've poisoned me!' he insisted, pressing hard. 'You've poisoned me because you knew I'd find you out! Braun had also realized everything, and that's why you and Hoffman killed him!'

Hugo felt a stab split his belly. He let go of Adele and ceased feeling any contact between his leg and the ground. He collapsed to his knees and found himself in the snow on all fours, like a defeated animal.

'Herr Fischer!'

Adele's voice was muffled, like the snow and the ash.

34

Adele was sitting on a chair, looking at him.

Hugo felt discomfort in his arm. Someone had tied him down.

He tried in vain to move. They must have secured him to a bed or something, because he was lying face up, and his arms and legs had probably been tied. They'd placed something heavy on his belly, something that pressed on his stomach and lungs and made him breathless.

He tried to move and a metallic sound echoed in his ears.

'Don't – you'll knock everything down,' Adele exclaimed.

Hugo felt anger rise to his temples. He had trusted her.

He tried to work out where he was, but could only see a flaking ceiling, the plaster swollen from the damp. She must have brought him to a secret room in Auschwitz with the help of an accomplice: the same one who'd killed Braun. And yet Berto was in prison.

'Where are we?' he mumbled.

He imagined himself lying on an autopsy trolley, in a camp cell where no one would ever find his body. They'd probably chop him up into such tiny pieces that taking him to a crematorium would be very easy. He'd turn to ash, the kind that lay beneath the snow in the camp, and all traces of him would be lost for ever. In Berlin, they would say that he'd run away, frightened by the failure of the Braun case, and would soon replace and forget him. These thoughts crammed into Hugo's mind and his head felt like it was about to explode.

He tried to free himself again. 'Where am I?' he asked.

'Herr Fischer,' Adele intervened, holding his arm still. 'You must keep calm.'

'Calm?'

'Don't get upset and all will be well.'

'What have you done to me?' Hugo tried to get up, breathing hard through his teeth.

'You'll knock out the drip!'

Hugo looked at the hollow in his arm and saw a needle stuck in his vein. He followed the long cannula to a small bottle from which transparent liquid was slowly dripping.

He was not tied down.

He was attached to a drip-feed that was injecting more drugs or a tranquiliser into him.

'Where have you brought me?' he asked, his mouth dry from the confusion.

'To the dispensary, in the officers' infirmary,' Adele replied with a sigh.

Hugo looked at his belly. The weight that kept him still was a hot-water bottle. He finally managed to turn his head and saw the room he'd already glimpsed when visiting the dispensary to look for phials of cyanide. There were five other beds, all empty. A photograph of Hitler hanging on the wall seemed to scrutinize him scornfully.

'What happened to me?' he grumbled.

Adele sniffed. 'You were expecting to bathe in icy water in December right after eating, with no side effects? You're severely congested. Fortunately, I came to find you to ask about the ring, or you'd be dead . . .'

'Congested?'

'Severely congested.'

'I thought—'

'I know what you thought. You told me.'

'I thought you'd poisoned me because I'd discovered everything about the Union . . .'

Adele knelt by the bed, her elbows on the mattress and squeezed his hand hard in a prayer.

'My life is in your hands,' she whispered in the dull half-light of the room. 'If you decide to tell what you know, I'll end up in front of a firing squad. I can't stop you and I certainly wouldn't have tried to by poisoning you. I'm not a murderer, even though I've stained myself with serious crimes by working for Braun. But I beg you, consider carefully the consequences of what you say—'

Hugo stopped her. 'I've no intention of talking.' His head was thumping ruthlessly. 'It's what I was trying to make you understand at dinner. I have no intention or interest in reporting anyone other than Braun's killer.'

Adele burst into tears of relief. She quickly wiped her eyes and huddled in her coat, as though to protect herself. She was still kneeling on the floor, her shoulders hunched, her face suddenly as small as a child's.

'There's a large network of subversives inside the camp and out,' she mumbled. Her voice was trembling like a tightened cord. 'We call it the Resistance. The prisoners have got organized as well as they can to have a better life. I do my bit. At the Kanada, I look for pens and paper, so they can keep a diary and write down their memories. When I can, I give them cameras so that they can secretly take pictures of the crematorium and the piles. When the war is over, Germany will explain what happened in the camps in its own way. In Berlin, they're building a museum with the finds the doctors send. Did you know that? They want to show our children why this place became *necessary*, why they *had* to cleanse the world of the inferior races that contaminate it. And have you thought of what would happen if we lose the war? There's already an active protocol for the destruction of the gas chambers and crematoria, and of any document that's inconvenient to high-ranking officers. Somebody will have to show people the truth: the photographs and stories of those who experienced this hell.'

Hugo took a deep breath. The hot-water bottle was resting like a boulder on his stomach. When had they reached this level of barbarism? When was the exact moment when everything had started to slide down the slippery slope?

The gunshot in the dance hall pounded in his ears. That had been his own personal moment, the instant he'd started to fall and hadn't ever stopped: the instant he'd turned his back on all his principles just so he could pursue his goals in peace. He wondered if he really hadn't known what was happening in Auschwitz. If his unconscious had really not already sensed it in the more or less veiled remarks that circulated in the department corridors, and if he'd decided not to listen to them because it was too inconvenient a truth . . .

He looked up at the ceiling. While he sheltered behind

a party with which he shared nothing, there were those who risked their lives for their principles every day, with a courage he now envied.

'What about the Union?' he asked. 'What's this got to do with the Union?'

'The Sonderkommandos need explosives,' Adele replied. 'I was acting as courier between them and the women who work at the factory.'

'Eighteen grams of explosive?'

Adele smiled, still shivering. 'You've not shown much acumen on this point, Detective. In camp language, "eighteen" is the secret code for alarm. The operation was aborted after Berto's arrest because it was no longer safe. They'll have to wait. It will take months for the Union women to carry out their intention – years, perhaps. Maybe it will never happen and they'll die first, but at least we will have tried.'

'The green triangles.' Hugo propped himself up on his elbows to make himself more comfortable, then pressed the scalding hot-water bottle on his stomach and felt relief. 'It was you who put the triangles under Berto's mattress, wasn't it?'

Adele shook her head. 'No. They belong to both of us. When we found ourselves in this place, we realized we had to do something. We couldn't just stand and watch, so we did what we did in Irsee . . .'

'What do you mean, in Irsee?'

'At the Irsee clinic, Berto's and my hands were tied and we had to obey orders, but we managed to erase the names of many children from the death lists. It was a risky operation, but no one ever noticed anything. We saved only a few lives, but every life is a huge victory.'

Hugo felt heat flare up in his stomach and temples. He thought of Gioele and his own inability to help him, to stop the piston that would flood his heart with phenol.

'Do you think Berto could have killed Braun?' he asked. 'Do you think his motive is strong enough?'

'I know Berto and I'm certain he would never have done it.'

'Berto and Bethany love each other. And Braun abused Bethany . . .'

'Even for love, he wouldn't have done it. What about the wedding band?'

'It was in the Brauns' swimming pool, but Brunhilde gave me a perfectly reasonable explanation for that.'

Hugo rested his head back on the pillows, exhausted.

He wondered if there was morphine in the drip, because he felt light – empty – despite his tiredness.

'Now rest, it's the middle of the night,' Adele murmured. 'You had a lucky escape.'

Hugo sighed. 'Maybe it would have been a just punishment.'

'Don't be silly.'

Adele leaned over to tuck him in. Their faces came close again. Hugo wished he could kiss her, lose himself in those soft lips, get drunk on that scent of salt and sand that reminded him of the tide in Wattenmeer.

Adele smiled and blushed. 'See you tomorrow, Herr Fischer.'

35

Auschwitz, 27 December 1943

'Berto Hoffman has confessed.'

Tristan Voigt woke him at dawn, which was softening the sky outside the infirmary window. His voice was like an echo shattering against the walls, snatching Hugo from his sleep.

Hugo sat up in bed and looked for Adele.

Her chair was empty.

Beyond the window, the sky was still mostly dark, a brilliant tone in the spot where the dawn was rising, but a strong smell of coffee substitute was already wafting from the floor below.

Hugo scratched his face and grimaced. The hairs were increasingly bristly.

'What do you mean, he confessed?' he grumbled in a daze. He searched for the stick standing against the bedside table and grasped it. 'What has he confessed to?'

'Braun's murder.' Tristan Voigt looked at him with eyes open wide.

Hugo felt the ground shift beneath his feet when he put them on the floor. Whenever he reached the end of a case, it was as though an avalanche had knocked him over. A strange melancholy would seize him and throw him down. It was like the end of a love affair.

Only this time he couldn't believe it.

'He has asked to speak to you,' Voigt added with urgency.

'Of course,' was the only thing Hugo managed to say.

Berto Hoffman was looking at him from his cot.

This time, now that the swelling had gone down, Hugo was able to see his eyes, pale and clear, beyond the folds of flesh.

'It was me,' was the first thing he said.

His voice resounded between the subterranean walls of Block 11. It blended with the saturated, pungent air, the dampness from the stone, the musty smell of an enclosed space natural light had never penetrated.

Hugo removed his hat. He took a chair, placed it against the wall and sat down. His body felt numb from the fever, and he had to repress a dreadful shiver that made his shoulders tremble.

'How did you do it?' he asked.

'I punched him in order to stun him, then I poisoned him with cyanide,' Berto replied.

'Where did you get the cyanide?'

'From the dispensary, when I was admitted.'

Hugo sniffed and coughed. He'd got chilled to the bone from his immersion into the frozen pool, and could feel the temperature rising to his temples, ready to overflow. It was in moments like these that the pains of his illness risked worsening. Despite the confusion he seemed to be floating in, he forced himself to keep lucid.

'Why did you kill him?' he asked.

Berto hesitated. 'You can't understand why I did it.'

'Then help me understand.'

Berto hunched over and was shaken from top to toe by a volley of coughing fits: proof that he was the man Gioele had heard with Bethany.

'Braun dragged me to hell,' he said, exhaling. 'First in Irsee, then here. Tell me, Herr Fischer, are we really in the twentieth century?'

Hugo froze at the question.

Berto laughed. 'The century of progress. I've seen things no man should ever see in the century of progress. One day, I dropped a canister of formaldehyde, so I opened the window and pulled up the wooden blind to get rid of the leftover smell. I looked into the prison courtyard. There was a family. A mother, a father and a child. The "strangler" knocked the father and mother to the ground and killed them. Do you know why they call them "stranglers"?'

'No . . .' Hugo's throat was dry.

'Because "stranglers" put an iron bar on the throat of the condemned person and jump on it. They balance on it until the bone in the neck snaps. They must have done something terrible, I thought, or they would have got a bullet in the back of the neck.'

'And the child?'

'He was a few months old. The executioner picked him up and slammed him against the ground a couple of times, like a freshly caught octopus. That's all.'

Hugo clamped his eyes shut. He saw the baby girl's crushed skull at the Jews' ramp. Heard that flaccid sound again. He felt dizzy and the air grew so thick he could almost grab it with his hands.

'That day I started to hate this place with my whole being,' Berto concluded. 'And I began my struggle with the help of green triangles.'

'How did you decide to murder Braun?'

'I lost my head, it happened during an argument.'

Hugo looked at him closely. Braun's murder hadn't been improvised, even if it had been triggered by passion. It had been premeditated, carefully organized, only the emotional component had caused many errors. And why would Berto have taken a note to the Kanada? Who was it for? Bethany was right next door to him, in Block 10, the same as his other colleagues.

'Did you kill him because of Bethany?' he asked.

Berto slowly looked up and rubbed his hands. He wasn't surprised, however. Somebody must have warned him that their relationship had been discovered.

'You're having an affair with a Jew,' Hugo added.

'I love Bethany and that's not a crime.'

'It is according to the law for the protection of the blood.'

'Those aren't *my* laws.'

'Did you kill Braun because he abused Bethany?'

'That pig forced himself on her,' Berto ground out.

He crumpled the fabric of his trousers at his knees. He was agitated, and when you're agitated, you make the worst mistakes and always reveal yourself. 'And he did worse . . .'

'What?'

'Bethany was pregnant. It could have been either mine or Braun's. But Braun couldn't have known about us, so he got very scared and wanted her killed. He had her shut here, in the bunker, but Adele and I told him that this would arouse more suspicion. He let himself be persuaded. Bethany had an abortion and promised to keep her mouth shut.'

'Was she losing blood because of the abortion?'

'No,' Berto replied icily. His voice was quivering with anger. 'Braun wholeheartedly rejected his attraction for Bethany but he couldn't control himself. Clauberg was aware of his weakness but has always kept quiet about it because he would never betray the only person he considered a brother. And so, two weeks ago, he suggested experimenting on Bethany. He attempted a new form of sterilization that would have prevented any further pregnancies.'

'What kind of sterilization?' Again, Hugo felt that sensation at the top of his stomach, as though a hand was squeezing it hard, preventing him from breathing. The snow over Auschwitz concealed the horrors buried beneath and he was digging at it with both hands, bringing up all the filth beneath the white coating.

'Radiation wasn't very effective and slow to act.' Berto looked drained. 'Clauberg devised a sterilization with liquid made from silver nitrate and formaldehyde mixed with a contrasting radiological substance. He injects it into the neck of the uterus in his guinea pigs and brags about being able to sterilize thousands in a single day. Imagine: Schering wants to buy the rights to the fluid . . .'

'What effect does it have?'

'Excruciating pain, heavy bleeding . . .' Hugo clenched his fists. His knuckles turned white.

Berto had called it 'the century of progress'.

'Bethany survived,' Berto murmured, 'but I could do nothing to spare her the surgery and the shame.'

'So you killed Braun out of revenge?'

'Wouldn't you have?'

'Not for a Jew.' Hugo squinted at him.

Anger leads you to betray yourself, he kept thinking, and he had to give this man enough rope to hang himself. 'You're an Aryan, how could you make such a mistake?'

As Hugo had expected, Berto shook his head, panting with anger.

'What does O A B mean?' Hugo asked.

Berto licked his lips anxiously and did not reply. And yet if he really had murdered Braun, then he must know that the doctor had tried to leave a note that made no sense.

'What can you tell me about the medallion?'

'The medallion,' he said as though waking up. 'The medallion's mine. My mother gave it to me years ago.'

'The inscription on the back is very moving. "You're my life",' Hugo recited, holding out his hand as though engraving the air with those words. Words that didn't exist.

'She loved me very much,' Berto said with a shudder, falling into the trap.

'There is no inscription on the back of the medallion.' Hugo leaned towards him and looked straight into his eyes.

Berto clenched his jaw, lost. He must have felt the ground vanish beneath his feet.

'You should have made sure you were better informed,' Hugo continued. 'You should have studied your part before handing yourself in. Now tell me who you're covering for. Bethany? Adele? Osmund?'

'I'm not covering for anybody. I'm just very tired and confused!'

'You did not kill Braun,' Hugo declared. He stood up and put his hat back on his head. He felt it throb in the grip of a migraine and the high fever, but decided to ignore it. 'You're trying to protect someone,' he said menacingly, 'and I'm going to find out who.'

'Accept my statement and get it over and done with!' Berto said furiously.

Confronted with that demand, Hugo felt momentarily suspended in mid-air. He could have ended it there, that was true. He could have accepted Berto Hoffman's confession, left this infernal place and returned to Berlin with all the honours. Nebe would have been pleased. Liebehenschel would have come to terms with it.

'Damn it!' he swore. 'I didn't become a criminologist for this!'

36

Gioele was sitting on a stretcher. A cannula was sucking out his blood and Hugo was happy to see that he was still alive.

'Hi,' he said.

The boy did not respond. He looked sleepy. The nurse gave him a slap on the back of the neck that practically toppled him, and he woke up.

'Good morning, Herr Fischer,' he muttered.

'How are you?' Hugo sat on the edge of the stretcher.

'Fine.' Gioele stared at him with his big eyes. 'But you look awful.'

'I ended up in the infirmary and I'm afraid I have a temperature.' Hugo rubbed his face. His temples were throbbing relentlessly. He wanted a hot cup of coffee, a bed and a morphine injection. Nothing else.

'Herr Fischer,' the boy whispered when the nurse moved away. 'I was thinking: if we manage to steal a green triangle and you find my father, we can get him out of Birkenau.'

'Gioele.' Hugo's tongue was dry because of the fever.

'We can do the same thing for my mum. If I find my mum, we'll all be better off. My brother, too. She's always the one who takes care of us when we're ill and I'm sure she'll know how to cure him of typhus.'

'Gioele,' Hugo said again. He closed his eyes, his head imploding, trapped in a vice of scalding fingers. 'I haven't been able to find them. The camp is too big and they're not listed in the records, so I'll need a lot more time. It's better if you stop thinking about them . . .'

'But why?' The boy opened his eyes wide. 'Why would you do that?'

Hugo withdrew into his shoulders.

'Do you have a mother?' Gioele asked.

'I did.'

'Did she die?'

'Yes, when I was thirteen. She fell while skiing.'

'Do you miss her?'

Hugo smiled. It tickled his heart to remember how beautiful she was. Tall and slim, with brown hair gathered at the nape, grey eyes like his. She smelled of ginger biscuits and when she played the piano, she looked like an angel and everybody would fall silent. When they went to the North Sea, she walked barefoot on the sand, carrying her sandals in her hand, leaving footprints he enjoyed following.

'Yes, I miss her very much,' he replied. 'I miss her even now I'm grown up.'

'You see? You can't forget your family.'

The nurse gave them both a surly look because of the intimacy of their chat, marched towards them, roughly snatched the needle from Gioele's vein and motioned for him to get off the stretcher.

'Did you want something, Herr Fischer?' the boy asked, adjusting his sleeve.

'I'd like to see the drawings of Braun's body again,' he replied.

Gioele nodded. He darted to the exit, but a dizzy spell made him rock like a top and fall on his bottom, and he let out a moan of pain.

'Don't they give you anything to eat after taking so much blood?' Hugo rushed to pull him up, hindered by his stick.

Gioele shook his head and got up, clinging to him. 'I have to wait for dinner, or for Uncle Mengele to bring me chocolate or biscuits.'

'But they took a lot of blood.'

'I know.'

Gioele went into the corridor, still swaying. Hugo followed him.

You could tell this child knew every corner of this block. It was his home, after all. Once they were in the dormitory, he opened the desk drawer and took out his drawings. 'Here they are.'

Hugo started looking through them one by one, hoping they'd suggest something to him, even if only a whisper.

He saw the drops of blood on the floor and remembered Bethany's haemorrhage. On the desk, you could make out the sheets of letterheaded paper and the fountain pen. O A B. Osmund, Adele and Bethany? Or Osmund, Anita and Brunhilde? What was the doctor trying to tell him just before dying?

'Give me Braun's portrait,' he commanded. Gioele obeyed. 'You've drawn the wound on his forehead very well,' Hugo remarked.

'How did he get it?' Gioele asked, bending over the drawing inquisitively.

'Someone struck him.' Berto had said he'd punched him, but it was obvious he was lying. 'Braun's skin is grazed, so it couldn't have been just a blow with bare hands.'

'I once saw a Pole have a fist fight with a kapo,' Gioele said.

'Here in the camp?'

The boy nodded. 'They organize matches in the roll-call square to have some fun, and it's the only time a prisoner can hit a kapo. We always root for the prisoners.'

'And do the kapos get beaten up?' Hugo laughed with a certain satisfaction.

'Sometimes, but the SS officers give the kapos knuckle-dusters.'

'Bastards.' Hugo picked up the drawings.

'Could the murderer have caused a wound like this with a knuckleduster?' Gioele asked, looking at the drawing.

Hugo shook his head. 'No. The wound would have been much larger with a knuckleduster and the skin would have probably been broken. They must have struck him with a much smaller object.'

'Did you find my drawings useful today, too?'

'They've given me a break. I needed a moment to think.'

'In that case can you reconsider my suggestion about the triangle?'

Hugo sighed. 'I can't.'

'I've heard Mengele say that there's going to be a "special delivery" this evening,' Gioele insisted. 'They've requested all the medical staff from Birkenau, the officers and even the Kommandant. We can take advantage of all the confusion to look for my father and give him the green triangle.'

'No, Gioele.' This time, Hugo's voice was hard and cutting. 'I'm sorry, but I can't do that. The Birkenau camp is huge.'

The boy's eyes widened with disappointment.

Hugo chose to be the target of his hatred rather than take him to a father who no longer existed.

37

The sky was dirty. An oblique, pale, almost stifling light was making everything ugly. If it hadn't been for the snow, the place would have looked ghostly. And yet the red-brick blocks were attractive to the eye, all orderly. The streets were clean and adorned with trees that glistened in the searchlights. Even so, Hugo could not view Auschwitz with the same eyes as on his first day here.

He took a stroll in the twilight. He needed a detail to unblock the jammed mechanism. Just one detail to nudge him in the right direction so that he'd stop fumbling in the dark.

He lit a cigarette, stopped on the threshold of Block 24 and leaned against the wall to smoke calmly. Questions were struggling against the fever that refused to drop despite the cold compresses in the infirmary.

The door opened that very second. Rose appeared and stared at him, with surprise at first, then with a faintly mischievous smile.

'I knew you'd come back to visit me,' she purred. 'Shall we go upstairs?'

'Thank you, but this isn't a good time,' he replied.

'No need to thank me. *Nix camela, nix travacho!*' she said in that incomprehensible *Lagersprache*. 'No food, no work. No work, no food!'

'I said this isn't a good time,' he replied dismissively. He took a long drag, and the smoke irritated his lungs. The fever made the tobacco taste sharp and unpleasant.

'Aren't we nervous today?' Rose put her hands on her hips and looked around. She welcomed the glances of a couple of prisoners shovelling the snow and smiled. Her role clearly afforded her significant freedom and a great deal of audacity. A Red Cross van drove past them and she followed it with her eyes. 'They're loading more.'

'More what?'

'They've come to pick up the bodies of the "syringed".'

'The syringed?' Hugo frowned and took another nervous nicotine-laden drag. He was feeling out of place now and found even the camp jargon hostile.

'I heard that in the beginning, the SS officers were very cruel with those who were sick,' she began. 'They killed them in random executions and in front of everyone, in the roll-call square. Now, they take them to the infirmary and the doctors give them a phenol injection right in the heart.' She mimed a piston with her thumb. 'They tell them they're injecting medicine so they don't catch typhus. Quick and discreet. In the evening, the van comes and takes away the bodies. This way, it's all much more "respectable".'

Her eyes were filled with bitterness.

281

'When I get out of here, I'm going back to Eggenthal,' she added. 'It's a wonderful place. If the war ever ends, you must come, too. The air is so fresh and clean in Bavaria.'

Rose closed her eyes. Hugo realized she was trying to escape from this hell even just for a moment.

'I can almost see it,' she murmured, 'with its sloped rooftops close together against the mountains. The sky's always blue. When I was a child, I used to run barefoot in the fields, among the cows.' She glanced at him. 'I don't know if you've ever run among the jingling of cow bells and their mooing . . .'

'I'm afraid I was born in the city,' he replied.

'Then you don't know what freedom really means,' she said defiantly. 'Or about the skill you need not to step into cow pats. You've no idea how humiliating it was to end up here and realize just how much shit you had to avoid . . .'

'I can imagine.'

'No, you can't. When I got off the train, I discovered that there were many Bavarians among the SS officers. Some from Eggenthal, even. I've known some of them since we were children, they'd try and chat me up at primary school . . . I was mortified.'

'Who are you talking about?'

'Tristan Voigt, for instance.'

'Did you already know each other?'

'We went to school together. He was always a cheerful boy, I liked him. When he saw me at the roll call, he advised me to accept the job Sigismund had offered me. He said it was the only way to survive with some dignity. I followed his advice and changed my name.'

'You changed your name?' Hugo felt a shudder under his skin.

'From Odalinde to Rose. I couldn't keep the name of the person I wasn't any longer.'

'I understand,' Hugo replied, remembering the letters in Braun's message.

'Voigt saved my life with that piece of advice. You may think this strange, but you have to compromise in order to survive.'

'What kind of man do you think Voigt is?'

'He's always been kind to me, but, like all the other SS officers, I've also seen him do cruel things. That's how it is in Auschwitz: the weak ones go under, even among the officers. How long do you think Liebehenschel will last, for instance? I've heard people say he's too soft.' Rose quickly touched her lips. 'Will you give me a cigarette?'

Hugo pulled one out and lit it for her.

She took a liberating drag and sighed.

'Tristan Voigt was such a cheerful boy,' she repeated with a note of sadness. 'But after his son died, he joined the SS and then he changed. This place is making him ugly, it's making him become like all the others . . .'

'His son died of pneumonia, right?'

'Yes, but maybe it was a blessing.'

Hugo gave her a puzzled look and gestured at her to carry on.

'He was a strange child,' she explained. 'He had fits of anger, he didn't speak, never looked anyone in the eye. Apparently, they'd had cases of schizophrenia in the family and the mother's also odd: she had some kind of rare skin disease. One day, the doctors came to take him for a programme of intensive therapy. But he never came home. He caught pneumonia at the hospital.'

'Are there any others from your home town here?' Hugo asked.

'Yes, and they're all officers. All of them courted me at one time or another and now they treat me like one more Communist prostitute who deserves to rot in jail and get fucked by kapos. They'd rather those whores in Block 10 take their blood samples,' she added, alluding to Betsy.

Hugo felt a shiver in his breastbone.

Something in what Rose had said had struck him between the eyes.

'Blood samples,' he stammered. In a second, a realization swept over him like an icy wave and left him panting. An electric shock travelled through his feet, up his legs and up to the back of his neck and throat, making him forget his fever. 'How could I have not seen this earlier? "O A B" are not initials at all!'

'What are you talking about?' Rose gave him a startled look. 'You're crazy . . .'

'I must make a phone call,' he said. 'Maybe I've got it!'

He grabbed his stick and headed quickly to the barracks where they sorted the post. They were bound to have a telephone there.

38

'I can't,' Hugo had said. Just like the other Germans, after all. He was only interested in himself and Dr Braun and, in the end, he hadn't kept his promise.

Gioele started kicking the chair.

He was furious.

If Hugo Fischer didn't take him to Birkenau, he'd find a way of getting there by himself.

He grabbed his jacket, left the dormitory, ran down the stairs two by two and rushed into the street, now dark from the twilight. He still didn't know how he'd get out of the Stammlager, but he'd think of something while walking in the snow. The cold weather never failed to reawaken his brain and help him shed that annoying lethargy he always felt after they'd taken blood from his arm.

Gioele cast a glance at the roll-call square, which would soon be filled, and thought back to when he and his family used to walk around the Piazza Maggiore, which in the evening was lit by the amber light of the lamp posts. They would stroll as far as the two towers that rose, crooked, at the end of the road, just before the ghetto.

He huddled in his jacket and skipped in order to warm up. His bare legs beneath the short trousers were livid, but he forced himself not to yield to the cold. He carried on down the street and saw Block 24, where Fischer was talking to a woman. He couldn't make out what they were saying, but at some point Fischer straightened up and headed towards him. Gioele hid behind a birch, where the beams from the searchlights were absorbed by the dark shadow projected by a wall.

Fischer didn't notice him in the gloomy twilight.

He continued to walk fast in spite of his stick and Gioele figured he must be in a rush. If he'd resolved all his problems at work, he thought, maybe he would finally have time to help him with his father.

He decided to follow him.

He shuffled close to the block walls, went past the kitchens and the roll-call square and slipped into the block where Hugo Fischer had just disappeared. He also went in, keeping his back to the wall, careful not to make a sound.

Hugo had entered a room and was talking to an SS officer. He was asking if he could use the phone.

Gioele crouched on the floor and leaned forward slightly, to look. It was a small room, full of shelving units and bookcases, with steel cabinets from which emerged a stack of papers. There were typewriters everywhere, wobbly stacks of letters and a strong smell of dust and ink.

The SS officer leaned back over the desk, resuming the correction of a letter. Bethany had explained that in the camp prisoners' letters were read and altered.

286

Gioele took advantage of the SS officer's distraction and hid under a desk.

Hugo Fischer was hunched over the telephone receiver. 'Exactly,' he heard him say. 'Can you read me the dates you see in the register? 4 December 1931 and 21 December 1939?' he added with a long breath, as though requesting confirmation of what he had just heard. 'Thank you.'

He put down the receiver and stood staring at the telephone attached to the wall.

'Have you discovered anything useful?' the SS officer at the desk asked.

'You can bet on it,' Hugo replied. 'Is Liebehenschel in his office?'

'He's in Birkenau,' the officer answered. 'All the officers are there this evening. There's just been a delivery of a lot of pieces.'

'Thank you, I'll catch up with him there.'

Hugo Fischer said goodbye and walked right past Gioele without seeing him, limping on his gammy leg. The boy remained crouching until he couldn't see his feet anymore, glanced at the SS officer to make sure he'd gone back to his letters and scurried out.

Once he was in the street, he looked around for Hugo, but the evening shadows had already swallowed him.

'What now?' he sighed.

He studied the street. There was a lorry outside Block 20, on which attendants were loading dead bodies. A shudder ran through him at the mere thought of what he was about to do, but there was only one way to get to Birkenau without Fischer's help.

Gioele clenched his fists and ran to the side of the truck,

287

entirely concealed by the wheel. He stood motionless until the prisoners disappeared into the block to pick up more bodies, then leapt into the back of the lorry.

No sooner was he in than he was petrified.

All the dead bodies were naked. The one nearest to him was so skinny, he could have counted his ribs. His eyes and mouth were wide open and he seemed to want to grab Gioele with his outstretched arm and open hand.

'Hurry up with that muck!' an SS officer yelled.

The prisoners threw in other bodies and Gioele was knocked over by one of them. He felt his heart dart into his throat and tears starting to flow. He freed himself from contact with that cold, damp body, crept into a corner of the truck and pressed his face hard against his knees. His heart was thumping in his chest like a drum and, for a moment, he thought that all he could see was whiteness, just myriads of colourless sparks that covered everything else in a deafening hum.

The lorry started and the body of a man slammed against him.

Gioele burst into tears. Sobbing, he lay down low so as not to be seen. As soon as they drove through the gate, the black inscription bade him goodbye.

The lorry clattered down the road and Gioele was knocked over by other bodies that smelled of dirt and sweat. He curled up and kept his eyes shut tight in order not to look at them.

'I'm going to get my family back,' he moaned to give himself courage.

He tried to imagine that the people next to him weren't dead. After all, it had been the same on the journey from Bologna to Auschwitz, the same smell, the same contact

288

with bodies. They'd travelled crammed in a livestock carriage, pressed against one another.

'I'm not getting into that carriage,' his mother had said when she'd seen it. 'They said it was an evacuation, so why are they putting us on goods wagons and not ordinary trains?'

But she'd been forced to board, prodded by German rifles. They'd positioned themselves next to a window because you could breathe better there, but soon even that small metal grille had proved to be insufficient, because they'd started to sweat despite the cold, and the bucket for physical needs was soon full and stinking.

After a few days' travelling, Signor Levi had died. He'd had a stroke, Gioele's father said. They'd put him at the back of the carriage, with his eyes closed and his arms lying along his body. At first he looked asleep, but then he'd started to smell.

Every so often, the train would stop and they'd be kept at the station all night, but they never removed Signor Levi's body. They could hear the Germans bivouacking outside, and he and his father would practise translating. One evening, Gioele had taken the empty water bucket, turned it upside down and climbed on it to reach the grating. He'd whistled to get the attention of an SS man. The other people in the carriage had looked at him in terror.

'He'll get us slaughtered like dogs,' a woman had hissed.

Instead, the SS man had started chatting to him. He was twenty-five years old and had a child of two waiting for him in a village by the sea, in Northern Germany. The war would end, sooner or later, and he would take him swimming. After an hour's conversation, the officer had given him some bread and a little cured meat, which Gioele had shared with everybody.

The lorry full of bodies stopped, snatching him away from his memories.

Gioele looked up. He recognized the dark outline of Birkenau, the walls and the barbed wire swept by the liquid glow of the searchlights.

The vehicle drove on through the gate, then stopped again.

The driver honked to get someone to move.

Gioele stuck his head out over the layer of bodies. He could now see the main watchtower, but from the inside of the camp. It was time to get off. He climbed over the bodies, gritting his teeth to stop himself from bursting into tears again, and jumped down.

He fell in the snow.

He was just in time; the lorry left, puffing in the frosty air.

Gioele looked around. Birkenau was huge and on the sides of the road there were so many sectors, all enclosed in a fortress of electrified barbed wire, that he felt lost: he'd never find his parents without Hugo Fischer.

'You!' an SS officer yelled.

He hit him in the back with the butt of his rifle and forced him to take two steps forward, towards the group of women and children walking like ghosts lost in the snow. They were looking around with bewildered eyes and terrified faces.

'Get back to your group!' the officer commanded.

Gioele obeyed. Maybe, if he followed this party, he'd be able to get into one of the camps. With any luck, his mother's camp, given all these women with children.

'Where are you from?' he asked a woman holding a newborn baby against her chest.

She responded with a long lament. She was rocking her child and looking around, distressed, her face completely congested from the cold.

'Have you got your tattoo?' he insisted, showing her his.

The woman looked at him in dismay. Gioele realized she must be new and didn't speak his language.

'Don't worry,' he said. 'It's all right.'

The day they'd got off at Auschwitz station, he and his father had had to translate for everybody. The Germans' tongue was rugged, harsh, and slashed through the air like a knife. They seemed about to gobble you up even when they weren't angry. It was a tongue for wolves, just like the Alsatians they walked around with. And so he'd had to tell his travelling companions that *alle heraus* meant they had to get out of the carriages. And that *schneller* meant they had to be quicker. The last word he'd had to explain was *Zwillinge heraus*.

A good-looking man with clean, white gloves had walked through the crowd shouting that word.

'What does it mean?' his mother had asked.

'All the twins out,' he'd replied.

Mengele had noticed him and his brother at a glance. He'd led them to a pillar and measured their height. Then he'd given them a sweet each.

'You must come with me,' he'd said. Then, addressing his parents: 'They'll be fine. We have a camp for twins, with lots of food and every convenience.'

An SS officer had put them with other children. Gioele had then asked in German if his mum and dad could also

291

go to the twins' camp. Hearing him speak his language, Mengele had turned abruptly, walked back, grabbed his chin and lifted his face to the beam of the searchlight. At that moment, Gioele had got all his attention.

'Your eyes,' Mengele had exclaimed, ecstatic. 'You have such rare eyes.' And so he'd gestured at an officer. 'These two aren't going to the camp. They're going to Block 10, in the Stammlager. Treat them with the utmost care.'

A month had gone by since then, but to Gioele it felt like a lifetime.

He walked on, mingling with the women and children with a Star of David sewn on their coats, and thought it would all have been so much easier if his eyes hadn't been so strange that Mengele had separated him from his parents.

'Quicker,' the SS officers were still yelling, but he didn't know how to translate it to the others.

In the stream of people they'd put him among, different languages were being spoken, but not Italian.

An officer slackened his dog's lead, and then there was no more need for oral commands to make them pick up the pace: all it took was bites at the ankles.

Gioele looked up.

The sky was heavy with snow.

Snowflakes began to fall slowly, like in a dance. One fell on his nose and immediately melted. The women were huddling together in the sleet like black, dismayed crows. The cold had turned their noses and cheeks red. The children looked around quizzically, dirty and perhaps hungry. He remembered well how hungry he'd been when he got off the train. The older ones were at the back, like the time he'd arrived, with the slow, swaying step of those who have to carry too much life on their shoulders.

Gioele turned and glimpsed Adele walking hurriedly among the other doctors. They recognized each other for a brief moment, then she looked away and vanished.

39

The SS officer at the camp entrance had said that Liebehenschel and the other officers were at the crematorium.

Hugo trod through the snow, putting a huge demand on his leg. Now that everything added up, every clue made sense and every motive seemed solid, he felt tension snapping at him all over, making him shake with a charge of adrenaline that made him sweat under his coat and hat, as if the fever blazing in his temples and drying his mouth weren't enough. He must have had the expression of a madman.

A lorry honked to make him shift, startling him. Hugo turned and saw a vehicle crammed with bodies puffing in the humid air. He stood aside, almost tripped, then limped faster along the Lagerstraße, asking more from his body, his lungs and his inner strength.

The air was saturated with smoke and the smell of burnt flesh grew stronger as he approached the crematorium. His taste buds and sense of smell now seemed to recognize the pestilent stench and somehow accept it.

He determined to keep walking and pay no attention to the Jews who were being made to walk in compact groups on both sides of the road. He couldn't afford to look them in the face, meet their eyes and see them as human beings. If he did, his strength would fail him and he'd collapse into a chasm from which he would never again resurface.

What he needed now was all the energy he had left in his body.

He reached the crematorium enclosure and showed the SS officer on duty his pass. He slid into the blinding light of the searchlights, looking for a familiar face among the multitude of SS officers aiming machine guns and dogs barking relentlessly.

It started to snow. Icy flakes, together with ash.

The gigantic edifice that appeared before his eyes was made of red brick, with a tall chimney that emitted smoke, and was in every way similar to the crematoria at the back of the Kanada. A flat, grey area stretched several metres to a staircase that plunged into its belly. In the layer of dirty snow, there were small, silent chimneys peering out.

Hugo made his way among the guards. He searched their faces but didn't recognize anyone. The person he was looking for could be anywhere in this immense complex. He stopped to ask if anyone had seen them. Everybody replied no.

'The Kanada,' he then muttered.

That's where they went. That's where they left their notes. That's where they were now.

There was nowhere else he could look in this confusion, he thought. He exited the Lagerstraße and headed towards a cluster of snow-covered birches that hid the other two crematoria from view.

The warehouse appeared in all its magnificence of thirty huts floodlit by the searchlights. The prisoners were working fast, carrying the suitcases of the newcomers from the Drancy camp. They were wheeling them on trolleys then carelessly tipping out the contents in wobbling heaps. The mounds were growing so tall and wide that there was practically no room to pass through: the lives of thousands of people, made up of everyday objects that told their personal history, were being thrown away and trampled without any respect.

Hugo walked past a heap and picked up the pace, gritting his teeth. He decided to focus exclusively on Braun and made an effort not to fall, once again, into the vortex of thoughts he was getting buried in.

He looked around, trembling. He knew in which hut to look.

He recognized the form he'd been searching for against the boards of a hut, and a sense of victory throbbed in his veins. He was sweating and his scalding skin was smoking in the frosty air. Even so, he confronted the black shadow that stood out against the blinding searchlights without even needing to put his hand in his pocket to find the phial of morphine. He had put off facing his demons for too long not to tackle the murderer now.

'I've been looking for you for a long time.'

'Can I help you?'

'I need to talk to you.'

'In that case, let's go somewhere quieter.'

'I'm coming, too,' another voice said from the massive shadow of the hut.

40

The birch wood was silent. The searchlights couldn't reach it, so the darkness stretched its blue fingers between the slender trunks and the thick undergrowth. The arms of bark extended towards one another, forming a blanket that almost concealed the sky.

The gloomy call of a night bird echoed among the branches.

The snowflakes were falling slowly, muffling everything, settling on the back of Hugo's neck and soothing the feverish heat. The person he'd been looking for throughout the camp was looking at him with cold eyes, two slits of metal just like the skull and crossbones grinning on his hat. His accomplice was clinging to his arm, as though afraid to fall.

'You should have contented yourself with Berto Hoffman's confession,' he said, raising the barrel of his pistol. A small, black, ruthless, cold mouth.

'It's not my style,' Hugo replied.

'How did you do it? How did you realize?'

'You left too many crumbs. Like in the Grimms' fairy

tale – remember? All I had to do was follow them. Where would you like me to start? With Dr Braun's message?'

The officer stared at him, inviting him to speak. Hugo could never understand why someone with their back to the wall would want to hear his explanations. It was probably to understand the errors they'd committed, to discover what or who had betrayed them, or out of some kind of smugness. Only this time the murderer wasn't sitting in a cell but pointing a pistol at Hugo's forehead.

'"O A B",' he said, swallowing the sense of danger as well as the excitement. 'At first, I thought they were initials, but I was wrong. In the note you tore up – without taking care to check that Braun hadn't pressed too hard on the sheet beneath – he left two essential messages. The first was a clue about the weapon: he knew you'd kill him with a phial of cyanide. The second revealed the identity of the killer.'

Tristan Voigt looked at him in shock. At his side, Anita Kunig shuddered.

'O A B are blood types,' Hugo explained. 'All the SS officers are obliged to have their blood type tattooed on their armpits. Osmund and Berto are not SS officers, but you are.'

Voigt laughed quietly and squinted, admitting Braun's brilliance. Anita Kunig, on the other hand, was pale and frightened, her eyes wet from crying. A gust of wind swept a lock of hair off her face, revealing the disfiguring tan stain: a skin disease, Rose had called it.

'On the evening of the murder, you asked Sigismund Braun to see you in his office to discuss something important,' Hugo continued, heedless of the pistol, which had come closer.

He closed his eyes and pictured the room where the doctor was listening to music from the phonograph, the armchair where he sat smoking his cigar, the microscopes, the lab coats hanging from the wall, and the Christmas tree giving off a festive scent.

'You joined Braun in his office and you spoke for a long time, like old friends, listening to music. Twenty-first December was an important anniversary for you: the day your son Bastian died. Braun couldn't have remembered it: he'd euthanised too many children to recall yours.'

Hugo imagined the unvoiced rage that must have come over Voigt and Anita the day they'd got themselves taken on at Auschwitz, when they'd finally come face to face with their son's murderer. They'd kept their relationship secret to avoid arousing suspicion; meanwhile, they had swallowed their grief and orchestrated their revenge.

'That evening, you showed him Bastian's medallion.' Hugo pictured the gold B glittering in the light of the desk lamp. Bastian's date of birth was engraved on the back: 4 December 1931. That medallion must have been returned to his parents in a little bag, together with his clothes and a document stating a fake cause of death: pneumonia. 'Nobody understood how special that little boy was, who never looked people in the face, never spoke to anyone and played in such an odd way,' Hugo continued, undaunted. 'The medical commission who'd taken him to Irsee didn't understand and neither did Braun, who killed him with cyanide because he'd run out of phenol supplies that day, but it was lunchtime, they couldn't wait and that little trick of nature had to die . . .'

Anita Kunig burst into tears.

Voigt kept pointing the pistol, but his grip wavered and

299

his face turned into a wax mask. Hugo pictured him taking the phial of cyanide from his pocket while ordering Braun to put on his lab coat. He was the doctor who'd euthanised his son, so he had to die as a doctor.

Braun had obeyed. 'Let me just write a farewell note to my wife,' he must have said while rolling up the white sleeves. He'd started to write, and Voigt had angrily snatched the note from his hand, read those incomprehensible letters and shoved it in his pocket. He would destroy it as soon as he was out of there.

'Now bite this,' he must have commanded, handing him the phial of cyanide, pointing the weapon at his head. 'And will you shoot me if I don't?' Braun would have asked defiantly. 'So everyone will hear?'

'You were determined to stay calm,' Hugo said, 'but Bastian's face came back to torment you right at that moment. You struck Braun in the temple with all your strength, to stun him. In the area where the skin collided with the skull and crossbones on your ring, the tissue immediately swelled and bruised, but it's only later that I realized that the injury was compatible with your ring. Then you grabbed him by the neck with your forearm before he could scream and squeezed him against you. The back of Braun's neck scraped the insignia on your uniform, got scratched, and his skin became impregnated with the scent of the cologne you wear every day.'

They'd stood like that, in that deathly embrace, for a few seconds. Hugo could picture them. Stunned by the blow, Braun must have been a dead weight. All Voigt would have had to do was open Braun's mouth, stuff the phial into it, keep it still with his finger and push the jaw shut. The phial would have broken and a shard must have cut Voigt's fingertip, making him swear. What Hugo had seen weren't fissures caused by Poland's harsh winter.

'The drops of blood fell without your noticing, in the heat of the moment.' Hugo stared at the barrel of the pistol, which was wavering. 'And the medallion flew under the Christmas tree at some point during the confrontation. You looked everywhere for it, but couldn't find it in the turmoil, and then you had other things on your mind: to remove the fragments of phial from the doctor's mouth and push a piece of apple in. The following day, you ordered the attendants to go through the room with a fine-tooth comb. Most importantly, you kept the promise sent to your wife that morning in a typewritten note. Braun is dead and you are now both free from the ghosts of the past.'

'Truly impressive. What do you want – a standing ovation?' Voigt took a step forward and pressed the barrel of the pistol against Hugo's forehead. Hugo felt the cold iron on his hot skin. 'On your knees,' Voigt ordered.

Hugo was forced to obey, defying his sick leg. The cold air made him tremble and his panting became an opaque cloud dispersed by the blizzard.

'It's my turn to speak now,' Voigt said, walking to Hugo's other side. The barrel of the pistol shifted to the back of Hugo's neck. The safety lock was released with a sinister click. 'You're right, Sigismund Braun didn't even remember my son's face or his name. He'd killed so many innocent creatures that he had no recollection of any of them as individual children.'

'That's true.' Anita Kunig's faint voice struggled against the wind. She stood still in the falling snow, looking like a ghost watching them from afar, from another world.

'When Mengele showed me that Jewish boy, Gioele, who looks so much like Bastian, I thought I would die . . .'

'I joined the SS-Totenkopfverbände after Berto Hoffman told me how my son died,' Voigt continued. 'We were childhood friends. He searched for me to tell me the truth.'

'Did you join the SS in order to kill Braun?'

'No,' Voigt murmured. His pistol quivered just for a moment, then returned firmly to the back of Hugo's neck. 'I didn't come to Auschwitz in order to murder him. I just came to look him in the face and to see for myself the things Berto told me about every time he managed to return to Bavaria. I couldn't believe his stories. This is not *my* Germany. I couldn't turn a blind eye the way I did with the racial laws and the boycotts: I couldn't stand it. We are the Resistance. We secretly help the prisoners, we limit their suffering, we keep them alive a few more months. I owe that at least to my Bastian . . .'

Hugo closed his eyes. This man's grief was penetrating him like a red-hot knife, reopening the wounds of his conscience.

'I had to tolerate Braun's presence every day,' Voigt added angrily, 'go to his parties, listen to his revolting anecdotes about Irsee, put up with his arguments about race. He once told me that a disabled person's entire lifetime costs the community at least sixty thousand Reichsmarks, and that being healthy is a moral duty towards the nation. As far as he was concerned, my son was a pointless expense. My hatred towards him grew day after day and Anita became increasingly embittered. Only, I made a mistake. I thought killing Braun would heal us, but, instead, I put the Resistance in grave danger . . .' Voigt grabbed Hugo by the hair and yanked him angrily. The pistol pressed into his skin so hard it hurt. 'A mistake I shan't repeat.'

The grip startled Hugo. 'Is that why you framed Berto Hoffman?' he asked breathlessly. 'To protect the Resistance?'

'No. Berto is also part of the Resistance and decided to take the blame for the murder of his own free will. He was afraid our clandestine network would fail. He's only a nurse, he has little power in the camp. If my support, the support of an SS officer is taken away, then there will be real trouble . . .'

'In exchange, you promised to take care of Bethany.' A drop of sweat trickled down to Hugo's collarbone. 'You had her transferred to the camp hospital even though she's Jewish, so she would get better treatment.'

'Accept Berto's confession.' Voigt bent over him like a hungry wolf. 'Go back to Berlin with a victory in your hands and don't meddle any more!'

'Did Berto give you the cyanide?' Hugo insisted. He had no intention of ending the day or his life without first shedding light on every single detail of this business.

'He took it from the dispensary when he was admitted for bronchitis,' Voigt replied. 'It was Adele Krause who suggested it. They wanted Braun dead as much as I did.'

Hugo stared. He felt the ground crumbling under his knees. Adele Krause, the young woman with fiery hair and eyes like leaves, who'd made his heart beat, knew everything. She'd helped only to throw him off the track and keep an eye on him so he wouldn't discover the truth. He suddenly felt like a fool.

'Adele would bring me notes from Tristan,' Anita Kunig intervened, wringing her hands. 'When I burned the note he'd sent me that morning, I was in a hurry. I was terrified

303

of being discovered. While I was destroying it, I heard voices behind me, so I ran away. A minute later, the branches of that damn tree came crashing down. I couldn't start looking for the note under the snow. It was too risky and there were too many SS officers about . . .'

Hugo laughed as the pistol pushed hard into his neck. They'd been right there in front of him all along, the accomplices to the murder, and he hadn't seen them.

'It wasn't supposed to end this way,' Voigt said accusingly. 'It's nothing personal, but unless you accept Berto's confession, I can't let you live. You know too much. Is there anything I can do before I shoot?'

Hugo sighed. 'I'd ask you for a dose of morphine, but a cigarette will do.'

Voigt inserted a cigarette between his lips. Anita lit it for him with trembling hands. The first match fell in the snow. The second managed to set the tobacco alight, making it sizzle.

Hugo inhaled the smoke and looked at the sky, swollen with snow, beyond the thick branches.

He heard the trigger squeak.

So this is how you felt when facing death. It was a little like being in Wattenmeer. Except that he'd got tired of waiting for the tide.

Hugo opened his mouth and the cigarette butt fell on the ground.

'Please,' he implored. 'Give me another one.'

Voigt seemed to hesitate, but then gave in and put another cigarette between his lips. He lowered the pistol for a moment to do so. Hugo knew that he was at a great disadvantage, with a leg that was sure to make him fall, but he also knew he had no choice. He dived forward with a sudden jolt of his back and headbutted Voigt in the stomach, falling on top of him. They both ended up in the snow while a shot went off, tearing through the silence of the birches.

Voigt was quicker. He grabbed him by the collar of his coat and pushed his face into the snow, holding it down to stop him from escaping. Hugo knew he couldn't compete with him physically, and the realization that he'd made the wrong decision swept over him like an electric shock. He felt Voigt's fingers dig into his hair and push down in order to suffocate him.

Hugo gasped for air, chewed the snow that had got into his mouth and tried in vain to shake Voigt off him. He felt the man reach out for the pistol and the cold barrel pressed his head again, this time with more anger.

'You piece of shit!' Voigt growled.

'Tristan, stop!' a woman's voice cried.

Hugo thought he recognized it. He lifted his face from the ground and saw Adele Krause among the birch trunks, breathless, her coat unbuttoned over her white uniform, her hair ruffled from running.

The pistol slowly came away from his neck.

Adele ran towards them, and Voigt let him go.

'What happened?' she panted.

'What happened is that you cheated me,' Hugo replied, grabbing his stick and getting up. 'All this time, you lied to me. You were watching my moves and reporting them to him!'

'I'm sorry,' she murmured. She glanced at Voigt and Anita, who were watching her, distraught, in the falling, silent snow. 'What we do here is very little, but also huge. Every day, someone survives thanks to us, so if I've lied to you, I did it in good faith.'

'What now?' Hugo picked up his hat and shook it. He put it on and looked quizzically at Voigt. 'How does it end? Aren't you going to kill me?'

Voigt squeezed the pistol handle nervously, but Adele appeased him with a gesture. She obviously wanted both of them to think.

'Berto decided to sacrifice himself for the Resistance,' she said. She'd gone to stand between them, to stop Voigt from using the pistol. 'It's his wish, Herr Fischer, and you must accept it and promise that you won't tell anyone what you've discovered.'

'Should I lie to Liebehenschel?'

'Yes,' Adele replied. 'You'll keep the secret, we'll continue our struggle and Officer Voigt will spare your life. Don't you find that a good compromise?'

Hugo shook his head. 'A compromise,' he whispered.

'A compromise that's better than the ones you've stooped to up to now,' she said.

Hugo felt her words slice through his flesh and thought he saw in her eyes those of the young woman in the dance hall. They were pleading with him as they had done then, asking him for a huge act of courage. He'd failed once before.

'A compromise,' he repeated, breathless.

Tristan Voigt lowered the weapon. He was now staring at Hugo, waiting for an answer.

'More lives will be sacrificed if you don't agree,' Adele warned him. There was a desperate urgency in her voice. 'A little while ago, I saw Gioele in the middle of a group of Jews heading to the crematorium. Don't you feel it's your duty to lie for a cause as important as this? Don't you feel the weight of what Germany is doing? If you lie about the Braun case, the Resistance can carry on with its work. If you don't, you'll have turned your back and shut your eyes for the umpteenth time.'

'Gioele is at the crematorium?' Hugo felt the snow sucking him into the muddy ground. His voice trembled and he felt as though he was standing on the edge of an abyss. 'Why didn't you stop him?'

'I couldn't. Would *you* have?'

Hugo felt a pain crushing his chest.

No symptom of his illness had ever been so excruciating.

41

The entrance to the building, Gioele thought, was like a hungry mouth.

The stairs unfurled like a terrifying tongue. He would never have gone there if he hadn't been forced by barking dogs and SS officers pushing him down the steps with the butts of their rifles.

'Don't get upset!' an officer behind him was shouting, except that the new arrivals didn't understand him. 'It's just a shower! Just a shower! Afterwards, you'll be fed and reunited with your families!'

'Silence!' another SS officer tried saying in the languages he knew. *'Taisez-vous!'*

The women and the old people were swarming from one side to the other, seeking an escape route, but in the end had no choice but to squeeze the shoulders of their children and push them down the stairs, as the SS officers commanded.

Gioele followed the crowd.

First the shower, he thought, then food. And, finally, your family.

He walked, pressed by the other Jews. At the bottom of the stairs appeared a long, cold room, illuminated by a light that made everything look grey. Prisoners in striped uniforms showed them benches with numbers and hooks for hanging up their clothes.

Gioele looked at the walls, which had signs in several languages. KEEP CLEAN, they stated. WASH! DEATH TO LICE! On a pillar, there was a sign with an arrow pointing to a metal door. TO THE DISINFESTATION ROOM, it stated.

A little boy with a limp and a hump that deformed his back was reading the signs in Italian, and Gioele's heart gave a jolt. He approached him, but a prisoner in uniform pushed them to the benches. They sat next to each other.

'Are you Italian?' Gioele asked excitedly.

'You, too?'

'Yes. Where are you from?'

'Rome. They first took me to the Drancy camp and now here. The children in Drancy say they take Jews to the Land of *Pitchipoi*. But I don't suppose we're in *Pitchipoi* at all, are we? What's this place – do you have any idea? Are there really showers?'

'Sure there are.' Gioele removed his worn-out shoes and stretched his toes.

'I've heard strange things about Auschwitz,' the boy whispered. His lips were trembling and he kept licking them. His hump seemed bigger now.

'It's not a nice place,' Gioele admitted.

'Yes, but I've heard some really awful things . . .'

Gioele took off his jacket and hung it up, then removed his sweater, vest, short trousers and pants. He remained naked, his teeth chattering from the cold, hugged his chest to warm up and hopped behind the people heading to the shower room. The woman in front of him had started to scream because she didn't want to go in and an SS officer slapped her to calm her down.

'*Judensau!*' he yelled.

'What does that mean?' the Italian boy asked.

'It's something nasty,' Gioele replied. 'A bad word.'

'I won't tell anyone if you translate it for me.'

'Jewish slut,' he said, paraphrasing. 'And they call us Italians *makkaroni*.'

Gioele followed the crowd into the disinfestation room. There were no tiles, only walls with damaged lime. There was a row of showers all around the room. Some, between the pillars that supported the ceiling, were just made of grating and an old man grasped one to see what was above it.

'What's the matter, grandpa?' the boy with the hump asked.

'It's what they said in Drancy,' the old man roared. 'The ceiling's connected to the outside . . .'

Gioele sensed that something about this place wasn't quite right. They kept bringing people in, cramming them all together, stark naked: how could they have a shower like this, all together?

'Hey, snotty nose,' the boy, crushed in the middle of the room, called out. 'Can you get to the wall and check if the showers work and if there are drains?'

Gioele nodded. He slipped between the legs of the women and skirted the wall to the showers. He looked on the ground. There were no drains for the water. His hand travelled along the wall: no knobs.

'There aren't any!' he shouted.

'We have to run away!' the boy replied. Gioele ran towards the exit to get some air, but the door suddenly closed with a terrible clang. The mechanism squeaked, the lights flickered and went out. A dreadful rumble tore through the sweat-saturated air. Everybody was crying and screaming. In the scrum, an elbow hit him in the temple, almost knocking him out.

'Stop it!' Gioele cried, trying to shield himself.

It was stifling. He was crushed by naked, smelly bodies and was struggling not to be carried off. He wanted to get out, tears pressing hard against his eyes. Something awful was happening, he could feel it. His heart was pounding with that awareness.

Suddenly, a metallic sound came from the pillars with the grating.

'They're killing us!' the old man clinging to the grille yelled.

Gioele felt the darkness suffocate him.

42

The enemy can see our lights. Put them out.

That was what the posters all over Berlin said. On the glossy paper, there was a monstrous skeleton astride a plane, ready to drop a bomb. Children would stare at that image in fear as they walked close to the walls, their faces would turn white and they would grip their mother's or their father's hand tighter.

When the first bombs began to fall, Hugo realized that the Germany Hitler had painted was crumbling. The beauty of buildings decorated with swastikas, the eagles soaring from the city's square pillars, the headlines applauding a country without poverty and free of beggars and any other kind of depravation, everything was breaking down because of this insane war into which the Führer had dragged them.

In the evening, as soon as darkness enveloped the city in a dangerous embrace, all the lights had to be turned off. Leaving one on, even to study or keep children's nightmares at bay, could lead to arrest. On those evenings, Hugo would lean out of the window and, in the liquid tar in which the Nikolaiviertel was immersed, he could no longer recognize Berlin. He could no longer recognize himself either.

But now he knew who he was.

While crossing Birkenau, his heart, throat and temples gone berserk, he had finally found himself and the courage to scream, rebel and save his soul.

'Open up immediately!' Tristan Voigt shouted, running downstairs like a fury.

Hugo followed him. He saw him push two Sonderkommandos and hurl himself at the metal door.

'What are you doing?' an SS officer yelled, taking up his machine gun.

'Open up immediately!' Voigt repeated.

'Are you mad? We can't: they're all already inside!'

'I don't give a damn!' Voigt cried. He grabbed Hugo by the shoulder and presented him to the SS officer. 'This man's son is in the gas chamber with Jews!'

'There'll be panic if we open!' the guard insisted.

Voigt seized him by the collar. 'Open this door,' he commanded. He tapped a finger to the insignia on his own uniform, then on the officer's clammy forehead. 'See these? I swear you'll get a bullet fired in your head if you disobey an order from your superior!'

The man trembled. 'Yes, sir.'

Voigt let go of him with a jerk.

Hugo watched the scene, motionless.

He could feel the fever burning his tongue, gouging his eyes, and fear biting every part of his body. He proffered the document, his thumb over the boy's surname. The terrified screams of the Jews could be heard through the door.

'Here, that's him,' he said, showing Bastian's photograph. The resemblance to Gioele was such that he suddenly realized how the Voigts must have felt over the past month.

'I must first give the order for the chimneys to be shut,' the guard said breathlessly.

You could now hear in his voice how urgent it was to avoid the death of a German, above all the son of a man very prominent in the Reich. He ran up the changing room stairs and disappeared in the densely falling snow.

Hugo looked around.

The room was full of clothes. The Sonderkommandos were removing them from the hooks and collecting them in sacks. These clothes would not be needed anymore.

'No rash gestures,' Tristan Voigt, standing in his straight military pose, whispered. 'We can save only Gioele. This is how you save lives here: you have to be willing to compromise, to sacrifice others.'

Hugo nodded. He sensed his anxiety turn to sweat, like tears that needed to find an outlet.

The guard returned with a group of SS officers. They shouldered their machine guns and one of them clicked open the lock of the airtight door. Bodies pressed against one another, trying to take advantage of the gap.

'Get back!' a guard yelled. 'Get back, you filthy Jews!'

An SS officer fired a volley of shots that riddled a woman. Her body jerked in a macabre dance before falling to the ground, her blood spreading in a puddle so red it silenced the people in front. Everyone slowly swarmed back.

Only one child was left standing on the threshold.

'It's him!' Hugo immediately said. He gestured at Gioele to come to him. 'Come, Bastian, come! Please, come!'

Gioele looked around with staring eyes, his face small and frightened. Hugo felt the tension rise. He prayed that fear wouldn't let him down, that he would come forward and run towards him.

'Are you sure it's your son?' the SS officer asked.

'He's confused!' Hugo said. 'Wouldn't you be, if you'd been dragged along with Jews and locked in a room, in the dark?'

The young guard withdrew into his shoulders.

Gioele opened his mouth. Hugo prayed again.

'Daddy!' he exclaimed in perfect German, his tattooed arm hidden behind his back.

Hugo felt the tension diminishing. He wished he could weep. Gioele was young and shrewd.

'Daddy, I'm scared!' he moaned again.

'Come on, let him out!' the SS man shouted. He pointed his machine gun at the other Jews, pushing them back in as Gioele ran out.

The guards dragged away the woman's body, leaving a scarlet trail on the floor, and the door slammed shut again with a metallic din that sounded like a grim dirge. On the other side of the thick door, the Jews started screaming and punching the door to get out. Hugo could hear every single voice, and every one was like a knife stabbing him.

'Daddy!' Gioele grabbed him by the legs. He was crying and shaking like a leaf. Hugo bent down to hug him and held his small, naked, frightened body close.

'I swear I'm getting you out of here,' he said breathlessly in his ear. 'I'm taking you away from all this filth.'

'I regret the incident,' the officer said apologetically. 'But you need to keep an eye on these children, you must put a sign around their necks or at least instruct them how to behave in such cases.'

'It won't happen again,' Hugo assured him. 'We're leaving tomorrow.'

43

Auschwitz, 28 December 1943

Mengele had received the news that Gioele had escaped to Birkenau on a lorry, that he'd ended up in the gas chamber, then in the crematorium, and that he was now nothing but a heap of ashes under the snow.

The news made him furious, Rabi said. And maybe sad, too.

'But I'm glad,' he whispered, standing on the threshold of Block 10. He sniffed and adjusted his glasses. 'It's better this way, Herr Fischer. Better go through the chimney than have your brain, your bones and your eyes end up in a Berlin museum – don't you think?'

'I think so,' Hugo replied. He was sorry to keep Rabi in the dark, but the fewer people who knew the truth, the safer Gioele would be.

'So in the end it was the male nurse who killed Braun,' Rabi said thoughtfully, glancing at the death block. 'He

317

seemed such a quiet person. At least the Kommandant will be happy now.'

Hugo nodded. 'He told me he'd always suspected Hoffman, but couldn't soil his hands and send a German to his death unless he was certain.'

'Don't you find it bizarre?'

'What?'

'That in Auschwitz a man should be punished for committing murder.'

Rabi looked around. His lively eyes came to rest on a lorry harvesting that day's crop: four bodies were being carried away from Block 10 and ten were coming from Block 20. A total of fourteen – unpunishable – murders.

'I hope I see you again someday,' Hugo said.

'Don't count on it.' Rabi smiled sadly. 'But if it does happen, I'll be pleasantly surprised.'

Hugo left him alone on the steps to the block and felt an excruciating hollow in his stomach. He knew he would never see him again. That Rabi would die in this accursed camp.

'Herr Fischer!' a voice called out.

He recognized it and smiled. It was coming from the end of the road and, for once, wasn't finding him in a pathetic condition.

Adele came up to him. Tristan Voigt was behind her, in his impeccable SS-Totenkopfverbände uniform. Hugo put his hand into the pocket of his coat, took out the gold medallion and placed it into Voigt's hand as soon as the latter had reached the steps to the block.

'Keep this safe,' Hugo said.

'Thank you,' Voigt replied, clasping it in his fist. 'I've issued orders to a trusted officer to drive you to pick your

318

son up from the hotel in the market square in town. I've also arranged this.'

Hugo took the document Voigt was handing him. The name next to his son's photograph had been skilfully changed to Bastian Fischer.

'Thank you,' Hugo managed to say, a lump in his throat.

'Thank *you*.' Voigt's eyes had a severe expression, but by now Hugo had learned to read them. 'You know that what you're trying to do is dangerous, don't you?'

'Yes.'

'If they find out, you'll end up in a camp like this one . . .'

'I'll take the risk.'

'Good. Now, if you'll excuse me, Liebehenschel has ordered me to make the arrangements for Berto Hoffman's execution.'

Hugo watched Voigt disappear through the door of Block 11 and searched Adele's eyes, which were filled with regret. In hell, you had to compromise.

'Berto and I started together,' she murmured, 'and now his life is ending.'

'Be there for Bethany,' was all Hugo could say. 'Get her out of here alive. Do it for him.'

Adele nodded. She took a deep breath that made her uniform quiver and looked at him with tearful eyes. 'We'll meet in Berlin, Herr Fischer. When all this is over, when this is just a distant memory, you'll take me dancing.'

Hugo laughed. It was a bitter laugh that had something of the tears in his heart, of injustice, of a horror against which he could do little. But even that little could be enough, so Adele Krause had taught him.

'See you soon,' she murmured.

The Kübelwagen, engine running, his suitcase already in, was waiting for him. Hugo headed towards it slowly with the help of his stick.

'Herr Fischer, one more thing!' Adele cried, making him stop and turn.

She ran to him, stood up on tiptoe in an abrupt movement that almost made him lose his balance and kissed him. It was a kiss that tasted of salt, of tides in Wattenmeer, of freshly picked shells.

Hugo smiled, embarrassed, when her lips parted from his.

The driver gave them a sly look.

'You may go now,' Adele said.

Hugo got into the vehicle, his heart in turmoil.

There's life even in this hell, he thought. As he abandoned that place, he turned just one last time to look at the dark inscription at the entrance. No word could describe what he'd seen there. He wouldn't ever be able to speak about this week even if he wanted to. And, above all, he would never be able to forget it.

The car rumbled down the snowy road, leaving the sad profile of the Stammlager behind them. They drove on to the town of Auschwitz, its snow-covered rooftops rising from the embrace of the countryside and beech forests, and stopped in the market square.

Gioele was standing by the hotel entrance.

He was waiting among snow shovelled into large mounds, his legs livid from the cold, his hair tousled under his beret, his eyes containing all the colours in the world. When he saw them arrive, he went towards them and got into the car.

'Hi, Daddy,' he called.

'Hi. How are you?'

'Fine – and you?'

'Fine.' Hugo smiled. 'I've just paid my debt to the past.'

The Kübelwagen drove off.

There would be time enough to tell Gioele what had happened to his mother, his father and his brother, and why he had to go with him to Berlin, change his name, make up new memories and hide for a while. But Gioele was a bright little boy, and perhaps he'd already worked that out.

Epilogue

There was a gash in the sky. A ray of sun filtered through a cloud and Berto Hoffman almost wept because of the beauty of that glow.

He slowly walked to the wall, the cigarette Tristan Voigt had given him between his lips.

He inhaled the smoke, at once pungent and sweet.

The black wall at the end of the courtyard was dirty and full of holes. It stank. As he got nearer, he was able to make out bloodstains from the previous execution.

'Have you finished with that?' the executioner asked.

'One more drag,' Berto pleaded.

He thought about Bethany. About her smile, her eyes, her laugh and the way she pronounced her *r*s in her French accent. She was alive and Tristan would watch over her. He would continue his silent, clandestine battle along with Anita and Adele.

He threw the cigarette butt on the ground and laughed. After all, ending up in Auschwitz had been the best thing that could have happened to him. He was the Resistance, and the Resistance was life in a place where everything withered.

'Are you ready?' the executioner asked.

'Never more ready,' he replied.

'Get down on your knees.'

'I'd rather die standing up, if you don't mind.'

Berto closed his eyes and let the sun warm him.

The warm rays kissed his skin.

He felt calm.

The barrel of the pistol caressed his neck and the trigger clicked.

There was peace and silence as he fell forward in the shimmering dust.

Acknowledgements

A book is much more than the story it tells: it's an encounter between lives, and each of them contributes to its birth.

My heartfelt thanks to Piergiorgio Nicolazzini for believing in this story and allowing it to find its place in the world after it was born. Thanks to all the staff at PNLA, to Alice and Antonio, and in particular to Arianna Miazzo for always being there.

Thanks to Michele Rossi for falling in love with Hugo and Gioele, and to Benedetta Bolis for her professional attitude and her kindness.

My thanks also to all those who, having touched my life, contributed to the development of this novel.

To Sebastian and to my sons, Samuel, Elia and Emanuele, for being the constant presence that fills my life with love and sweet chaos.

To my father and mother, for being the best parents one could wish for. My stories would not be here if it weren't for you.

To my sister Fernanda, Arturo and my nephews for always supporting me.

To my aunt Maria Antonietta, the first person to teach me to love reading.

To my grandmother Mina, whose eyes speak more than her mouth ever could, and to my grandfather Pasquale who's here even if he is no longer here.

To Aunt Cherubina, to my cousins and Uncle Tonino, who, on hearing that I wanted to become a writer when I grew up, gave me a book by Stephen King.

To Uncle Angelo, deported to the concentration camp in Nuremberg, a witness of the horrors of the *Lager*. Thank you for telling me your story.

To Alessandra, Marcella and Grazia, distant but close sisters.

To Scilla, for always being there, like a soul mate, and to Elisa, a travelling companion in this wonderful literary world.

To the 'Ancelle', for sharing one of the best periods of my life, and for still being there for me.

To Ida and Incoronata, because whenever I see you, it feels as though time has stopped.

To Carlo Petruzzelli and Alberto Lo Margio, for external consultancy.

To Luca, Anna and Alessandro for always being there. You're my second family.

To Marietta, who taught me that you can go a long way even in a wheelchair.

To the sisters Esposito and Rosetta, present since my childhood.

To Francesca Barra, who loves Berlin as much as I do,

and to Giselda and her wonderful family who welcomed us to Berlin with exceptional warmth.

To Franco Forte for his teachings and his guidance through the literary world and to everyone at Collettivo 28, full of friends as well as colleagues.

Finally, thanks to Berlin for adopting me and revealing its history to me.